DARK MOON

RED MOON SERIES, BOOK THREE

ELIZABETH KELLY

EK PUBLISHING INC.

Cover art by
EK Designs

DARK MOON

(BOOK THREE, RED MOON SERIES)

Will her love set him free?

Sophia Williams, a powerful and strong-willed Lycan, never thought she would fall for a human. Yet, she cannot deny the instant attraction she feels for Bree's brother, Kaden. Used to getting what she wants, Sophia pursues him, determined to prove that she can be trusted.

Beaten and enslaved by Lycans, Kaden wants nothing to do with the family of Lycans his sister is marrying into. But his lust for Sophia is undeniable. As lust turns to something deeper, he begins to question everything he believes about the Lycans.

When a mutual enemy threatens to destroy their growing relationship, Kaden must put aside his distrust of Sophia's family to save her.

CHAPTER 1

"He is a handsome man, is he not?"

"I hadn't really noticed."

Avery smiled at Sophia and stroked her dark hair. "Dani seems quite taken with him."

"Aye, she does." Sophia stared out her bedroom window. Kaden and Dani were standing next to the barn, and she watched as Dani threw her head back and laughed before resting her hand on Kaden's arm.

"It's driving your Uncle Marshall crazy."

"Why? He is married to a human. Why should he be bothered that his child is infatuated with a human?" Sophia asked.

Avery shrugged. "I think it's the fact that Kaden hates Lycans."

"Dani is as human as he is."

"True. But her father and her brother are not."

Sophia didn't reply. Kaden's sister Bree was engaged to her half-brother James and like it or not, Kaden would soon have a very close relationship with the Lycans. She sighed. She understood why Kaden hated the Lycans. He and Bree had been kept as slaves by a Lycan named Draken. James and

Nicky had stumbled onto Bree in the forest after she had been attacked and hunted for sport by Draken and his pack, and James had used his healing powers to save her life.

It had not taken long for Bree and James to fall in love and when Draken had come after her, bringing Kaden with them, Bree had offered herself in exchange for Sophia's sister Leta. The young girl had been captured by the powerful Lycan, and Draken had quickly agreed to the exchange. Kaden was stabbed and left for dead by Draken, but James and Avery healed him. Once he was healed, they set out after the pack of Lycans to save Bree.

Sophia shivered. It had only been two weeks since she nearly died at the hands of Draken and she couldn't seem to shake her fear.

Everything went according to their plan. Kaden offered Sophia in exchange for his sister and Draken, instantly taken with Sophia and eager to make her the mother of his pups, agreed. Once Bree and Kaden were safe, James and the others attacked the Lycan's camp and saved her.

That's not exactly true. Kaden saved your life. He killed the Lycan about to tear your throat out, and he stopped you from shifting with that silver collar around your neck. If it hadn't been for him, you'd be dead right now.

"Sophia? Are you all right, my love?" Avery's warm hand stroked her back through her shirt and Sophia took comfort from her touch.

"Aye, I am fine."

"Are you sure? Leta said she heard you crying out last night."

Leta's bedroom was next to hers, and Sophia forced herself to smile at her mother. "I'm fine, Mama. I just had a bad dream."

Avery squeezed her waist. "Tell me about it."

Sophia hesitated. The dream had been awful. She was back with Draken, the hideous silver collar around her neck, and his hot breath blowing on her face as he leaned over her.

"You're mine, Sophia." He'd smiled down at her as his teeth lengthened and sharpened. "You're mine."

She'd woken from the dream, sweating and afraid, and couldn't fall back asleep. She laid in her bed, staring out the window as the darkness faded and the sun rose in the sky. She supposed it didn't help that Draken had escaped before they could kill him. The Lycan was out there somewhere and it would be foolish to think that he would not attempt to take his revenge.

She shook her head. "No, Mama. It was nothing."

She watched, her stomach tightening with what she refused to admit was jealousy, as Dani took Kaden's arm. He glanced briefly at the house - she could have sworn he was staring directly at her - and then followed Dani into the barn. Sophia had kissed Kaden in that very barn, had felt his erection against her abdomen and his hand on her breast, and try as she might she couldn't forget the way it had felt.

It was ridiculous. The man hated Lycans and she had never once mated with a human. Not that she was opposed to the idea of mating with a human, she had just never met one that interested her.

Kaden interests you.

She snorted angrily. That might be true, but Kaden had made it perfectly clear he wanted nothing to do with her. He'd kissed her in the barn because she had practically thrown herself at him. It hadn't taken him long to come to his senses, and since the moment he pushed her away he hadn't spoken a single word to her.

She realized Avery was still watching her and she cleared

her throat. "Dani will be upset when Kaden leaves tomorrow."

"If he leaves," Avery said.

Sophia stared at her. "He will, Mama."

Avery shrugged. "He may not. He loves his sister very much. He may find it more difficult to leave her than he realizes. He has been here two weeks and even he has to admit that Bree is very happy with us. He has seen for himself that not all Lycans treat humans the way that Draken did."

"He hasn't spent any time with us. The last two weeks he's been with Bree or Dani, or in the barn helping Ian with the horses. He's been actively avoiding anything to do with our family."

"That's true," Avery said. "But the last few days, Bree has gotten him to agree to eat dinner with us. It's a step in the right direction."

Sophia snorted. "He stares at his plate, eats his dinner, and leaves. He won't speak a word to any of us unless he has to."

"He just needs more time. You remember how Bree was the first moon she was here. She was terrified of anyone she thought to be a Lycan."

"Aye, but she was only frightened of us. Kaden hates all of us."

"Does he? I'm not so sure about that," Avery replied.

Sophia frowned at her. "What do you mean?"

AVERY STARED THOUGHTFULLY AT SOPHIA. SHE HAD SEEN the way Kaden looked at her child when he believed no one else was watching. And Sophia might avoid Kaden more than any of them, but Avery wasn't blind. The others had attempted to gain Kaden's trust over the last two weeks, even Nicky had been friendly and polite, but Sophia hadn't bothered. In fact, to anyone watching, she projected a clear dislike for the large human.

Avery smiled a little. Sophia might have fooled her father and her brothers, but she couldn't fool her mother. The slight reddening of her cheeks, the frequent subtle glances at Kaden whenever he was near her, and the way her eyes darkened when she watched Dani and Kaden together were unmistakably clear. Something had happened between Sophia and Kaden, and both were doing their best to keep it from the others.

"What do you mean, Mama?" Sophia said again.

"Nothing, my sweet. Only that perhaps Bree will still be able to change his mind." Avery stretched up to kiss Sophia's forehead. "Come, it's almost dinner. Let us join the others."

KADEN SMILED AT THE YOUNG GIRL STANDING NEXT TO HIM. He liked Dani, she had a happy, bubbling personality that was infectious, but he was growing distinctly uncomfortable with the way their relationship seemed to be turning.

She touched him at every opportunity, just small presses of her hand against his arm or his back, but he recognized it for what it was. Last night at dinner she had wormed her way into a seat beside him and spent the entire meal brushing her thigh against his. He had subtly shifted further and further to his left until he was practically sitting on his sister's lap.

Bree had given him an odd look but rather than try and explain with Dani's father staring suspiciously at him across the table, he had just hurriedly finished his meal and excused himself to the barn.

He grinned a little to himself. It was painfully obvious that Dani's father Marshall did not approve of his daughter's crush. Kaden was almost tempted to sleep with the girl just to anger the Lycan.

He stared down at Dani's pretty face. Who was he trying to fool? The girl was an innocent, and he wasn't the type of man who would use a woman in that manner. Besides, pretty as she was, she wasn't his type. Her slender body and blonde hair did nothing to stir his lust. He liked his women dark haired, with full and lush curves a man could get lost in. Wide hips to hang on to when the sex turned frantic and rough, and full breasts that overflowed in his hands.

Sophia's face flashed in his head and he automatically looked at the wall of the barn. He had pushed her back against that wall, had kissed her full mouth and ground his cock against her. He could still remember the feel of her breast in his hand, the way her nipple had tightened against his palm, and her low voice moaning his name.

He looked away quickly as his cock started to harden in his pants. Gods, he was going crazy. Thinking about having sex with a Lycan was pure madness. Besides, he was leaving tomorrow. He would never see the Lycan again.

Dani was chattering to him and he smiled and nodded, only half-listening as his thoughts turned to Bree. He couldn't convince her to leave with him. He had, in fact, known it was useless after the first few days and stopped pressuring her.

Bree loved the redheaded Lycan and, as much as Kaden hated to admit it, it was obvious that James loved her. Bree spent much of her time the last two weeks with Kaden and he was surprised by James' lack of objection. He'd given Bree her space and her freedom to visit with her brother, and Kaden had no sense that the Red was doing it as a way to win his favour.

He told Sophia that James was trying to control his sister, but he realized his mistake after only a few days. It was clear, even to him, that the Lycan would do anything his sister asked. It would have amused Kaden to no end that his tiny baby sister had such a powerful Lycan wrapped around her finger, had it not been for his deep-seated hatred for Lycans in general.

And fear, a voice deep inside his head whispered. *You can deny it all you want, but you fear them as well.*

He nodded at something Dani said and stared down at her blankly. He did fear the Lycans. He hated that he did, knew that it made him weak, but he had spent two years as their slave and his entire body was proof of their cruelty. His chest, back and thighs were covered with the reminders of their whips and their claws. Even now, away from Draken's home, he could feel a shudder run through him at the memory of being chained to the pole like a dog.

His hand rubbed at the skin on his throat. The band of pale skin, the only reminder of the collar he had worn around his neck for over two years, was still there. He wondered if it would ever go away or if it would brand him forever as a Lycan slave.

"Kaden?"

He realized Dani was staring at him oddly and he made himself smile at her. "Aye?"

"Were you listening to me?"

"I'm sorry, I was, uh…"

He was saved from replying by the appearance of Leta at the barn door.

"Uncle Marshall is looking for you," she said to Dani. She was holding Tia in her arms and she frowned when the small dog barked excitedly and wiggled from her grip. Tia

7

ran to Kaden and he scooped her up, petting her head as she wagged her tail and licked at his hands.

Dani sighed. "What does he want?"

Leta shrugged. "I don't know. He just asked me to come find you."

Dani frowned and then turned to Kaden. "I'll see you at dinner?"

"Aye."

She hesitated and before Kaden could step back, she stood on her tiptoes and kissed him lightly on the cheek. Blushing a little, she hurried past Leta who stepped out of the way but didn't follow her out of the barn. She kept a careful distance from Kaden and stared at him warily.

"I still don't like you," she said.

He grinned. "No? Why not? I'm not taking Bree away from you."

"I know! Bree would never leave me – she loves me. And my brother." She added as an afterthought.

His grin widened. Despite the fact that she was half-Lycan, he liked the girl. Other than Sophia, she was the only Lycan who had made no effort with him at all in the last two weeks. Although she refused to leave Bree's side the first few days, she'd spent most of the time glowering at him as he visited with his sister. After a few days she mysteriously disappeared, and he had questioned Bree about it.

His sister smiled a little. "She's in trouble for being rude to you. Avery and Tristan aren't allowing her to spend time with us until she learns better manners."

He laughed. "How long before she cracks and starts being nice to me?"

Bree giggled. "You have no idea how stubborn Leta is. When her parents told her what they expected of her, I guess she vowed she would never be kind to you and that she couldn't wait until you left, and she never had to see your ugly human face again."

He had snorted laughter as Bree poked his side in a friendly way. "She lost horse-riding privileges for a week and was sent to her room without supper for that little outburst."

"So that's why I haven't seen her glaring at me in the barn lately." He had grinned.

Now, he crossed his arms across his chest and arched one eyebrow at her. "Why such a dislike for me, young Leta?"

She pursed her lips together and stared silently at the ground. He'd decided she wasn't going to answer when she suddenly blurted, "Because you're making Bree sad."

He frowned. Bree hadn't said a word to him about leaving. She had seemed to make her peace with the fact that he wouldn't stay, and she had not appeared upset to him. Her acceptance had hurt his feelings and, in a way, made it easier for him to leave.

"It's true." Leta mistook his silence for disagreement. She forgot herself and moved deeper into the barn to stand in front of him. "She cries when you're not around."

"What do you mean?"

"She cries! She cries to Mama and to James almost every day. She's sad because you won't even stay for the wedding."

She gave him a cautious look. "I wasn't spying. Don't you tell Papa that I was spying because I wasn't. I just – just happened to hear them when I was playing in the closet in Papa and Mama's room."

"I won't," he promised.

She stared gravely at him. "You're not a very nice person. I thought you would be nice like Bree but you're not."

Surprisingly, her words stung him a little. "I am a nice person, Leta."

9

"No, you're not," she insisted. "You won't even stay for your own sister's wedding. That's mean. You're mean!"

"Leta!"

The young girl whirled around. Sophia had entered the barn and she frowned at her younger sister. "What did Mom and Dad say about being respectful to Bree's brother?"

"He's mean!" Leta was starting to cry. "He's making Bree sad and he doesn't even care!"

Sophia started toward her and Leta backed away until she bumped into Kaden. He steadied her with a hand on her back, and she turned and growled at him.

"Leta!" Sophia said and the young girl slumped to the ground and began to cry. Sophia sat beside her and gathered her into her arms. "Hush, Leta. Don't cry."

She glanced up at Kaden. "I'm sorry, she isn't usually like this. The thing with Draken frightened her very much, and things have been different around here lately. She's excited about the wedding and I think she's overtired and over-stimulated."

Leta crawled into her lap and continued to sob. "Please don't tell Papa I was bad, Sophia."

Sophia stroked her dark hair. "Honey, you know that Dad told you specifically to be respectful to Kaden. You weren't. There are consequences for your actions."

"They won't let me ride again for another whole week!" Leta wailed. "I'll die, Sophia. Die!"

Kaden sighed. The girl's dramatics would have been funny if it wasn't so obvious that she was truly upset. He crouched beside them and touched Leta's shoulder lightly. "It's all right, Leta. I know you didn't mean to be rude. You were just being honest, right?"

She sniffed and nodded. "Aye."

"I'll make you a deal. I'll ask Sophia not to tell your

father if you promise to help Ian brush the horses after I'm gone. There are too many for him to brush by himself."

She eyed him carefully for a moment and then nodded again. "I promise."

"Good." He straightened as Sophia kissed Leta's cheek gently and then stood, pulling the young girl to her feet.

"Dinner is ready, my love. Go and wash up."

Leta left the barn and Sophia turned to Kaden. "Um, dinner is ready," she said awkwardly. "Will you be joining us tonight?"

"Aye."

It was the first time they had been alone together in days, and his gaze flickered to the wall where they kissed. He cleared his throat and glanced back at Sophia. She'd followed his gaze and was staring at the barn wall. Her cheeks were pink, and her tongue darted out to flick nervously at her upper lip.

She looked at him and her blush deepened. He stared silently at her and after a moment, took a step towards her. She backed up a step and smiled uncertainly at him.

"Is it true what Leta said? Is Bree upset?" he asked.

She gave him an odd look. "Of course, she is. You're her brother and she wants you to stay."

"For what? She has your brother now. She has no need for me." Even he could hear the jealousy in his voice.

She stared impatiently at him. "Loving my brother does not mean she doesn't need you, Kaden. You don't strike me as a stupid human but you're certainly acting like one."

He glared at her. "I'm not being stupid. I'm being realistic. Bree no longer needs my protection. Why would I stay?"

"You stay because she loves you. You stay because it's foolish of you to leave when you have no money and no place to go. My parents are willing to hire you to work with Ian in the barn. You could earn a wage, be a free man, and have protection from Draken."

He scoffed. "Another reason Bree should be leaving with me. I know you believe that your family can protect us from Draken, but you don't know him the way that we do. His pack is large and he's crazy. And now," he stepped closer and took her arm in a firm grip, "it's not just my sister and me he wants, but you as well."

He rubbed her arm with his thumb. "You think you're safe. You believe that Draken cannot harm you but you're wrong. Your family has no idea what he's capable of."

"All the more reason for you to stay," she replied. "You can help us. You know what he's capable of."

"Aye, I do," he whispered. He was standing so close to her now that his chest brushed against her magnificent breasts.

"Do you want me to stay?" he said.

She nodded.

"Why?"

"I – what?" she said.

He lowered his face to hers and she parted her mouth for his kiss. Instead of kissing her, he rubbed the ball of his thumb across her lower lip. She moaned, her breath warm against his face, and he stared mesmerized at the hint of her straight, white teeth. "Why do you want me to stay?"

"Because Bree wants you to stay," she whispered.

"Is that the only reason?" He slipped his thumb between her lips and she closed her mouth around it and sucked.

He made a quiet groaning noise and slipped his other hand around her to cup the back of her head. He slid his thumb back and forth in her mouth, feeling the wet heat of her tongue and lips holding him firmly inside of her.

His cock was rock hard, his breath coming in harsh pants,

and he couldn't look away from her dark eyes. They were changing, flecks of green appearing, and he watched fascinated as the dark brown changed to a light, clear green.

"Is there another reason you want me to stay, Sophia?" he said.

He started to pull his thumb from her mouth, and she tightened her lips around it, stroking it roughly with her tongue until he groaned again.

"Tell me," he whispered as he pulled his thumb out of her mouth.

"Kaden, I -"

"Gods be damned, it's cold out there tonight. You sure you want to leave when it's this cold?" Ian came ambling through the doors at the far end of the barn and stopped short when he saw Kaden and Sophia locked together.

Sophia pulled away from Kaden and ran to the door. "Dinner is ready," she called hoarsely before disappearing into the darkness.

Ian stared shrewdly at Kaden. "Sophia's a pretty girl."

"Aye." Kaden started for the barn door, ignoring the grin on Ian's face. "Are you coming for dinner or not?"

"Aye, I am." Whistling softly, Ian followed him out of the barn.

CHAPTER 2

"**A**re you awake, Kaden?" Ian's voice drifted up the ladder of the hayloft.

"Aye, come up," Kaden called.

He'd been uncomfortable staying in the house with the Lycans and he wondered if Avery had sensed it. After only a couple of days she brought him out to the barn and showed him the hayloft.

"Ian used to stay here," she said. "He moved into the house a couple of years ago. I know it isn't much but you're welcome to use it if you like."

She was right. The loft wasn't much, just a bed, a dresser and a couple of overstuffed armchairs, but he had grunted his thanks and moved in that night.

Ian climbed the ladder and stood in the middle of the room, a small grin playing on his lips. "I haven't been up here in years."

"Why did you move into the house?" Kaden asked.

Ian sat down in one of the armchairs. "When you get to be my age, you'll understand the importance of having a bathroom close by." He laughed. "It's a lot easier in the middle of the night to walk down the hall to a bathroom with running water, than it is to scale a ladder and use the outhouse behind the barn."

Kaden grinned and settled his large body into the armchair opposite of Ian. "Aye, you have a good point."

He shifted in the chair and waited for Ian to ask him exactly what he had been doing with Sophia in the barn before dinner.

"Still planning on leaving tomorrow?" Ian asked.

Kaden nodded. "I am."

"I imagine your sister is upset about you leaving. Maybe some other people too," Ian said.

Kaden didn't reply and Ian stared down at his hands. He picked at one dirty and broken nail thoughtfully for a few moments. "I have a sister."

His smile was sad. "She was a real firecracker. As a child, Sophia reminded me quite a bit of her actually. Melinda was very," he paused, "strong-willed and opinionated."

"Sounds more like Leta," Kaden said.

Ian laughed. "Aye, Leta definitely knows what she wants. Of course, Sophia was quite the strong-willed child herself. Still is, as I'm sure you've noticed."

"Aye," Kaden said. "Where is Melinda now?"

"She died just after her eleventh year."

"I'm sorry, Ian."

"Aye." The old man sighed heavily. "She drowned. We weren't much for swimming, but it was a hot day and she wanted to cool off. She was supposed to have someone go with her when she went to the river, but I guess she couldn't find anyone. She went off by herself and the current was stronger than she thought."

He stared at the floor, lost in thought for a moment, before looking up at Kaden. "It's been years since her death, but I still wonder what would have happened if I had been with her that day instead of off causing trouble with my friends."

"You can't blame yourself."

"Aye, I don't. She knew the rules," Ian said. "I still miss her. I think about the woman she would have become. When I married my Anna, I hoped we'd have a little girl first. Thought maybe she would be like Melinda. But Anna never took with child. The gods didn't see fit to bless us that way."

Kaden nodded. He knew that Ian's wife Anna had died many years ago. He'd been spending quite a bit of time with the old man, and Ian wasn't much for staying quiet.

"The point I'm trying to make is that you're making a mistake," Ian said. "The odds of both you and Bree surviving Draken's pack were nearly impossible, yet here you both are. If you leave now, you're throwing away the precious gift the gods have given you."

"Lycans beat us and nearly killed the both of us, Ian. I can't stay with them."

"You're not a stupid man Kaden, but you sure are making stupid decisions."

"Why does everyone keep saying that to me?" Kaden gritted out.

"Perhaps because it's the truth." Ian grinned at him before sobering. "I lost my sister and never got the chance to see her grow up, to marry the man she loved, and to have children. You have that chance. Bree is the only family you have left. Why would you walk away from her?"

"I told you, the Lycans -"

Ian held up his hand. "I know what the Lycans did to you, Kaden. But it wasn't these Lycans who whipped you and chained you and hunted your sister. Tristan and his family are good people and they respect humans. They believe that

17

everyone is the same, no matter if they're Lycans or humans. You could try giving them a chance to prove that to you."

Before Kaden could reply, Ian stood and stretched stiffly. "I know you have your mind set on leaving but do me a favour and think hard tonight about your decision. At the very least consider staying for your sister's wedding, will you?"

Kaden nodded and stood up as Ian approached him. The old man held out his hand and Kaden shook it firmly. "It's been good getting to know you, Kaden. If you do leave, I'll miss your help around the barn. You're a good worker."

"Thanks, Ian."

Kaden waited until Ian had descended the ladder before stripping off his clothes and blowing out the lantern. He climbed into the bed and stretched out on his back under the cold sheets. He stared sightlessly into the dark. Until this morning he'd been sure of his decision to leave. Now, with Leta's admission that Bree was upset he was leaving and Ian's belief that he should stay, he was second-guessing his decision.

Is that the only reason?

He turned on his side and pulled the covers up to his chin. The memory of Sophia sucking on his thumb had his dick hardening. He reached down and stroked it back and forth. He closed his eyes as he remembered the way Sophia's lips had looked around his thumb. Her mouth had been warm and wet, and her tongue soft against his skin.

He stroked harder, picturing her mouth not around his thumb, but his throbbing cock. Gods, it would feel good to have that soft tongue of hers licking his cock. He wondered if she had thought about it. If she had imagined herself on her knees before him, his hands threading through her hair as he pushed his cock deep into her mouth.

His dick was hot and heavy in his hand, and he squeezed

and rubbed it as he panted harshly. Her mouth would be so warm, and she would use her lips and her tongue to –

He snorted and abruptly stopped touching himself. He was an idiot. Sophia was a Lycan and if he did find her on her knees in front of him, he'd be lucky if she didn't use her sharp teeth to bite off his cock. He winced, his cock deflating at the thought, and twisted onto his back. He was tired but he had a feeling he would get very little sleep tonight.

"GOOD MORNING."

Kaden glanced up from the large, brown horse he was petting. Tristan was standing in front of him, and he gave the Lycan an uneasy look. "Hello."

"You've really made a difference for Ian the last couple of weeks," Tristan said.

"If you're looking for Ian, I don't believe he's awake yet. You'll probably find him at the house," Kaden said.

"He's eating breakfast with the others. Bree was wondering if you were going to eat breakfast before you left. I told her I would find you and ask."

"I'm not hungry."

It was true. He had lost his appetite at the thought of saying goodbye to his sister.

Tristan leaned against the stall next to Kaden and pointed to the horse. "I've told Ian that you'll be taking Bandit with you."

Kaden blinked in surprise. "What do you mean?"

"You'll need a horse. Bandit is young and healthy, and Ian says you're fond of him."

"I don't have money to buy a horse from you," Kaden said.

"Consider him a gift."

"That's generous of you."

Tristan shrugged. "With Bree marrying my son, you're part of our family now." He gave Kaden a small grin. "Whether you like it or not."

He straightened and pulled an envelope from his back pocket. He held it out to Kaden who frowned but took it.

"What's this for?" Kaden stared in confusion at the wad of bills in the envelope. Before Tristan could reply, he shoved the envelope at him. "I don't need your charity."

"It isn't charity," Tristan said patiently, refusing to take the envelope back. "It's your wages."

"Wages?"

Tristan nodded. "Did Bree not tell you that we pay wages to the people who work for us?"

"Aye, but -"

"Ian says you've been invaluable to him the last two weeks. He has nothing but good things to say about you. Even though you're not staying, you still deserve to be paid for the work you've done for us," Tristan said.

He held his hand out and after a moment's hesitation, Kaden shook it.

"It was good to meet you, Kaden. I'm sorry you're leaving. We could use someone like you to work in the barns. If you change your mind, we'd be glad to hire you on permanently."

Kaden didn't reply and Tristan nodded to him before leaving the barn. Kaden stared down at the envelope of cash before tucking it into the pocket of his pants. He reached out and stroked the side of Bandit's neck. The horse chuffed and Kaden leaned against his warm neck.

"I PACKED YOU SOME FOOD." BREE, LUGGING A LARGE leather bag behind her, climbed the ladder to the loft in the barn.

"Thank you." Kaden was sitting in one of the armchairs and, leaving the bag on the floor, Bree crossed the room. She dragged the other armchair close to his and sat across from him, her knees touching his lightly.

Kaden stared at his sister. Even he could see that she had been crying.

"You look tired," she said.

"So do you."

She sighed deeply. "I had trouble sleeping last night. Where will you go?"

He shrugged. "I haven't decided yet. Maybe the city."

"You told me once that you could never live in the city. Too many people you said."

"I could find work in the city."

"You could have work here," she replied. "The Lycans would pay you to work in the barns."

He didn't reply and she sighed again. "What if Draken goes hunting for you?"

"It's more likely he'll return here."

"I know."

"But does your boyfriend?" he asked.

"Aye," she said. "They're not stupid, Kaden. They know Draken will be back."

"They don't know what he's capable of, Bree."

"All the more reason for you to stay." She echoed Sophia's words to him.

"Bree -"

She reached out and captured his hands in hers. "Please don't leave, Kaden. I'm sorry. I told myself I wouldn't beg and that I would respect your decision, but I don't want you

21

to leave. I can't imagine getting married without you there. If you're gone, who will give me away?"

"I'm sure your boyfriend's father would," he replied.

"I don't want it to be him. I want it to be you." She started to cry, and he squeezed her hands.

"Don't cry, Bree. Please."

"I can't help it," she sobbed. "After everything we've gone through together, you would just leave me? I know you hate the Lycans, but these ones are different. I swear to you, Kaden."

He sighed. "I know."

He stared at the floor for a moment and then raised his gaze to hers. "I will stay until after the wedding."

She gasped. "Truly?"

"Aye." He smiled at her. "It's not every day my baby sister gets married."

"Oh, Kaden!" She jumped on him and hugged him enthusiastically. "Thank you so much!"

She kissed his cheek and then rested her forehead against his. "You've made the right choice. You can earn some money and get to know our new family. Who knows, you might even start to like them."

He snorted. "When is this wedding day anyway?"

She returned to her seat. "I told James I didn't want anything fancy. I thought maybe just a small party with his family and some of their friends, and that the sooner we did it, the better. He agreed but we were overruled by the rest of the family. Dani is especially adamant that we have a proper wedding."

He rolled his eyes and she poked him affectionately. "She said we need at least two months to properly plan the wedding."

"Two months?" He frowned. "That long?"

She gave him a hesitant smile. "You could make a decent amount of money in two months."

"I'm not staying for the money, Bree. I'm staying because of the wedding, and because I want to be here to protect you when Draken returns."

"Do you believe he'll return that quickly?" she asked.

He shrugged. "Honestly, I do not know. He was surprised that the Lycans were able to defeat him so easily. I could see it in his eyes. He's surrounded himself with Lycans he can control and humans he can rule, for many years. It shook him badly to be around his own kind that did not blindly follow him and instead, went after him. That may buy us some time."

"Perhaps." She was quiet for a moment and then gave him a soft smile. "Can I ask one more favour of you, Kaden?"

"What?"

"Will you try with the Lycans? Will you give them a chance over the next couple of months?"

"I have been," he protested. "I've spent two weeks with them, and I've been pleasant and -"

She squeezed his hands. "You've avoided the Lycans for the last two weeks and you know it."

"I haven't." He frowned. "I've spent time with Dani and Leta and -"

"Leta doesn't count. She's the one Lycan here, who isn't trying to be your friend. And Dani is human, you know that."

He gave her an innocent look. "Is she?"

She laughed. "Don't even, Kaden. You know she's human. She has a crush on you."

"Aye, I know."

She stared curiously at him. "What do you think of her?"

"I think she's a sweet girl who is much too young for me."

23

"She's not that young. She's over twenty."

"Aye, and I am nearing thirty. Besides, she is not my type."

It was Sophia he was thinking of. Those dark eyes and curvy body of hers that begged for his touch.

Bree jerked. "It is almost your birthday!"

"Is it?"

"Of course, it is! I can't believe I nearly forgot. It's in less than two weeks. We should have a party!"

"No," he said immediately. "I don't want a party."

"We have to celebrate," she said.

"No, Bree. I'm serious."

"Fine." She pouted a little. "No party. But I'm telling Avery and asking if we can do something special for dinner that day."

He rolled his eyes. "You drive me crazy, you know that right?"

"I do." She grinned at him. "And I'm so glad you're staying. I love you."

"I love you too," he said. "Now go on, tell your new family they'll have to put up with me for a while longer. I'm sure they'll be thrilled."

"They will be. They want to get to know you better," she said. "Especially James."

He laughed. "I doubt that."

She stood and kissed his forehead. "Thank you, Kaden. You won't regret staying, I promise you."

CHAPTER 3

"I'll be right back." Bree patted his arm and left the common room.

Kaden stared into the fire. It was later that afternoon and although he didn't regret his decision to stay, he wasn't sure he could do what Bree asked of him. Just the thought of trying to get to know the Lycans made him anxious and uncomfortable. They might be different, but it didn't mean he wanted to be their friends. The idea of ever fully trusting them was completely foreign to him.

"Hello, Kaden." Avery walked in and sat down gracefully in the chair next to him.

He nodded to her. "Hello, Mrs. Williams."

She laughed. "Please, call me Avery."

They sat in silence for a few moments and then Avery smiled at him. "We're so happy you decided to stay for the wedding, Kaden. We're all anxious to get to know you better."

He shifted uncomfortably in his chair and didn't reply.

"Sophia told me that you're injured. You have a bruise on your side."

"It's fine."

"Would you show it to me?"

"Why?" He gave her a suspicious look.

"You know why." She smiled at him.

"It's nearly healed."

"I know that Nicky gave you the bruise. I would feel much better about what he did, if you would allow me to finish healing it."

He stared into the flames and then stood abruptly and pulled off his shirt so that Avery could examine it.

"I'm sorry that Nicholas did this to you," she said.

"He thought I was hurting his sister."

"Aye, he told me. I've asked him to apologize to you."

He shrugged. "It doesn't matter. I would have done the same if I thought that someone was hurting Bree."

She smiled. "There are many similarities between humans and Lycans when it comes to their loved ones."

She reached out to touch him and he stepped back, his hand automatically covering the fading bruise.

"I won't hurt you, Kaden," Avery said.

He dropped his hand. Avery reached out and placed both of her hands on the bruise, covering it completely. He gave her a questioning look as warmth tingled through his side.

"How do you do this, Avery?"

"I do not know. I have had this ability since I was a teenager. My father's grandmother had the same gift."

Avery studied the scars on his chest. "Would you allow me to try something?"

He felt like he should say no but there was something about the Red that was very comforting, and he was finding it pleasant to stand next to her while she touched him.

"Aye."

She smiled and moved her right hand to his chest. She

rested it against one of the smaller scars that ran just above his right nipple and pressed hard against it.

"Mama, you have to speak to Dani." Sophia stormed into the common room. "She's completely taken over the wedding. Poor Bree isn't making any of the decisions and it's her wedding! Dani told me this morning that the colours are pink and cream. Pink! I do not wear pink, Mama. The gods help them if they try and make me -"

She stared wide-eyed at her mother and the half-naked Kaden. "What – what are you doing?"

"Healing Kaden's bruise," Avery replied.

"I'll leave you alone," Sophia said.

"No, my sweet, stay for a bit. Kaden won't mind if we talk wedding while I heal him." She smiled up at him. "Will you?"

"No," he said.

Sophia stood next to her mother and examined his naked chest. He wasn't much to think about his appearance but having Sophia's frank gaze on him was making him a little self-conscious. She was still staring at him and seemed particularly fascinated by the random tufts of hair that grew between the scars on his chest. She stared for a long moment at the thin line of hair that grew below his navel and disappeared beneath the waistband of his pants.

She finally glanced up, realized both he and her mother were staring at her, and cleared her throat. "Why are you touching his chest? Was he hurt there as well?"

Avery shook her head as she removed her hand from Kaden's side. Kaden glanced down at his ribs and grunted with surprise. The bruise was gone.

Avery smiled at Sophia as she pressed her other hand next to the one still pressed against his chest. "I'm trying an experiment."

27

"What kind of experiment?" Sophia's grandmother, Kaden thought her name was Vivian, entered the common room. Leta trailed after her and, after checking that Avery wasn't looking, stuck her tongue out at him.

Kaden grinned at the young Lycan as Vivian circled around him to examine his back. "Gods," she said disgustedly, "this Draken gives all Lycans a bad name."

"I thought I would see if perhaps my abilities could heal his old scars." Avery told her mother-in-law.

"Does it work that way?" Sophia said.

Avery shrugged. "I do not know. It doesn't hurt to try though."

He jerked a little when Vivian touched his back. He was starting to feel distinctly uncomfortable by the stares of the women surrounding him. Leta kicked at one of the chairs before collapsing in it and staring moodily at him.

"How come you're not skinny like Bree was?" she asked.

He hesitated, not sure how much he should say to the young girl, but Avery gave him an encouraging look and he decided to be honest. "The Lycans who held us as slaves valued those of us who were – were naturally strong. They wanted us strong and well-fed so that we could," he hesitated again, a strange look coming over his face, "provide them with manual labour. They made sure we were fed."

He looked down at the floor. "Slaves like Bree, who were only needed for housework and -"

He stopped abruptly and stared at the floor. He was absolutely not saying what slaves like Bree were often used for in front of Leta.

Avery gave him a sympathetic look as she continued to press against his chest. He took a quick glance at Sophia. She had a sick look on her face, one that suggested she knew what the slaves were used for.

"They weren't given much food," he finally said. "And they would not let me give her my share of food."

He glanced at Sophia again. He wondered if she judged him for being so healthy when Bree had nearly starved to death. "I tried to give her my food, but they would not allow it," he said again.

"Aye, we believe you," Sophia said softly, and relief flooded through him.

Vivian traced the scars on his back before peering around him at Avery. "If it were to work, then you would already know. James would have healed Bree's scars."

"Bree didn't have any scars," Avery replied.

Vivian poked him in a not unfriendly way. "So, the Lycans who held you as slaves at least had the decency not to whip the women then?"

Kaden shook his head. "No, they whipped them."

Vivian frowned. "Avery, are you wrong? Perhaps James had healed her scars before he brought her home. We should ask him if -"

"Bree wasn't whipped," Kaden said.

"Why not?" Vivian asked.

Kaden didn't reply. He was staring at Sophia again and she made a small moan of dismay.

"You took her beatings," she said.

He remained silent and Avery stared up at him. "Kaden? Is that true?"

"She was too little." He looked away from Sophia and gazed into the fire instead. "If they had whipped her, it would have – have killed her. Whenever they went to punish her, I convinced them to let me take her place."

There was a long, drawn-out silence, and he looked at Avery when her soft hand touched his face. He was surprised to see tears in her eyes as she said, "You sweet boy."

He was oddly embarrassed by the way they were all staring at him. Allowing Draken's pack to capture them was his greatest shame. He had failed to keep his baby sister safe. Taking her beatings had been his only way to protect her.

Avery patted his cheek gently and then dropped her hand back to his chest. She pressed again and stared questioningly at him. "Do you feel anything, Kaden? Warmth or tingling?"

He shrugged. "I'm not sure. I don't think so."

He glanced at Sophia again. She was biting at her lower lip and giving him a look he didn't quite understand. She had her long, dark hair braided today, and she was wearing a plain grey shirt with a pair of black pants. The shirt hugged her full breasts and her pants clung enticingly to her firm thighs. Her pants were tucked into leather boots that rose to her knees and he watched as she ran her hands nervously down the front of her thighs.

He made himself look away when he realized Avery was watching him watch Sophia. She gave him a deliberately innocent grin, and he groaned under his breath when Dani entered the room.

"What's going on?" She stared with bright interest at the group of women surrounding the half-naked Kaden before joining them. She linked her arm through Kaden's and pressed the side of one small breast against his arm. "Hi, Kaden!"

"Hello, Dani." He looked away, his gaze automatically returning to Sophia. She was staring at Dani, and he wondered why her eyes were lightening. Her nostrils were flaring and there were two red spots high on her cheeks.

"What's going on?" Dani repeated.

"Mama's trying to heal the human's scars," Leta said from her spot in the chair.

She dangled her feet and pouted when Avery gave her a

stern look. "His name is Kaden, not 'the human'. Behave yourself, Leta."

"Sorry, Mama."

"Leta," Avery prompted.

"Sorry, Kaden," she muttered.

He winked at her and shifted away from Dani. She followed him, pressing herself even more tightly against him, and he sighed. He would have to speak to her soon about her crush. Avoiding her was obviously not working. Maybe he could ask Bree to speak to her for him. He had no wish to hurt the girl's feelings.

"Is it working?" Dani asked.

"Let's find out." Avery removed her hands and everyone, even Leta who had slinked over to stand by her mother, leaned in to stare at Kaden's chest.

The small scar was still there, and Avery wrinkled her nose in disappointment. "I'm sorry, Kaden."

"It's fine. Uh – thank you for trying."

"Aye," she said distractedly before staring at Vivian. "Perhaps if I held him every day? What do you think? Maybe it's just a matter of them needing time to heal."

"It might work," Vivian said. "Or maybe we should ask James to try. He is more powerful than you and -"

"No," Kaden said. "The scars don't hurt."

Vivian suddenly laughed. "Aye, I'm being a silly old Lycan. I suppose it would be a bit awkward to have James hugging you." She laughed again at herself and Dani giggled.

"I wish I had the healing ability." She rubbed her hand over Kaden's chest. "I'd be fine with touching you every day." She blushed at her own boldness but let her hand drift toward his flat stomach. "Maybe we -"

She was interrupted by a low growling and Kaden and the others turned and stared in surprise at Sophia. She was glaring at him and Dani, and the growl that was radiating from deep within her chest was growing steadily louder.

"Sophia?" Vivian said. "What is wrong?"

Sophia quit growling and gave her grandmother a horrified look. "Nothing, Grandmamma. I am just, uh…"

"She is just tired," Avery said. "And perhaps a bit disturbed by the prospect of wearing pink for the wedding."

She reached for Dani's hand and pulled her gently away from Kaden. "Come girls, let's find Bree and discuss some wedding ideas."

"I was going to visit with Kaden for a bit," Dani protested. "I haven't even had the chance to tell him how happy I am he's staying." She smiled brilliantly at him as Avery tugged her towards the door.

"I'm sure Kaden has work to do in the barn," Avery replied.

"Aye, I do," Kaden said with a quick grateful look at the Red. "Ian will be wondering where I am."

He grabbed his shirt and walked quickly from the room, nearly running into his sister.

"Kaden? What's wrong?" She frowned at the look on his face as he shrugged into his shirt.

"Nothing. I need to go and help Ian in the barn. Avery and the others are looking for you. They want to discuss wedding plans."

She grinned. "Aye, I heard a rumour that Dani has chosen pink and cream for my colours. I need to let her know that's not going to happen."

"Sophia will be happy to hear that," he said.

She gave him a strange look. "How do you know that?"

He shook his head. "Never mind. I'll talk to you later, all right?"

She nodded and disappeared into the common room.

CHAPTER 4

Sophia was crossing the yard when she heard Leta scream. The sound was coming from the barn, and she turned and raced toward it. Her heart thumping in her chest, she drew her sword and burst into the barn as Leta screeched again.

"Stop it, Evan! Stop it right now or I'm telling Mama!"

Kaden appeared in front of her and Sophia ran into his broad back before she could stop herself. He twisted quickly and caught her before she could fall, wincing when the flat of her sword hit him across the thigh.

"Gods be damned! Are you trying to cut off my leg?" He glared at her and released her. She stumbled back, nearly falling again before catching her balance.

She brushed past him as Leta squealed loudly. "I mean it, Evan!"

"What in the gods name is going on here?" She pushed into the empty stall that Evan and Leta were standing in. She had to suppress her shudder of disgust at the creature in Evan's hand. It was a rat, dead thank the gods, but still a rat. She hated the vile things, had since she was a small child, and she kept a careful distance even as she reminded herself not to show Leta her fear. Evan was swinging the dead animal by its plump, pink tail and grinning at his younger sister.

"Sophia! Make him stop!" Leta cried, cringing when Evan swung the rat closer to her.

"Evan, enough," Sophia said sharply. "You know better."

She turned to her younger sister. "Honestly Leta, it's only a dead rat. You're screaming like you're being tortured in here."

"It's gross, Sophia! And Evan touched me with it!" Leta cried.

Evan laughed and swung the dead rat in a large circle over his head. Revulsion mixed with fear crossed Sophia's face. She masked it quickly when she realized Kaden was staring at her. To her relief, he stepped forward and plucked the dead rat from Evan's hand.

He dropped it into the large garbage can at the end of the stall as Evan frowned at him. "Hey, that was mine. Give it back."

Sophia smacked her brother on the arm. "Really, Evan?"

Evan stared down at the floor of the barn as Leta ran to Sophia and put her arms around her waist. "You're so mean, Evan!"

"Calm down, Leta. It's only a rat – they're more afraid of you than you are of them," Sophia said. She patted the young Lycan's back as Evan crouched in front of them.

"Sorry, Leta." The look on his face suggested he wasn't sorry at all, but his voice was sincere enough. He held out his hand. "Come on. Let's find Marian and see if she made fresh bread this morning."

Leta took his hand and the two of them left the barn. Sophia rolled her eyes. "One minute they're at each other's throats, and the next they're best friends."

"Why do you not want Leta to know you're afraid of rats as well?" Kaden asked.

"I'm not afraid of rats." She gave him a dirty look.

"No? That's good, because there's another one right there." He pointed to the floor and she looked down to see a rat scurrying past her foot.

She shrieked and launched herself at Kaden. She climbed his body like he was a tree, hooking her legs around his waist and wrapping her arms around his head.

"Gods!" She shuddered and looked down at the floor, trying to see where the rat had disappeared.

"Not afraid of rats, huh?" His voice was muffled, and she realized with embarrassment that his face was buried between her breasts.

She leaned back as his hands circled around her and cupped her ass. She searched the floor again and didn't notice the way his hands kneaded her firm flesh. She shuddered and tightened her legs around his waist when she caught a glimpse of the rat's long tail disappearing into the stall.

His body was shaking with laughter and she flushed and glared at him. "Stop laughing! This isn't funny. Go and kill the rat, please."

He laughed again. "You can't expect me to catch it with my bare hands. You'd have better luck shifting into your Lycan form and hunting it down that way."

She made a small noise of disgust and pressed herself against him. "I'm not going anywhere near that thing."

"It's just a rat. He's probably more afraid of you than you are of him," he mocked her lightly.

"Shut up!" she muttered before looking around again. "I don't know how you can stay in here. You probably have rats crawling across your body while you sleep."

"Luckily, I'm not afraid of rats."

She imagined he could pinpoint the exact moment she forgot about the rat and realized he was cupping and rubbing her ass. A mixture of desire and apprehension crossed her face.

"Stop that," she whispered.

"Stop what?" His hand slipped down the curve of her ass and the tips of his fingers nearly brushed against the soft flesh between her thighs.

"That," she moaned.

He squeezed her ass, pressing her against his firm stomach. "You seem to like it."

She didn't reply and he squeezed her ass again. "Tell me you don't like it, and I'll stop."

"What's going on?"

Kaden dropped her so quickly at the sound of Nicholas' voice that she nearly landed on her ass. She stared guiltily at James and Nicky as they entered the barn.

"Nothing. There was a rat," she said.

Nicky gave her a suspicious look, but James grinned. "I can't believe you're still afraid of rats. You know you're a Lycan, right?"

"Shut up, James." She grimaced and picked up her sword from where she had dropped it in her mad scramble to get away from the rat.

"Why are you here?" she asked as Nicky looked from her to Kaden.

"You're late," Nicholas replied.

"Sorry. Evan was teasing Leta and I needed to intervene."

"Late for what?" Kaden asked.

"Jeffrey is waiting for you. We thought you had forgotten." Nicky scowled at her.

"I said I was sorry, Nicky, and I'll apologize to Jeffrey," Sophia said.

She was walking toward the door when Kaden caught her by the wrist. "What are you doing with Jeffrey?"

She wondered briefly if it was jealousy she was hearing in his voice.

"Take your hand off my sister," Nicky growled.

Kaden's hand tightened around her wrist. "And if I don't?"

Nicholas growled again, his eyes going from blue to yellow, and Kaden stiffened behind her. "What are you going to do, Lycan? Hmm? Do you believe that you can -"

"Stop it," Sophia snapped. She turned to her brother. "Calm down, Nicky."

He ignored her and she gave James a pleading look. He took Nicky's arm. "She can take care of herself, Nicky. You know that."

Deciding the best course of action was to distract the two of them, Sophia turned to Kaden. "We've been keeping watch for Draken. It's my turn."

He frowned. "How long have you been keeping watch?"

"Since we returned. We've been keeping guard in the trees just beyond our home at all times."

"Why wasn't I told? I want to be involved in this," Kaden said.

"You're useless at keeping watch," Nicholas replied. "Unless you have suddenly developed the ability to smell the Lycans like we can?"

Kaden glared at him and Nicky laughed. "I didn't think so. C'mon, Sophia. Jeffrey is waiting."

"Just wait," James said. "Kaden would be helpful. We guard in pairs. As long as he's with a Lycan he can take his turn on watch."

"Really? And which Lycan would we put him with? He

avoids all of us like we have the sickness," Nicholas said through gritted teeth.

"I'll go on watch with whoever you put me with," Kaden said.

James clapped Nicholas on the back. "See? Kaden is willing to help and so we'll let him. It'll take the strain off the rest of us to have an extra person."

Nicholas snorted and Sophia tugged at Kaden's hand until he released her.

"I can take my turn right now," Kaden said suddenly. "I could – I mean I don't mind taking a shift if Jeffrey has something else to do."

"Oh, um…" Sophia could feel herself starting to blush as James stared at them silently.

"He's already there, waiting for her," Nicholas said. "Don't worry, human. You'll get your turn."

He took Sophia's hand and led her from the barn as James stared at Kaden. "Thank you for staying for the wedding. It means a lot to Bree," he said.

"Aye," Kaden replied.

They stood in uncomfortable silence for a few moments until James cleared his throat. "I was just about to join Bree in the house for a bite to eat. Would you like to join us?"

Kaden nodded. He had promised his sister he would make an attempt to get to know the Lycans, and her future-husband was probably the best one to start with.

"YOUR BROTHER LIKES MY SISTER."

Bree, sitting on the bed and brushing her long hair, paused and stared at James. "What? How do you know?"

"I can smell it on him." James pulled his boots off with a

soft grunt. "And Nicholas and I walked into the barn this afternoon to see him with his hands on her ass."

Bree gaped at him. "No! Does Sophia like him?"

James shrugged. "I don't know if she *likes* him, but she's attracted to him." He made a face. "I can smell it on her."

"It must be so weird to smell your sister's attraction to someone," Bree replied.

"More gross than weird. Although honestly, most of the time we can just block it out." James shrugged out of his shirt and dropped it to the floor before sitting behind Bree on the bed.

"Poor Sophia. I couldn't imagine growing up with brothers who could smell when I liked someone."

"You get used to it." He kissed the back of her shoulder. "Anyway, it's why Nicky's having such a hard time warming up to your brother. He's always been protective of Sophia."

"Well I hope those crazy kids get together." Bree smiled at him and he took the brush from her hand. He ran it through her soft hair as she clasped her arms around her knees and stared into the fire.

"They would make a cute couple don't you think?" she said. He grunted in reply and she craned her neck to look at him.

"And their children would be adorable." She wiggled her eyebrows at him, and he laughed and kissed her nose.

"You just want them to get together so that Kaden will stay."

She sighed. "A little, I suppose. But mostly, I just want him to be happy."

"And you think Sophia would make him happy?"

She nodded. "I do. Kaden needs a woman who's strong and can handle his occasional bad behaviour. Sophia wouldn't put up with his bullshit."

He blinked. "Did you just say bullshit?"

She giggled and covered her mouth. "It seemed appropriate for the situation."

He kissed her throat. "And here I thought I was marrying a lady."

She smacked him lightly on the arm. "My bad language doesn't seem to bother you when we're in bed."

He nipped her neck. "I do like it when you beg me to fuck you."

She blushed and he slipped his hand inside of her nightshirt to cup one small breast. He kneaded it softly, rubbing his thumb over her nipple, as she stared into the fire.

"I think we should have Sophia come with us when we go into town to look for wedding stuff. Kaden will be going with us to pick up some clothes, and it would be a good opportunity for them to get to know each other."

He pinched her nipple lightly. "Can we talk about this later, little one? I'm trying to make love to you."

"Don't you mean fuck me?" she whispered before pressing her ass against him.

He grinned. "Aye, that's exactly what I mean."

CHAPTER 5

"Any trouble in the night?" Sophia asked.

Martine shook her head no and yawned as Leo stretched tiredly.

"It was quiet all night," Martine answered. "Gods, it's cold out." She shivered prettily.

"Thank you for helping us, Martine," Sophia said. "I know that you have a crush on my brother and -"

Martine held up her hand and gave her a dry look. "It was only a crush, Sophia. I'm happy for James, truly. Although I still don't understand what he sees in humans. Is it because he's half-human himself, do you think?"

Sophia shrugged. "I don't know."

She didn't believe it had anything to do with that. She was a full Lycan and she wanted a human desperately. And he wanted her. He could deny it, but she could smell it on him every time they were close to each other. It made it harder for her to control her own need for him.

She scoffed to herself. Kaden may want her, but he neither liked her nor trusted her. She would be smart to remember that. Sleeping together might lessen their need, but she wasn't going to degrade herself by sleeping with someone who hated her. Regardless of how long it had been since she had mated, or how much she wanted the human.

Leo stretched again, groaning as he placed his hand in the small of his back, before smiling at her. "Who are you on watch with this morning, Sophia?"

"Ian. He's not here yet?" Sophia asked.

"No." Leo looked in the direction of the house, obviously anxious to get to its warmth, and Sophia smiled at him.

"You and Martine go on. I'm sure Ian will be here soon."

"No." Martine shook her head. "We'll wait until he arrives. You know your father's rules as well as I do, Sophia. No one is out here alone."

Sophia opened her mouth to protest and then stiffened. She inhaled deeply and anxiety and anticipation washed over her.

Kaden stepped into the small clearing. "Good morning."

"Hello." Martine gave him a hesitant smile. "How are you today?"

"Fine, thanks." He nodded to her and Leo as he stopped next to Sophia.

"Why are you here?" Sophia asked.

"I'm on watch with you this morning."

"It's supposed to be Ian. Where is he?"

Before he could reply, Leo and Martine said their good-byes and disappeared in the direction of the house.

"Where is he?" she said again.

"He wasn't feeling well this morning."

"Not feeling well? What's wrong with him?" Sophia asked. "Did he go to see Mama?"

"He said it was just a headache. He didn't sleep well and wanted to rest a while longer. I'm sure he'll be fine by this afternoon."

They stood in awkward silence for a moment. Kaden glanced around the woods. "So, what do we do?"

Sophia shrugged. "We stand here and keep watch."

"Sounds like fun."

"If you don't want to do it, just say so. We've been doing it for weeks without you."

He scowled at her. "Only because you didn't tell me."

She didn't reply and he gave her a hard look. "What's your problem with me today, Lycan?"

"I don't have a problem with you," she said.

"Could have fooled me," he muttered.

She rolled her eyes. "Are all humans this sensitive or just you?"

"Are all Lycans this rude or just you?" he replied.

Sophia sighed harshly and stared into the trees. She *was* being rude, but at least it had stopped the smell of need coming from Kaden. She didn't think she could stand out here for an entire four hours, smelling how much he wanted her, without trying to have sex with him.

"WHY ARE YOU LOOKING AT ME LIKE THAT?"

Sophia jerked. It had been two hours, and she hadn't realized she was staring at Kaden until he had looked over at her with barely-concealed irritation.

"I wasn't looking at you." She scowled at the ground.

"You've been staring at me for ten minutes. Why?"

"Fine!" She glared at him. "I was just thinking that for siblings, you and Bree are oddly different looking."

"Nicholas doesn't look anything like you or your other siblings," he countered.

"Nicky is my half-brother."

He raised his eyebrows at her. "He's not Tristan's son?"

"No, he is not."

"Does he know?"

"Of course. Papa and Mama sat him down when he was ten and told him."

He gave her a questioning look and she scuffed at the frozen ground with her boot for a moment. "When I was two, my mother left my father and went to the city. She had grown up there, and I guess she hated living in the country. Papa went after us and spent weeks searching, but the city is large, and my mother had hidden us well. I did not see my father again until I was seven years old."

"Why did the leeches take your mother?"

"You remember me telling you that?" she said in surprise.

"Aye."

She stared into the trees. "I – I don't really know. Papa said that she made friends with the wrong people, and that eventually she was given to the leeches as payment for something those people did."

He frowned. "That's all you know? Tristan hasn't told you more?"

"I don't think he knows more. My mother had a cousin in the city and after she died, the cousin sent word to Tristan. He immediately left for the city and took both Nicholas and me home with him."

"Where was Nicholas' father?"

"I have no idea. My mother had many," she paused, "friends. I don't even know which of them might have been Nicky's father. If he was one of them, he certainly didn't stick around after the leeches killed my mother."

"I'm surprised that Tristan took in a child who was not his," Kaden said.

She smiled a little. "I like to believe that he took Nicky

because of me. That he knew how much I loved him. But the truth is - Nicky was a very sick baby. I think Papa believed that he wouldn't last much longer anyway."

"What was wrong with him?"

"I don't know. Papa was right though. He would have died if it had not been for Avery."

"Did she heal him?"

"Aye. On our way home, Papa stopped at a slave house to purchase some more house staff and a nanny for Nicky and me. Avery convinced him to take her sister Maya as our nanny."

"How did Avery end up with you?"

"I wanted her. I was fascinated by her hair, and I begged Papa to buy her as well." She smiled to herself. She could still remember the way Avery's hair had glowed in the light from the window. She studied her index finger for a moment.

"I had cut my finger and it wasn't healing. Avery healed it right there in the slave house, just by kissing the wound. That, and the combination of her red hair, made me determined to take her with us."

"So, your father bought himself a slave and ended up with a wife?" Kaden said.

She frowned at the disgust in his voice. "My father may have had slaves at one time, but he treated them all very well. I know it doesn't make it right, but he didn't realize how wrong it was to keep slaves."

"Why did he stop then?"

"Mama feels very passionate about all people having the same rights and freedom. She convinced Papa that he shouldn't have slaves."

"Do you ever miss your real mother?" he asked.

"No. I barely remember her."

She was lying. She remembered her mother very well.

Her mother's wild mood swings, her childish outbursts and her habit of slapping first and asking questions later, had made her impossible to forget.

"Are you all right?"

She glanced at Kaden. He was staring at her, and she had the oddest feeling that he knew she was lying. She cleared her throat and nodded. "I'm fine."

She walked a few feet away and leaned against a tree. She inhaled deeply, searching for any scent of Draken and his pack, and relaxed slightly when she smelled nothing. She wanted to tell him more. She wanted to tell him how afraid she had been all the time. How she had often pretended that her mother was not actually her mother, and that her real one would arrive to rescue her. She snorted softly. She had shared too much with Kaden already. It made no sense to share anything personal with the human. It wasn't what he was interested in.

"Bree is my half-sister." His low voice was directly behind her and she turned to face him, her eyes wide with surprise.

"She doesn't know." He stared into the trees and crossed his thick arms over his chest.

"Why not?" she asked.

He shrugged. "I didn't think there was any reason to tell her. My father died when I was five. My mother remarried and when I was ten, Bree was born. Two years later they were both dead, and it was just Bree and me."

"Gods," she muttered, "how on earth did you take care of a two-year-old? You were only a child yourself."

He shrugged. "I was big for my age and strong. I did a lot of manual labour in exchange for food and shelter for us both."

"Bree said your parents were robbed and murdered. Did they ever find the men who murdered them?"

He was giving her a strange look and she could see shame deep within his eyes.

"What?"

"I – I told Bree that story, but it isn't true," he said.

"What really happened?" She was being nosy, but she couldn't help herself.

He looked at his hands. "Bree's father fancied himself an adventurer. He was always coming up with wild schemes to make money. If he did actually manage to make some money, he would immediately disappear for months on his grand adventures. He would leave my mother with barely enough money for food. Even after she became pregnant with Bree, he still left. He cared about no one but himself. I started working when I was seven, odd jobs that people in the village would give me out of pity, just so we had enough money to buy food."

He snorted in disgust. "It didn't matter how many times he left, or how many times we nearly starved while he was gone, my mother always welcomed him home with open arms. She was so weak."

"How did they die?" she asked.

"When I was twelve, Arden got it into his head that he needed to see one of the old cities."

She gave him a look of horror. "That's suicide."

"Aye. He had met a man in our village - a stranger who was just travelling through. He convinced Arden that he had gone to the city and survived. He told Arden that he had a magic pill that protected him from the sickness. The fool didn't even ask for proof, just blindly believed him, and eagerly bought the pills."

He rubbed his hand angrily through his hair. "He started

planning for the trip and I was happy. I knew that this time his foolishness would cost him his life, and I wanted him to die. Only, he decided this time that my mother should go with him. Eager to please him, she agreed."

"Oh, Kaden," she whispered.

"They left for the city within the week. Two months later they were back. They had made it to the old city, had gone deep within it, and both had the sickness."

He lapsed into silence and Sophia suddenly hated that she was forcing him to tell her what happened. She touched his arm. "Kaden? You don't have to tell me anything else."

WHEN SOPHIA TOUCHED HIS ARM, HE STARED DOWN AT HER blankly.

"Kaden?" she said. "You don't have to tell me anything else."

"I want to," he said.

He took her hand and linked their fingers together, needing some type of connection. "It was late at night when they arrived home. Bree was sleeping, thank the gods. My – my mother was bleeding from every orifice in her body, and Arden wasn't much better. They had lost their teeth and their hair. Shortly after they arrived home, my mother lapsed into a slumber that I couldn't wake her from, and Arden was babbling incoherently about the old city. He had a small bag filled with jewels and other items they had picked up. I sold those jewels and made enough money from them to keep our home, and food in our bellies, for the first year after they died."

She stroked his hand with her thumb and made a soft sound of comfort. He tightened his grip on her hand and closed his eyes. "They had to travel through the village to get home and people had seen them. They showed up at our home the next morning to drive my mother and Arden to the outskirts. They were too late though. Both had died in the night. Once the money ran out from the jewels, we lost our home and Bree and I were forced to leave the village so that I could find work."

"Was there no one in the village who was willing to take you in?" She was horrified that so many people had turned their backs on two children.

"The people in the village and surrounding area were barely surviving themselves. The whole village was dying out, people were just giving up and moving on, and I couldn't even find enough odd jobs to keep Bree and me fed."

"Why didn't you tell Bree the truth?" She squeezed his hand gently.

"Bree does not remember our mother, but she adored her father. She was only a toddler when he died, but she says she remembers him very well. I'm not surprised. He was a selfish man, but he could be very charming and loving when he wanted to be. He treated Bree more like a pet than a daughter, but she doesn't remember that."

He studied their linked hands. "Thank the gods. Anyway, I didn't want Bree to know that her father had essentially murdered her mother, so I made up the story about them being killed by thieves."

He gave her a pleading look. "I know I shouldn't have lied, but I couldn't stand the idea of her being more upset by their deaths than she already was. Was that so wrong of me?"

She shook her head immediately. "No."

He looked down at the ground and she reached up and cupped his face, stroking her thumb across his cheek. "You

49

did what you thought was best, Kaden. You took care of your sister, you protected her and -"

"I got her captured by Lycans and watched her starve." He could hear the helpless anger in his voice.

"You took her beatings. You kept her from being abused by the Lycans," she pointed out.

"And then they decided to use her in their hunt, and I was helpless to stop them." He shuddered as he remembered the fear and panic that had flared in him when they had brought Bree out the morning of the hunt. He had gone crazy when they wouldn't agree to let him take her place. He had attacked the nearest Lycan and ripped its throat out with his bare hands before they could stop him.

Shame burned through him at the memory of Bree on her knees, begging Draken to spare his life. They had chained him to the wall in the slave's quarters and left him there for three days. On the morning of the fourth day, they had finally released him. Certain that Bree had died at the hands of the Lycans, he had been shocked when the pole they placed the head of the hunted on, was empty. His relief that Bree had survived was so great, he hadn't even felt the daily beatings Draken had bestowed upon him in retaliation for his sister's escape.

Sophia was still stroking his face and he gave her a haunted look. "I failed her. If it had not been for your brother, Bree would be dead."

"You can't think that way, Kaden. You did everything you could to protect her, and to keep her alive. She would have died as a child if it had not been for you. It's amazing that both of you survived. You were only a child yourself, remember."

He didn't reply and she made him look at her. "It's not your fault, Kaden."

He shocked her by hugging her. He buried his face in her throat and wrapped his arms around her waist as a shudder went through his large body.

SHE HADN'T EXPECTED KADEN TO HUG HER BUT THE MOMENT he did, his big body trembling against hers, she returned his hug. She ran her hands over his back and crooned soft, meaningless words of comfort in his ear.

She threaded her hand in his hair and tugged gently until he was looking at her. She rubbed her hand across his face, feeling the rough stubble under her palm. He turned his face and kissed the middle of her palm. A spasm of pleasure gripped her belly, and she bit at her bottom lip before suddenly reaching up and placing a soft kiss on his mouth.

"It's not your fault," she repeated before kissing him again. He groaned and returned her kiss. She opened her mouth and their tongues touched delicately, before he stroked his tongue against hers in a rough movement that made a shiver run down her back.

She moaned, her hands gripping his neck, as he explored her mouth hungrily. His large hand wrapped in her braid and he tugged her head back so he could nip at her throat. He licked the hollow of her throat, his tongue stroking and exploring the soft skin, as his hand cupped her breast through her jacket. He made a muttered curse and pulled impatiently at the buttons of her coat.

Sophia stared up at the sky. Glimpses of it could be seen through the thick canopy of trees, and she made another soft moan of need when his hand slipped inside her jacket to knead at her breast through her shirt.

She took a deep breath, smelling the sweet scent of pine

trees and Kaden's desire for her. Her eyes widened and she pushed at his broad body until he released her. She stumbled away, leaning against a tree and breathing heavily. Gods, they were supposed to be out here standing watch. She took a deep breath, searching for any scent that didn't belong, and breathed a sigh of relief when there was nothing. She had put her entire family in danger because she had an itch that needed scratched.

"Sophia?" Kaden was moving up behind her and she staggered away before he could touch her.

"Don't," she gasped out. "We shouldn't be doing this."

The smell of his need dropped away immediately, and she turned to look at him. He was staring at her with hurt and confusion and she sighed. "Don't look at me like that, Kaden. I only meant that we're supposed to be -"

He held his hand up. "It's fine, Lycan. You're right – this is wrong. I don't mate with animals."

Anger and hurt rushed through her and she lashed out at him. "Probably a smart idea, human. You wouldn't be able to handle me."

She turned away and stormed deeper into the woods before he could spit out a retort. She stared angrily into the trees. She was an idiot for believing that Kaden would ever think of her as anything more than an animal.

CHAPTER 6

"Sophia?"

"Hello, Bree." Sophia smiled at her before continuing to rub the oil into her boots.

Bree sat down next to her on her bed. "Are you all right?"

"Just fine. Why?" Sophia gave her a puzzled look.

"You've been even quieter than usual lately."

Sophia shrugged. "There's nothing wrong."

"Did something happen between you and my brother?"

Sophia gave her a careful look. "Why would you ask that?"

"James said that yesterday when he and Jeffrey took over on watch, both you and Kaden seemed upset."

"Nothing happened." Sophia poured more oil on the side of her boot and studiously rubbed it into the soft leather.

"I know my brother likes you."

"He doesn't," Sophia said.

"He does," Bree insisted. "And I know you like him too."

"Bree, please. I don't want to talk about this."

"It helps to talk about it. You made me talk to you when I was upset about James."

"It's not the same," Sophia muttered.

Bree laughed. "It's exactly the same, Sophia. What you and Kaden are going through is what James and I went through. I fought my feelings for James because I was afraid of the Lycans, and afraid of what Kaden would think of me. Kaden is fighting his feelings for you because -"

"Because he hates the Lycans," Sophia said. "You only feared us. Kaden hates us. Don't try and deny it."

"I think he's starting to realize that not all Lycans are like Draken."

"He won't stay, Bree," Sophia said abruptly. "I know you want him to, but he won't. He thinks we're animals and after what Draken did to him, I don't blame him. Honestly, I'm not sure he should stay with us. Sooner or later, we'll do or say something that will prove to him he's right. He should leave before that happens. If he doesn't, your relationship with him will suffer. Do you really want that?"

Bree didn't reply and Sophia sighed. She had spoken too honestly, and she obviously had hurt the young woman's feelings. "Bree, I'm -"

She was surprised when Bree hugged her hard. "You're wrong about my brother, Sophia. He'll learn to love you the way I learned to love James."

Sophia blinked at her. "Bree, we aren't -"

"We're leaving tomorrow for town and I want you to come with us. We'll be doing some dress shopping for the wedding," Bree said.

"I don't know. I'm not -"

"You have to go, Sophia. You're my maid of honour." Bree smiled and squeezed her arm.

"Are you sure you want me to stand up for you, Bree? I know you and Dani have grown close, and I'm sure she would love to be your maid of honour."

Bree shook her head. "No, I want it to be you. Dani is happy to be a bridesmaid." She hesitated. "Unless you don't want to?"

"Of course ,I do," Sophia said. "I just - I was surprised when you asked me."

Bree stared at her solemnly. "You saved my life, Sophia. You went willingly to Draken, knowing what could happen, just to save me. I will never forget that."

Sophia gave her an impulsive hug. "I would do anything for James and for you. I'm glad you asked me to stand up with you, but I'm not wearing pink."

Bree laughed. "How do you feel about blue?"

"I like blue." Sophia grinned at her.

"Good. Make sure you pack an overnight bag. We're going to stay the night at the town. We're taking the wagon and it's such a long ride, James thought it would be best if we stayed the night. Better safe than sorry, right?"

Sophia nodded. Neither of them needed to say it, but they were both thinking of Draken and his pack. They were still out there and underneath the excitement over the wedding, there was a growing tension among all of them. Not knowing when or how Draken would attack, was putting them all on edge.

"Are you going to tell me what's wrong, or just keep glaring at your food?" Ian asked.

"There's nothing wrong," Kaden replied. He hadn't wanted to join the others for dinner tonight, and Ian had brought their dinners to the barn without commenting.

Ian leaned over and scraped the carrots from his plate on to Kaden's. "Seems like there's something wrong."

Kaden pushed at the pile of carrots. "I'm just tired."

"Sophia seems to be upset as well," Ian said.

Kaden glared at him. "Drop it, old man."

Ian stared steadily at him. "You'll feel better if you talk about it."

"What's there to talk about? I find Sophia attractive and I'm disgusted with myself because of it."

"Why?"

"Why?" Kaden gave him an impatient look. "Because, Ian, she's a Lycan."

"Aye, I'm aware of that," Ian replied in amusement.

Kaden put his plate down. "I know you've worked for the Lycans a long time, but they can't be trusted."

Ian shook his head. "You're wrong, Kaden."

"I'm not," Kaden insisted. "Lycans aren't like you and me. They're – they're animals."

Ian gave him a sharp look. "No, they're not. They have emotions and feelings just like humans and they love as deeply, if not deeper, than humans."

Kaden didn't reply and Ian sighed harshly. "Listen closely to me, Kaden. I like you. You're a good man and I consider you a friend. Do you think of me as a friend?"

Kaden nodded. "Aye, I do."

"Good. I hope that you'll take what I'm about to say to heart. It is not just the Lycans you believe untrustworthy. It's everyone."

Kaden stared at him in shock. "That's not true."

"Is it not? Name one other person, besides Bree, that you have trusted."

Kaden opened his mouth and hesitated as Ian gave him a knowing look.

"Your life has not been easy, Kaden. I don't blame you for not trusting, but I promise you that these people, these Lycans that Bree has learned to love and respect and trust, are worth getting to know. You have a wall around yourself and I understand why you do, but you're hurting no one but yourself by building it higher."

Ian sighed. "Bree has found her mate. She loves him and she trusts him with her life, and it upsets you. Your entire purpose since you were a small boy, was keeping her alive. Not having to do that anymore has left you floundering and unsure of yourself. You're allowing your distrust for Lycans, for people in general, to keep you from seeing the truth. Sophia and the others are worth getting to know. You promised Bree that you would try."

"I am trying," Kaden replied.

"Try harder." Ian clapped him lightly on the back and left him to his supper.

"Please, Mama. Please, please, please." Leta gave her mother a pleading look and Avery smiled at her.

"They're going overnight, Leta. You've never been away from your father and me overnight before."

"I'm ten now, Mama. It's old enough."

"Aye, I know, my love." She kissed Leta's forehead as the little girl stared anxiously at her. Avery glanced at Tristan who gave her a small nod.

Avery smiled at Leta. "You'll have to ask your brothers. If they -"

"I already asked Nicky and he said it was fine with him. Please, Mama, I want to pick out my own dress for the wedding."

"Leta, you're Bree's flower girl. I imagine she'll have a specific dress she'll want you to wear."

"She already told me I could wear whatever I wanted as long as it had blue in it. Oh, please, Mama – I haven't been to town in forever." The little girl sighed dramatically.

"You need to listen to your brothers and your sister and obey them without question. Do you understand me?"

Leta nodded eagerly as Avery stroked her hair back from her face. "And you cannot wander away at all. You must have your brothers or your sister with you at all times."

The little girl nodded again, and Avery held her chin firmly in her hand. "I'm serious, Leta. If you disobey them or wander away, it will be a very long time before you're allowed to leave my sight again."

"I understand, Mama." Leta said solemnly.

"Good. Now, go quickly to your room and pack a bag. They're leaving soon."

"It's already packed!" Leta said brightly. "I packed last night!"

"Of course, you did." Tristan laughed and swung the little girl into his arms. "Run and get your bag, my sweet." He kissed her soundly on the cheek before rubbing his scruff against face.

She giggled and pushed him away. "Stop it, Papa!"

He set her down gently and she skipped out of the room as Avery sighed. Tristan put his arm around her and kissed her on the mouth. "She'll be just fine."

"I know." Avery ran her fingers over his mouth. "You're looking very handsome today, my lord."

He grinned and kissed her again. This time he probed at her lips with his tongue and she opened her mouth so he could explore it lightly.

"I'm not on watch until this afternoon," he whispered against her mouth.

"Is that right, m'lord?" She slid her hand down his back and squeezed his ass. "What did you have in mind?"

"You know exactly what I have in mind, girl," he growled playfully.

She smiled and ran her hand through the grey that was just starting to show in the hair at his temples. "Again, my lord? You had me up half the night."

"Aye, I remember. Are you tired?"

She kissed him on the mouth in reply, and he pulled her against his hard body. He was reaching for her breast when Nicholas and Sophia walked into the room.

"Gross." Nicky rolled his eyes as Maya and Dani joined them.

"I'm so excited!" Dani grinned at the others. "I can't wait to try on dresses and look at decorations and -"

"Dani, remember that it's Bree's wedding," Maya chided.

"I know, Mama," Dani replied. "But it doesn't mean I can't make suggestions."

Avery laughed and led the others towards the door. "I'm sure Bree will be very happy for your help, Dani."

———

"KADEN? ARE YOU READY TO GO?" BREE CLIMBED THE ladder to the hayloft and peered into the room.

"Aye. Just packing my things." He grinned at her and showed her the empty bag.

She laughed. "It'll be nice to get your own clothes, will it not? James' clothes fit you fairly well, all things considered, but your pants are a little short."

He looked down at his legs. "You don't like the look of my ankles?"

Bree laughed again as she climbed down the ladder. "Hurry, Kaden. We're leaving in ten minutes."

He followed her down the ladder and stared at Bandit's empty stall. "Where is Bandit?"

"I believe Ian has already saddled him for you and brought him into the yard." Bree opened the barn door as Kaden joined her.

He stiffened when he saw Sophia swinging into the saddle of her own horse. "Why is she going with us?"

Bree smiled. "Because Kaden, she is my maid of honour. I need her with me."

"I'm not going." Kaden turned and headed toward the hayloft. Bree grunted in frustration and ran after him. She grabbed his arm and swung him around. He blinked in surprise at the look of anger on her face.

"Stop being such a baby, Kaden!" she huffed at him.

"Bree, what -"

"You cannot avoid Sophia forever. I don't know what happened between you two but if she's willing to put it aside for the wedding, then my own brother should be able to do the same."

He stared at her for a moment and then grinned before tugging on her hair. "What has happened to my timid baby sister?"

She slapped at his hand. "Nothing's happened to me. I am just tired of you being a pain in my ass."

He laughed out loud and she shrieked with surprise when he suddenly lifted her and dumped her over his shoulder. "I never thought I would say this, Bree, but living with these Lycans might actually be good for you. It's nice to see you with a bit of spirit."

She bit him on the back, and he flinched before setting

her back on her feet. He rubbed at his back. "So, the Lycans have taught you to bite?"

She stuck her tongue out at him. "Let's go, the others are waiting."

He followed her towards the door, and she gave him a warning look. "I want you to play nice, Kaden."

He stared at the way Sophia's dark hair gleamed in the light. Playing nice with Sophia was something he dreamed about on a nightly basis.

CHAPTER 7

"Bree, are you sure you don't want to get married in a church instead of at the house? There's a lovely one in the town we're going to. We could decorate it so beautifully, and there's a small building next to it that we could have a dinner in and dancing." Dani smiled eagerly at her.

"No, I want to be married at home," Bree said.

"Can Lycans even go into a church? Don't they just, I don't know, burst into flame?" Kaden raised his eyebrows.

"It's leeches who burst into flames if they go into a church," Leta said solemnly.

"No, they don't, Leta. That's just an old ancients' tale. Leeches can go into a church as easily as Lycans and humans," Sophia said. "And Kaden is only teasing – he knows that Lycans can go into churches."

Leta gave him a suspicious look and Kaden winked at her. He was riding Bandit, and Leta was sitting in the back of the wagon with Dani. He watched as James, sitting in the front of the wagon next to Bree, handed her the reins.

She took them carefully and he kissed her forehead. "Just like I taught you, little one."

She nodded, and he stretched and glanced at Nicholas who was riding his own horse in front of them. "There was that time in Windora when Nicky and that girl -what was her name again, brother?

"Minta," Nicholas said.

"Right, Minta. The people at that church certainly thought they might burst into flames. Of course, that had nothing to do with them being Lycans and more because Nicky was -"

"Hold your tongue, brother," Nicky said warningly, "unless you want Bree to know what you were doing in the church that day?"

James flushed and Bree raised her eyebrow at him. "Care to share, my lord?"

He shook his head innocently. "Honestly, my love, I can't remember a single thing that happened to me before I met you."

She laughed and handed the reins back to him. "Wise answer."

"Bree." Dani tugged on her arm impatiently. "What about flowers? Have you thought about the kind you would like?"

Bree frowned. "There are no flowers this time of the year, Dani. It is too cold."

Dani smiled. "I keep forgetting that you haven't been to town before."

"I have," Bree replied. "I went with Sophia and Tristan and Mama."

Sophia smiled at her. "You did, but we did not take you to very many of the shops in the town. You didn't see the flower shop."

"Flower shop?" Bree frowned.

"It's a store that sells fresh flowers all year around," Dani explained.

"Really?" Bree blinked in surprise and Kaden's stomach twisted with guilt.

Growing up, he had purposely kept Bree away from towns and cities as much as he could. He had been terrified that someone would realize how young he was and try to take Bree away from him. Because of that, Bree was sadly naïve, and his stomach twisted again.

"Aye, really," Dani replied. "Of course, they don't have nearly the selection that the ancients used to have. Did you know that before the Great War, there were hundreds of thousands of different flowers?"

"That can't be true." Bree stared wide-eyed at her.

"It is," Dani said. "The poison the ancients used in the Great War killed many of the flowers and plants and animals. Only a small percentage of them survived."

"Why didn't they just grow them again?" Bree wondered.

"They couldn't. It was many years before humans and Lycans could even begin to grow their own food again. The races were on the brink of extinction before the earth and the air finally healed itself. Why, I bet even a hundred years ago we could not have grown food in the land like we do now." Dani said. "We are too close to the old city."

"Too close to the old city?" Bree frowned. "It has to be at least a month's ride to the old city." She looked to James for confirmation and he nodded.

"Aye, I know," Dani answered. "But the poison spread far."

"How do you know all of this?" Bree asked.

"Mama taught me. She taught all of us," Dani said.

"How did a slave learn it?" Kaden asked.

Dani smiled at him. "Mama and Aunt Avery weren't always slaves. As children, they were very wealthy. My grandfather was James Hendrin."

"What?" Bree stared flabbergasted at her. Even she knew the name of the man who brought light back to the world.

"It's true!" Dani said gleefully. "Mama used to have a ton of money. She said they used to go to parties nearly every month, and that their house had a room in it that was just for books. My grandfather taught them lots of stuff about the ancients."

"James?" Bree looked at the Red and he nodded.

"Aye, it is true. I am named for my grandfather."

"Mama says that Grandpa was obsessed with the ancients. He wanted to learn everything about them so that we didn't repeat their mistakes," Dani said.

"How did Mama and Maya become slaves?" Bree asked.

"Their father died, and their mother sold them into slavery," Sophia said.

Bree gave her a horrified look. "That's terrible. Why would she do that?"

"She needed money for drugs," Sophia said.

"That's awful," Bree whispered.

"Aye, it is." Dani was quiet for a moment. "But Mama always says that if her mother had not sold her to the slave house, she would never have met Dad. She says the gods knew what they were doing when they brought Uncle Tristan to the slave house."

The group was quiet for a while, the only sounds were the creaking of the wagon and the soft snorts of the horses, before Dani smiled at Bree again. "So, what type of flowers do you want, Bree?"

Bree shrugged. "I don't know. It seems silly to buy flowers when you could just pick them in the fields for free."

"It's too cold," Dani reminded her.

"Aye, but do we really need flowers? It's a waste of money," Bree said.

"You don't need to worry about money anymore, Bree," Dani said airily. "James is rich, remember?"

Kaden could see Bree squirming uncomfortably on the wagon seat. He had an idea that although Bree knew that James was wealthy, she hadn't really thought about what it would mean when she married him.

James squeezed her hand reassuringly. "If you do not want to spend money on flowers, then we won't. You can put the money toward your dress instead."

"I don't want an expensive dress," Bree said. "I don't want to spend a lot of money on the wedding."

James smiled at her. "You can have whatever kind of wedding you want, little one."

Bree kissed his cheek and Dani sighed loudly from the back of the wagon. "Well, I want lots of flowers and a big party and a gorgeous dress for my wedding."

"You don't even have a boyfriend," Leta pointed out.

"Not yet." Dani smiled at Kaden. He glanced quickly at Sophia. She was staring impassively at the road ahead, but he thought he saw a muscle twitch in her jaw.

"WELL, I HAVE GOOD NEWS AND BAD NEWS." NICKY STEPPED out of the large white building and walked down the steps towards the others.

"The good news – they have rooms available for the night. The bad news – there's only three. We'll have to share."

"I want to stay with Sophia," Leta said. She took her sister's hand and Sophia squeezed it before smiling at her.

"That's fine," Dani said cheerfully. "James and Bree can

take one room, Sophia, Nicky and Leta can share another, and Kaden and I will share the third."

"No," Nicky, James and Sophia all spoke at once.

Dani gave them a look of frustration. "You're not the boss of me."

"Aye but before we left, your father asked me to watch out for you," Nicky said. "And if you think I'm going to let you share a room alone with the human, you're crazy."

"Shut up, Nicky," Dani said furiously. "You're embarrassing me."

"Nicky's right," Sophia said. "Your father would not want you to share a room with Kaden, and you know that."

"My father isn't here." Dani gave her a look that clearly told her she wanted Sophia to stay out of the conversation.

Kaden cleared his throat. "I don't think it's a good idea, Dani."

She gave him a look dripping with hurt and crossed her arms over her chest. "Fine, whatever."

"Dani, you can stay with Sophia and Leta in their room, and Nicky and Kaden can share the other," James said.

"No," Kaden snapped.

"Like hell I will," Nicholas growled.

Dani raised her eyebrows. "I'm looking like the better option now. Aren't I, Kaden?"

He flushed and Bree rolled her eyes. "Oh, for the gods sake! Nicky and Dani will share the second room, and Kaden, Sophia and Leta can share the third."

She took James' hand in her small one and before anyone could argue, said, "Now, are we going shopping or not?"

She glanced at the darkening sky above her. "I'd like to get some shopping done before it's time for dinner."

"Kaden!" He turned at the sound of Dani's voice and waited patiently for her, as well as Sophia and Leta, to catch up to him.

"Did you find some clothes before the store closed?" Dani asked.

"Aye. I was just looking for Bree," Kaden said.

"James took her into that store over there." Dani pointed across the road and then slipped her hand into the crook of his arm. "They won't be too much longer. They told us to go ahead to the restaurant and they would meet us there."

She tugged on his arm and he followed her as Sophia and Leta trailed behind them. "Have you ever been in a restaurant before, Kaden?" Dani asked.

"No," he admitted.

"Then this will be a treat for you." Dani smiled at him as she stopped in front of a small building with weathered and greying boards.

"Do you think they'll have the peach pie?" Leta asked Sophia as they stepped into the building.

Sophia shook her head. "Probably not. The season for peaches has passed. They might have apple though."

"I don't like apple pie," Leta sighed.

"Where's Nicholas?" Kaden asked as Dani led them to a long wooden table. When they had split up after the flower shop, Nicholas had been with Dani, Sophia and Leta.

Dani sat on the wooden bench that ran along the wall behind the table and urged Kaden to sit beside her. "He had a few things to pick up for Uncle Tristan. He said he would join us for dinner."

"I'm starving," Leta moaned.

"It won't be much longer now." Sophia was sitting across from him and Kaden stared briefly at her. She looked tired,

69

but she smiled at Leta and stroked her hair affectionately as a man approached their table.

"Good evening."

"Hello." Dani smiled at the man as he handed each of them a single piece of paper.

"We'll need three more menus please," Sophia said.

The man nodded and left the menus stacked neatly on the table. After a few minutes he returned. He was balancing a round wooden tray, filled with glasses of water, on his muscular forearm. He set a glass down in front of each of them and smiled at Leta. "Are you ready to order or will you be waiting for the rest of your group?"

"We'll wait," Sophia replied.

Leta moaned and grabbed at her stomach. "I'm so hungry, Sophia. Do we have to wait?"

"Aye," Sophia said. "Drink some water."

Dani looked up from the piece of paper she was reading. "What are you going to have to eat, Kaden?"

Kaden looked down at the paper in front of him. It was filled with meaningless scribbles and he could feel sweat breaking out on his forehead. He had never learned to read or write, but he was too embarrassed to admit it in front of Sophia.

"Kaden?" Dani prompted.

SOPHIA STARED CURIOUSLY AT KADEN. HIS FACE WAS RED, and he looked both embarrassed and angry as he scanned the menu in front of him. When Dani patted him gently on the arm, he jumped a little and gave her a weirdly nervous look. "I'm not sure yet."

He glanced quickly at Sophia and she was puzzled by the

look of shame in his eyes. What was going on with him? Why was he so –

Understanding washed over her and she quickly looked down at the menu.

"Leta, what do you feel like having?" she asked loudly. "They have chicken on the menu today with potatoes and turnips. The roasted duck might be good. Or do you feel like having bear? We haven't had bear in forever, and it comes with biscuits and gravy."

Leta grinned happily. "I'm going to have bear. I wish when we went hunting, we'd go after a bear. It's always boring old deer."

Sophia looked up in time to see Kaden giving her a look of gratitude mixed with embarrassment.

"I'm going to have the chicken," Dani said. She smiled at Kaden. "Have you decided yet?"

"Aye. I think I'll have the bear as well. I've never had it before."

"Never had it before?" Leta forgot about her dislike for him and leaned closer. "Not even once?"

He shook his head. "Not even once. But I have eaten rat."

Leta's eyes widened. "You haven't!"

"I have." He grinned at her. "If you want, I'll catch one in the barn so you can try it."

Leta shuddered. "Gross! No way! I'm never trying rat."

He laughed and took a drink of water as Leta hesitated and then said, "What do they taste like?"

He leaned across the table until his large head was only inches from hers. "They taste like..." Leta stared mesmerized into his eyes as he paused dramatically.

"Chicken." He tapped her gently on the nose, and she squealed in surprise and nearly fell off her chair. She stared wide-eyed at him, and then burst into loud peals of laughter.

There was an older couple sitting a few tables away, and they frowned in disapproval at Leta's loud laughter. Sophia squeezed Leta's hand lightly. "Hush, Leta."

She giggled and nodded before looking at Kaden. "Why did you eat rat?"

He wiggled his eyebrows at her. "Because the bear I was chasing didn't feel like being dinner that night."

LETA'S LAUGHTER MADE HIM GRIN. BUT THE GRIN FELL FROM his face when he caught a glimpse of Sophia's face. She wasn't smiling. In fact, she was giving him a clear look of pity that both unsettled him and made him a little ashamed. He didn't want her pity. The Lycan had no idea what real hardship was, and he was suddenly furious with her. So what if he had eaten rat to survive. He had done worse things to keep both himself and Bree alive. Their different backgrounds were yet another reason for him to ignore his attraction to her.

He knew he was overreacting, knew it was his own sense of shame at the things that he had done to survive that was making him so angry, but it didn't stop him from glaring at her. "What?"

"Nothing," she said.

"Do you have something you want to say?" He clenched his hands into fists under the table as she gave him a confused look.

"No. Kaden, what -"

She was interrupted by the arrival of James, Bree and Nicholas. Nicholas sat down beside her and ruffled her hair affectionately. She smacked his hand away and rolled her eyes at him as Bree, nearly glowing with happiness, slid onto the bench beside her brother. Dani leaned over Kaden, letting her small hand rest on his thigh under the table.

"Why so happy?" she asked Bree.

Bree smiled at James and then held her left hand out. Kaden winced when Dani squealed shrilly into his ear before grabbing Bree's hand. "It's beautiful!"

Sophia leaned forward and admired the ring on Bree's finger. It was a simple gold band with a large blue stone embedded into it. The stone shone in the dim light of the restaurant and Sophia traced it gently with the tip of her finger. "It's lovely, Bree."

"Thanks, Sophia. James actually picked it out." She flushed a little. "I had my eye on a smaller one, but James liked this one best."

"It matches your eyes." James kissed her gently on the forehead as Nicky made a gagging noise.

"You're like a lovesick puppy, James," he teased. "Next you'll be spouting poetry and writing love songs for Bree."

Bree snickered loudly and Sophia laughed as James reached across the table and punched Nicholas in the arm.

Kaden's faint smile disappeared when Dani placed her hand on his thigh. She rubbed slowly and he glanced at Sophia. She was staring at Dani, a look of jealousy spreading across her face. Feeling oddly guilty, he shifted closer to Bree, dropped his hand under the table and tugged Dani's hand from his leg.

She gave him a disappointed look, but Sophia's look was pure triumph when Dani placed both of her hands on the table and stared at her menu.

"Can we order now?" Leta asked. "I'm starving."

Nicholas reached around Sophia and tugged on Leta's hair. "Let me guess – you're having the bear."

CHAPTER 8

Nicholas stood on the sidewalk and breathed deeply of the cold air. "Come on, baby brother, just one drink. The night is young and I'm handsome. There's bound to be a human female who is curious about the size of a Lycan's -"

"Nicky!" Sophia said.

She stared down at Leta who was looking at Nicky curiously. "The size of a Lycan's what, Nicky?"

"Boots, Leta," Sophia replied.

Leta shook her head. "Who cares about the size of a Lycan's boots? Human females are stupid."

She suddenly gave Bree and Dani a horrified look. "Except for you guys."

Bree and Dani laughed as Sophia glared at Nicky.

"Sorry." He grinned and winked at her. "I forgot Leta was with us." He turned back to James. "Well, brother?"

James gave Bree a quick look. She smiled at him and squeezed his waist, and he dropped a kiss on the top of her head. "Fine, Nicky – one drink." He glanced at Kaden. "Would you like to join us?"

Kaden hesitated. Given the choice between going back to

the hotel room he was sharing with Sophia or going drinking with two Lycan brothers who didn't particularly like him, he would choose the safer option. "Aye, I'll go."

He groaned inwardly when Dani latched onto his arm. "I'll go as well!"

Kaden gave his sister a sideways look of desperation and Bree stepped forward. "Really, Dani? I was hoping you would come back to the hotel with me. There's still so much planning to do for the wedding, and I really need both you and Sophia with me to go over the details."

Dani hesitated, obviously torn between her desire to go with him and her desire to help with the wedding.

"Please?" Bree gave her a pleading look and Dani relented.

"Of course." She linked arms with Bree. "It'll be fun. Are you sure you really want blue and cream? Because I was thinking that pink would go so nicely with our blonde hair and -"

Leta took Bree's other hand. "I don't like pink."

Bree smiled down at the young girl as Dani, still chattering, led the two of them toward the hotel.

SOPHIA LAGGED BEHIND THE OTHERS AS THEY PASSED THE darkened store fronts.

Kaden was still acting cool toward her and it was driving her crazy. She cursed herself. What did she care if he didn't like her? A few kisses and grope sessions didn't mean anything. She sighed with annoyance. How many times would she have to remind herself why it was not a good idea to lust after him? The back and forth was driving her mad.

"Spare a few coins for an old woman, young miss?"

Sophia looked down at the dirty, skinny woman huddled against one of the buildings. Her head was bowed against the cold, and she could see the woman's scalp through her thinning, white hair. She stopped and reached into her pocket.

"Oh, you're a kind one then to help an old starving woman." The old woman smiled at her, revealing blackened gums, as Sophia crouched down and pressed the coins into her palm. As the woman made the coins disappear within her jacket, Sophia took a better look at her. She looked oddly familiar to her and she leaned forward, staring closely at her. She inhaled sharply as the woman's eyes, milky with age, widened with nervousness.

"Mrs. Lanning?"

The woman jerked all over and drew her tattered coat closer around her. "Who's asking? Who are you?"

"My – my name is Sophia. Do you remember me?"

The woman stared suspiciously at her for a moment before breaking into a wide toothless grin. "Aye, little Sophia. Look how big you are now."

"It's good to see you again." Sophia tried to keep the horror from her face as Mrs. Lanning reached out with a trembling hand and latched on to her shirt.

"You're the lord Williams little girl, are you not?"

"Aye, I am." Sophia held her breath as the smell of urine washed over her.

"I always enjoyed working for the lord Williams. He treated us well, he did." The woman suddenly cackled loudly, and Sophia winced when it turned into a coughing fit. Spittle flew from her toothless mouth and she spat onto the ground before peering up at Sophia.

"Until he married the witch, that is." Her fingers tightened on Sophia's shirt. "Tell me, child, is he still married to that dirty Red whore?"

"Don't speak about my mother that way," Sophia said.

Mrs. Lanning laughed nastily. "Mother? She's not your mother. She's a witch who seduced your father and drove me from my home."

"It was not your home," Sophia said sharply. "You worked for my father, nothing more."

"Aye, I worked for him for nearly twelve years. Served him faithfully I did, and how did he repay me? By letting his Red witch whore drive me out."

"You chose to leave, Mrs. Lanning," Sophia replied. "My father and my mother both tried to convince you to stay."

Mrs. Lanning shook her head. "She's a witch. She used her spells to enchant your father and weaken his mind."

The old woman leaned closer still. Her face was only inches from Sophia's, and Sophia stared into her eyes with a combination of fascination and disgust. "I tried to warn him, child. I tried to tell him that only a witch could have her kind of power."

She stroked Sophia's face with one shaking, grimy finger. "I had to leave. I've seen her kind before. I have seen the terrible things they are capable of. I can see she's fooled you as well. Your eyes betray your love for her. Don't you under- stand, child? It's not love but magic. She's tricked you into believing she's normal. But don't you worry. Mrs. Lanning is here to show you the truth."

"What do you mean?" Sophia said.

"There is still hope for those who have fallen under a witch's spell. It requires only a small sacrifice."

Too late Sophia saw the small dagger in Mrs. Lanning's hand. She grunted in shock when the blade sliced across her cheek. She touched her face and stared at the blood on her fingers.

"Do you see the light now, sweet Sophia? Has the blood

I've drawn from you opened your eyes to the Red witch's terrible power?"

Sophia inhaled deeply. How had she missed the scent of the woman's insanity? "You've lost your mind."

The old woman frowned and, with surprising strength, pulled Sophia back down when she tried to stand. "It's been too long," she said in a soft, sing-song voice. "You cannot be saved. I will release you from her spell and bring you to the light, sweet Sophia."

She raised the dagger over her head and thrust it at Sophia. Sophia grabbed the old woman's wrist and twisted sharply as a pair of hands grabbed her under her arms. She was yanked out of Mrs. Lanning's grip and onto her feet.

Mrs. Lanning gave a harsh cry of pain, the knife dropping to the ground at her feet, as Sophia inhaled the familiar scent of Kaden. She peered at him over her shoulder. "I'm fine."

He scowled and turned her around as the others gathered around them. "You're bleeding." He circled one arm around her waist, tipped her chin up with one finger, and examined her cheek.

"It's only a scratch."

"It's more than a scratch." He touched the cut and then showed her the blood on the tip of his finger. She could feel liquid sliding down her cheek as Nicholas grabbed her arm and pulled her away from Kaden.

"Sophia? What happened?" He stared in alarm at the blood on her face. "James! Sophia is hurt."

"I'm fine. It'll heal by morning. James, I don't need -"

Ignoring her, James placed his hand on her cheek. "Hold still."

Nicholas stared down at the old woman rocking and muttering softly to herself. "Do you know this woman, Sophia?"

"Aye. It's Mrs. Lanning. She used to be the head of our household. You wouldn't remember her, Nicholas. You were just a baby."

He squatted and pushed lightly on the old woman's shoulder. "Look at me, you old hag."

"Nicholas, don't," Sophia said as Mrs. Lanning raised her gaze to him.

Bree gave a soft gasp and Dani pulled Leta closer to her as Mrs. Lanning hooted loudly. "Burn the witch! Burn the witch!"

"Shut up!" Nicholas leaned closer and glared at the woman. "Touch my sister again and I'll kill you. Do you understand?"

"Nicky, stop," Sophia said. "She's gone insane. You can smell it on her. She doesn't know what she's saying."

"Does she know who you are, Sophia?" James asked.

At the sound of his voice, Mrs. Lanning raised her head and squinted at him. Her mouth dropped open with horror and a low keening noise, it sent shivers down Sophia's spine, rose from deep within her chest.

"Another Red witch," Mrs. Lanning moaned. She staggered to her feet and made the sign of the cross at James before backing away. "Stay away from me! I know what you are! I'm warning you – stay away or I'll see you burned at the stake!"

She stumbled back toward Leta and Dani. Leta broke free of Dani's grip and ran to Nicholas. She wrapped her arms around his waist, staring wide-eyed at Mrs. Lanning before whimpering, "Nicky, what's wrong with her?"

"She's just sick, Leta. It's all right." Nicky put his arm around her.

Mrs. Lanning backed toward the alley to her left. "Stay

away from me!" She screeched before staggered into the alley and disappearing into the darkness.

"Sophia?" Bree put her arm around her waist. "Are you all right?"

Sophia nodded as James removed his hand and peered at her cheek. "It's healed."

"Thank you, baby brother." Sophia squeezed his hand.

Nicholas ran his hand through his short blonde hair. "Gods, why the hell would Dad hire a crazy old woman like that?"

"She wasn't like that before, Nicky," Sophia said. "She was a mean woman, but she wasn't crazy. She hated Mama, thought she was a witch, and she treated her terribly when Papa first brought her home."

"Really?" Bree asked.

Sophia nodded. "Aye. Mama wouldn't talk to me about it, not even when I was older and questioned her, but Laura told me all the mean things Mrs. Lanning did to her. She even beat her once. She took a stick and beat Mama's back until it was bruised and bleeding."

"Are you kidding me?" Nicholas replied. "Why didn't Dad do anything about it?"

Sophia gave him a dry look. "You know as well as I do that Mama is too soft-hearted for her own good. I guess she told Papa that it was a misunderstanding and refused to tell him why Mrs. Lanning did it or even confirm that she was the one who did it."

She suddenly scowled. "Laura said she overheard Mrs. Lanning threatening Mama that she would tell Dad that Aunt Maya was a witch as well, and she would convince him to burn them both."

Dani frowned. "That's ridiculous."

"Aye, I know. But you know Mama would do anything to

protect Aunt Maya. I only remember Mrs. Lanning as being quite strict, she used to say mean things about my birth mother as well, but Laura said she was actually very nasty."

She hesitated, glancing briefly at Leta before lowering her voice. "She said that Mrs. Lanning forced Mama to go out into the woods alone one night to gather berries, and that Mama was nearly killed by a leech. It was a full moon and Papa was hunting. He smelled the leech and saved Mama before it could drain her."

The rest of them were staring at her with rapt interest. Sophia glanced at Leta again. The little girl was studying the alley and didn't appear to be listening. "I don't know if this part is true or not, Laura swears it is, but the rumour was that Papa was going to banish Mrs. Lanning to the outskirts after that."

"Uncle Tristan would never do that," Dani said. "He's too," she groped for an appropriate word and settled for a weak, "nice."

Sophia shrugged. "Laura says that Mama pleaded with him not to do it. Papa didn't send her to the outskirts, but he made Marian head of the household and Mrs. Lanning became one of the house staff."

"What happened to her then?" Bree asked.

"She left after Papa married Mama. They tried to convince her not to go, but Mrs. Lanning refused to stay. She was convinced that Mama was a witch."

"I say good riddance." Nicky squeezed Leta's shoulder. "Come, little one, it's getting late. We'll walk you to the hotel."

"I want to go for a drink too," Leta said.

Nicky laughed. "You're too young, Leta. Can you imagine what Dad would say if he found out I gave you wine?" He picked the little girl up and kissed her loudly on the cheek. "Besides, you need to help Bree plan her wedding, remember?"

"BREE, CAN I ASK YOU SOMETHING?" SOPHIA ASKED.

Bree folded her legs under her as she sat on the bed next to the sleeping Leta. They had spent the last couple of hours visiting and discussing the wedding until Leta had fallen asleep. After tucking her into the bed, the three of them had talked for a while in hushed tones until Dani, yawning tiredly, had left for her own room.

"Of course." She smiled at her.

"How is it that you know how to read and write but Kaden does not."

"Did he tell you he didn't know how to read or write?" Bree asked.

Sophia shook her head. "No, I guessed it."

"I thought you must have. Kaden is ashamed of it, and I would have been surprised if he told you," Bree said.

She ran her hand over the quilt on the bed. "Before we were captured by Draken, we worked for a human family. They didn't pay us, but they fed us and gave us beds in the slave quarters. We weren't exactly slaves. We could leave anytime we wanted, and they were kind enough to us."

"How did you get hired by them?" Sophia asked.

Bree shrugged. "I don't know. Kaden arranged it. Anyway, I became friends with one of the other girls who worked in the kitchen, and she taught me how to read and write. I had started to teach Kaden, he knows the letters and the numbers, but then we were captured by Draken."

She gave Sophia a look of shame. "I've been meaning to start teaching him again but honestly, I don't think I'm a very good teacher and I've been busy with James and the wedding and… I feel like I'm not being a very good sister right now."

"What do you mean?" Sophia asked.

"It's always just been Kaden and me and now – now I have James. As much as I love Kaden, I feel like a part of me is missing when I'm not with James. I want to spend all of my time with him, but I'm worried that Kaden will feel like I'm neglecting him. I want my brother to stay for longer than just the wedding, and so I should be spending as much time with him as I can, you know? I need to convince him that he should stay. Only, there's a part of me that just wants to be with James."

She traced the ring on her finger. "Your brother has been so good about how much time I'm spending with Kaden, but sooner or later he's going to get tired of being in second place and maybe he'll change his mind about marrying me."

She gave Sophia a miserable look. Sophia reached out and took her hand, squeezing it gently. "Trust me, Bree. you don't have to worry about James changing his mind. My baby brother loves you and would do anything for you. He understands how important Kaden is to you."

"Do you really think so?"

"I know so," Sophia said.

Bree sighed. "It would be good if Kaden could find someone as well. I want him to be with someone who loves him and wants to make him happy."

She gave Sophia an innocent look and Sophia snorted softly. "Aye, I imagine you do. My cousin Dani is hoping for the same thing. I'm sure she and Kaden will be very happy together."

Bree grinned. "We both know that Kaden is not interested in Dani."

"Aye, but my cousin can be very persuasive when she

puts her mind to it," Sophia said. She suddenly felt sick to her stomach at the thought of Kaden in Dani's bed, and it must have shown on her face because Bree reached out and took her hand.

"Sophia, if you ever want to talk about -"

"There's nothing to talk about." Sophia made herself smile at the young woman. "I do have an idea though. Aunt Maya taught all of us to read and write, she's an excellent teacher, and I bet she'd be more than happy to teach Kaden. Do you think he would be willing?"

Bree squeezed her hand excitedly. "Aye, I know he would. He's always wanted to learn how to read."

"Good. I'll mention it to Aunt Maya and ask her to talk to him." Sophia glanced at the sleeping Leta, and Bree slid off the bed.

"I think I'm going to go to bed. I imagine James and the other two will be back any time now." She hesitated and then quickly kissed Sophia on the cheek. "Thank you."

"For what?"

Bree shrugged. "I know planning the wedding isn't your idea of fun, and I appreciate how patient you've been about it."

Sophia smiled. "I'm enjoying it. I swear."

Bree smiled. "Good night, Sophia."

"Good night, Bree."

"WHY DO YOU WEAR SWORDS?" KADEN TOOK A DRINK OF HIS beer as James set his empty mug down.

"For protection," James replied.

Kaden rolled his eyes. "As if you need them for protection."

Nicholas laughed. "He has a point, James. Honestly, I use mine mostly for chopping up firewood."

James shrugged as Nicholas snickered. "And let's not forget the ladies love seeing a long, thick sword on a man."

"Gods Nicky, you're drunk already," James grunted.

"Am not!" Nicky took a gulp of beer. "I've only had six. And it's been watered down so much, it hardly tastes like beer." He banged his empty mug on the top of the bar and the bartender wandered over and picked up his empty mug to refill.

"Can I get you another as well, my lord?" She gave Kaden a slow and inviting smile.

"No thanks." He glanced disinterestedly at her but didn't fail to notice the way James looked over his head and raised his eyebrows at Nicholas.

Nicky stroked the dark-haired woman's arm. "What time are you done work, my lady?"

She looked him up and down, apparently found him wanting, and returned her gaze to Kaden. "I'm done in an hour or so. Perhaps you would care to stay and have a drink with me?"

Kaden stared, really stared, at her for the first time since they had sat down. His gaze lingered on her mouth and the way her breasts nearly spilled out of her shirt. She leaned against the bar, giving him an unobstructed view down her top. He gave her a polite smile. "No, thank you."

She frowned as Nicholas snorted.

"What?" Kaden asked as the woman turned away to pour Nicholas another beer.

"Nothing," Nicky said.

"The swords. Why?" Kaden prompted.

Nicholas eyed him closely. "Our mother is human. Dad thought it would be wise if she knew how to protect herself."

"She's a healer," Kaden said. "Any wound she received would quickly heal itself."

James smiled a little. "Our father believes in being cautious when it comes to our mother. Some might accuse him of being overprotective."

"Aye," Nicky agreed. "A trait my brother has inherited when it comes to his woman. I, on the other hand, understand that a woman craves her freedom and can take care of herself."

He winked at the bartender and she rolled her eyes before setting the beer down in front of him.

James laughed. "I'm sure Sophia would have something to say on the matter. You hover over her like a protective mama bear."

Nicholas scowled at him as Kaden grinned.

"Anyway," Nicholas continued, "Dad hired a human to teach Mama how to use a sword. She picked up on it quite quickly and encouraged our father to learn it as well. So, she would have someone to practice on, she said."

He took another drink before continuing. "When Sophia and I were old enough, Dad decided to teach us to use the sword."

"Nicky turned out to be an exceptional student," James said. "He's better than all of us combined. Once Dad realized that, he allowed Nicky to take over the training for the rest of us. He's teaching Evan and Bree right now and eventually when Leta is bigger, he'll train her as well."

"But why?" Kaden asked. "I can see why he would want your mother to learn, but you can easily protect yourself without a sword."

James shrugged. "There's no harm in learning and," he paused and lowered his voice, "it helps us blend in with the humans."

Kaden looked curiously at him. "You would hide your true nature?"

Nicky shook his head immediately. "No. But we're not going to go around announcing it. We already have enough issues with Mama and James being Reds. We don't hide the fact that we're Lycans but for some reason, seeing us with swords eases their minds. Perhaps it makes us more human in their eyes."

James grunted and spilled some of his beer as he was jostled from behind. Nicky made a low, snarling noise deep in his throat.

"Easy, Nicky," James said.

The large and foul-smelling man had bumped into James for a record third time, and Kaden had no doubt that he was doing it on purpose. The man sneered at James as he reached for the jug of beer the bartender had set down on the bar.

"S'cuse me." He grabbed the jug and returned to the table of men waiting for him.

"If he does it again, I'll be forced to teach the idiot a lesson in manners," Nicky said cheerfully. He downed his beer and raised his hand for another.

"Ignore him," James advised. "He's just looking for a fight and it's better if we keep a low profile, you know that."

"Why?" Kaden asked. "I thought this town didn't have a problem with Lycans."

James shrugged. "For the most part they don't, and we'd like to keep it that way."

Nicky sipped at his fresh beer. "In this case, it's not the Lycan thing anyway. It's the red hair."

Kaden gave James a thoughtful look and James grinned at him. "We Reds are witches, remember?"

Kaden grimaced. "Nothing but an old ancient's tale. I cannot believe there are humans who still think that way."

"There are still more humans who believe it than those who don't." Nicholas took another drink.

There was loud laughter from the group of men at the table, and Nicholas stiffened when the voice floated over to them. "Aye, he's a big one, but the Reds all scream the same when they burn."

Nicholas drained his glass and set it down on the bar. He slid off the stool and as he walked toward the table, weaving just the tiniest bit, James sighed loudly. "Here we go."

"Good evening, gentlemen." Nicky smiled at the group of men.

They stared at him in sullen silence and his grin widened. "Do you have something you wish to say to my brother?"

"If I were you, I would not confess to having a Red for a brother." The foul-smelling man said peevishly.

"Aye, but you're not me, are you?" Nicky replied. "Frankly, I would rather have a Red for a brother than an overgrown goat like you."

The man stood up. "You dare to insult me?"

Nicky laughed. "Insult you? That was hardly an insult. Now, if I *was* going to insult you, I would have said something about your smell. Tell me - do you actually bathe in horse shit, or do you just sleep in it?"

The man roared with anger and charged at him. Nicky grinned fiercely and swung sharply to his left. He stuck his foot out and the man tripped and went sprawling on to the floor. Nicholas leaned down and smacked him lightly on the ass. "Ready to apologize to my brother, you stupid goat?"

The man's face turned bright red as he staggered to his feet. He turned and lunged at Nicky, who sidestepped neatly and laughed when the man fell into his table of friends.

Nicky turned to Kaden and James. "I thought goats were nimble."

"Nicky! Watch out!"

James' warning came too late. The glass pitcher of beer came crashing down over his head and drove Nicky to his knees. Blood and beer ran down his face as he shook his head to clear it. He was yanked to his feet and two men pinned his arms to his side as the man he had tripped stood in front of him.

"Not so much of a smart mouth now, are you?" He drew his fist back.

Before he could punch Nicky, his arm was grabbed, and he was swung around to face James.

James squeezed his arm and the man screamed as the bones in his forearm cracked. He dropped to his knees, and James gave him a look of disgust before he turned to the men who were holding Nicky.

"Let him go," he said quietly.

Movement flickered to his left and he turned just as two more men jumped him. They knocked him to the ground, and the three of them began to fight and roll on the floor of the bar as one of the men holding Nicky brayed loud laughter.

Nicholas turned and smiled at the man on his left before head butting him in the face. There was a sickening crack as the man's nose broke. He howled with pain and dropped to the floor, his hands covering his gushing nose.

The second man threw his arms around Nicky's neck and squeezed. Nicky drove his elbow into the man's stomach, and the man made a thick, coughing wheeze but didn't relax his grip.

Another man appeared in front of them and cocked his arm back. Before he could land the blow, Kaden grabbed the man by his shoulders and threw him to the ground before kneeling on his chest and punching him repeatedly in the face. The man made a loud grunting noise and his eyes rolled up in his head as he sagged against the floor.

Kaden stood and looked around in disbelief. The bar had erupted into chaos. All around him men were shouting and fighting. He watched as Nicky wriggled free of the man holding him around the neck and punched him hard in the stomach. The man collapsed and Nicky, grinning ferociously, grabbed the bartender who was cowering against the wall and pulled her against him.

He dipped her with a flourish and pressed a kiss against her lips before pushing her to safety under one of the tables. He made a sound that was half-laugh, half-howl, and then dove at the group of men who were piling onto his brother.

Kaden groaned loudly and followed.

CHAPTER 9

"Gods, what a night," James muttered. They were standing in the hallway of the hotel and he stretched and cracked his back. "We need to be on our best behaviour tomorrow, Nicky."

Nicky shrugged. "They started it."

"Yeah, well you're just lucky the bartender was willing to vouch for us with the lawman."

"It's because I kissed her. The women can never resist me once they've had a taste." Nicholas laughed loudly.

James punched him on the arm. "Quiet, Nicky."

Weaving unsteadily, Nicky turned to Kaden and clapped him hard on the back. "You know, for a human you're pretty good in a fight. Thanks for your help back there."

He slung his arm around Kaden's shoulder and squeezed roughly. Kaden winced and James tugged on Nicholas' arm. "C'mon, Nicky. Time for you to get your drunk ass to bed."

"I wasn't too drunk to save your ass back there, was I?" Nicholas snickered a little and then grabbed Kaden's head and planted a loud kiss on his cheek. "Welcome to the family, Kaden."

Singing softly under his breath, he meandered down the hallway to his room. James and Kaden stood uncomfortably in the hallway for a moment before James nodded to him.

"Good night, Kaden."

"Good night."

They were asleep when he slipped silently into the room. There was only one bed, but Sophia had made a bed of blankets and quilts on the floor in front of the fireplace for him. He stopped next to the bed. Leta was burrowed under the covers, he could see just the top of her head poking out, and he gazed at Sophia's face for a few moments. A thick strand of her dark hair was lying across her cheek and he carefully brushed it back, making sure he didn't touch her soft skin.

She didn't move and he sighed and walked to his bed on the floor. He took off his shirt, wincing at little at the bruising and swelling on his ribs, and crawled under the thick quilt. He rested his head on the pillow and carefully touched the swelling under his eye.

James had offered to heal him, but the idea of being hugged and touched by his future brother-in-law was a little too awkward for him. He had declined with a rough thanks. He sat up and peered at the bed again. He could just make out Sophia's face and he stared at her for a few moments before lying back on the blankets. He rolled to his side and stared at the glowing flames.

———

SOPHIA OPENED HER EYES AND STARED AT THE CEILING before sitting up and looking to the fireplace. Kaden was in his bed on the floor. His back was turned to her and she checked quickly on Leta before sliding out of the bed.

She guessed it was close to dawn. The room was dark and

cold, the fire had died down to embers, and she wondered if Kaden was warm enough. She wasn't cold, even in her thin nightdress, but Kaden was a human. They didn't retain their body heat the way Lycans did. She moved quietly to the fireplace. She would build the fire up so that he didn't catch a chill.

She knelt on the cold stones of the hearth and glanced at Kaden. His arm was over his face, but she could see the dark bruising on his ribs. She leaned in and ran her hand lightly over the bruising, frowning to herself. How did he –

His arm came off his face, his hand gripped hers, and he yanked her down onto the blankets next to him. He threw his leg over hers and placed one large hand on her stomach.

"Why is it that I keep waking to find your hand on me, Lycan?" he rasped.

She flushed. "I thought you might be cold. I was trying to be nice by building up the fire."

He cocked his eyebrow at her. "You need to touch me to build up the fire?"

"I saw the bruising." She raised her hand and tentatively brushed it across the swelling under his eye. "How did this happen? Did one of my brothers do this?"

He shook his head. "No. There was a bit of a…misunderstanding at the bar between some humans and your brothers."

She sighed deeply. "Tell me we'll be able to go shopping tomorrow without a mob going after us."

He grinned. "Aye, we smoothed it over. Besides, they started it. We were only defending ourselves."

"That's usually how it happens with my brothers." The sarcasm was thick in her voice.

His hand rubbed a slow firm circle on her flat stomach, and she swallowed nervously. "Why did James not heal you?"

"He offered. I declined." He dipped his head and buried his nose in her hair. "Your hair smells good."

"Thank you," she whispered. "You should have allowed my brother to heal you."

"I'm used to pain." His hand moved higher and rubbed just below the swell of her breasts. "If I allow your brother to heal me every time I'm hurt, I fear it will make me weak and," he nuzzled his face into her neck and inhaled again, "unable to handle any type of pain."

"That won't happen," she breathed.

"Perhaps not."

She was trembling and he pulled her closer, his large thigh pressing her legs into the blankets. "Are you cold, little Lycan? Maybe you should climb under the quilt with me."

She shook her head. "That's not a good idea."

"Why not?"

"You know why," she murmured. "Besides, I am not cold."

"Aye, the Lycans do seem to run hot." He bent his head and pressed his mouth against the soft skin of her throat.

She moaned when he licked the rapidly-beating pulse he could see fluttering under her warm skin.

"Your pulse beats so quickly, little Lycan," he whispered. "Are you afraid of me?"

"You know I am not," she replied.

"Then why do you tremble so deeply?"

"I should go back to my bed," she said.

"Aye, you should." He brushed his mouth against hers, and she returned his kiss hungrily.

He groaned into her mouth and sucked on her tongue when she thrust it between his lips. She lost track of how long they kissed for. He explored her mouth with a lazy kind of need, his tongue stroking and tasting and darting in and out.

When her entire body was shaking and trembling beneath him, and she was gripping his arms so tightly her nails were digging into his skin, he pulled his mouth from hers and stared down at her.

Her mouth felt swollen and her wolf had pushed forward until her eyes were the colour of jade. She closed her eyes, knowing he would be disgusted by the sight of her Lycan side.

"Open your eyes, little Lycan."

"No," she said.

"Why?"

"Because I know you don't like seeing my eyes turn green."

His big hand cupped her jaw, his thumb rubbing across her lips. "Open, I said."

She couldn't resist his command. She stared up at him and he studied her eyes for a long moment. "You're wrong, Sophia. I like it when your eyes turn green. Do you know why?"

She shook her head, the tip of her tongue flicking out to brush against his thumb.

He groaned and moved his hand to rest against her ribs. "When your eyes turn green, it means you're losing control. Does it not?"

"Perhaps," she whispered.

He stared at her mouth, his nostrils flaring when her lips parted. Instead of kissing her, he said, "I like it when you lose control."

His hand tightened on her ribs before moving to the buttons of her nightshirt. He unbuttoned it to her navel and pushed it open, baring her breasts.

He took a deep breath, his eyes burning with lust, as he stared down at her full breasts with their hardened nipples. He dipped his head and captured one nipple between his lips. She made a soft moaning sigh and tugged restlessly at his hair. He sucked hard on her nipple, pulling and tugging on it with his lips and teeth as she arched her back.

Sophia moaned low in her throat. Kaden's firm lips on her breast were driving her crazy with need. She gasped when he kissed his way to her other breast and licked the tight pink bud with flat strokes of his warm tongue.

He nipped at it with his teeth, a sharp bite of pain that he quickly soothed with his tongue, before moving his hand up to cup and knead her other breast. He pulled on her nipple, rolling it between his fingers until it was aching and throbbing with need.

He pulled one last time on her nipple with his mouth and then licked his way to her ear. "Open your legs, little Lycan," he demanded in his low and raspy voice.

She spread her legs and he smiled his approval before sucking on her earlobe. Her fingers dug into the warm skin of his back as he moved his hand down to her thigh. He stroked the outside of her thigh with the tips of his fingers and reached down to trace her kneecap before he ran his fingers up the inside of her leg. He was almost to her aching, wet pussy when Leta sat straight up in the bed with a loud growl.

They froze and Sophia gave him a wide-eyed look of dismay before glancing at the young girl. Leta was staring directly at them, and she could feel Kaden pulling her shirt closed as she smiled guiltily at her younger sister.

"Leta, honey, it's late. Go back to sleep."

"Papa, make the bear stop dancing so I can eat him," Leta said.

Sophia blew her breath out in a relieved rush. She pushed at Kaden's broad shoulders and he leaned back as she scrambled to her feet. She buttoned her nightshirt hurriedly and crossed the room to Leta.

The little girl was staring through her and Sophia pushed her back gently onto the bed. "You're dreaming, Leta. Go back to sleep," she said.

"Thank you, Papa," the little girl growled again. Her teeth lengthened and her eyes glowed briefly before she made a soft snorting noise and closed her eyes.

Sophia climbed over her and crawled into the bed beside her. Her heart was pounding, her cheeks were flushed, and her lower body was throbbing with need. She glanced at Kaden. He was sitting up in the blankets, staring hungrily at her, and another throb of lust went through her.

"I – we should probably get some sleep. We have shopping and then it's a long ride home. Plus, Leta is, um, a light sleeper," she said.

"Aye," he agreed.

She swallowed down her disappointment and nodded at him before lying down in the bed. She pulled the covers to her chin, turning her back and staring at the wall. Leta curled up against her, her small body warm against her back, and flung her arm around her waist.

She stared into the darkness, listening to Leta's soft snoring and wondering if Kaden was lying awake as well.

THE ALLEY WAS QUIET AND DARK. HE MOVED SILENTLY DOWN it, blending into the shadows when he thought he heard the noise of humans. When no humans appeared, he moved on, his eyes glowing in the dark.

The old woman was huddled in a doorway. Her frail body was curled up under a ragged blanket, and her face was tucked into her arm. He stared silently at her before crouching down and closing his eyes. When he opened them again, they were back to their faded hazel colour.

He reached out to shake her awake, but she twitched and sat up before his hand touched her. She stared at him with wide, frightened eyes, and he gave her a reassuring smile. His white teeth shone faintly in the darkness and she pressed herself back against the door behind her.

"Fear not, old woman. I will not harm you." His voice was low and gravelly, and he showed her his empty hands.

"Spare some coins for a starving old woman, my lord?" she recited automatically.

"Aye, I could do that." He reached into his coat pocket and pulled out a large coin. She watched as he flipped it across his knuckles and then reached for it with a trembling hand.

He pulled the coin out of her reach. "But first, I want to ask you a question."

She blinked at him and he leaned in, his nose wrinkling at the smell of mud and urine. "The woman you spoke with earlier. What do you know of her?"

"She is the lord Williams oldest child. Sophia is her name. I used to be their housekeeper many years ago. Until the witch arrived." The old woman licked her lips and stared at the coin.

"How often does she come to town? Does she ever go alone?"

"The witch is never alone. The lord Williams knows she would be burned at the stake."

He sighed irritably, his hand tightening around the coin. "Not the witch, the dark-haired one."

Mrs. Lanning frowned. "Sophia? What do you want with her?"

"That's none of your concern," he snapped.

She shrank back and he made himself smile at her. "Have you seen her in the town before?"

"I – I've only been here a few days." She stared again at the coin. "I have not seen her for many years. I did not know that she had fallen so deeply under the witch's spell. Are you – do you want to release her from it?"

"Aye, we do." The man tossed the coin into her lap and she grasped it eagerly.

"It will be very difficult, my lord. The Red witch has her completely under her spell. I – I could help you."

The man laughed. "We have no need for the help of an old woman."

She bristled and straightened. "I could win my way back into their household. They would trust me, they would -"

He laughed again. "You're a fool if you think they would take you back. I saw the interaction between you and the woman earlier. I can smell your madness and so can she."

The woman's wrinkled cheeks flushed, and she staggered to her feet. "You have no right to speak to me that way!"

The man looked around warily. The old woman's voice was rising, and he made a shushing gesture with his hand. "Quiet, you stupid old cow."

"I am not mad! The world needs to be cleansed of the Reds. They are growing more powerful by the day and if they are not stopped, they will destroy us all!"

The man sighed irritably. The woman was screaming now, and he moved quickly. His hand clenched around her thin shoulder, and she gave a thin wavering scream as her collarbone snapped under his hand.

He shoved her back against the wall. His eyes were glowing, and his face was covered in a thick layer of hair. She screamed hoarsely as fangs protruded from his mouth.

"No! Do not -"

Her scream of terror turned into a gurgling moan as he bent his head and tore her throat open. Thick and salty blood flowed into his mouth and he growled low in his throat as he ripped into her thin flesh.

He released her and she collapsed to the ground. He wiped his mouth and walked out of the alley. He looked around carefully, saw no one, and shed his clothing before shifting into his wolf form. He loped through the streets and disappeared into the forest that surrounded the town, as the sun rose over the horizon.

***

"IT'S GORGEOUS," SOPHIA SAID AS BREE STOOD NERVOUSLY in front of her.

"Do you like it?"

"I love it." Sophia smiled at her as Dani squealed, took Bree's hands, and made her twirl around.

"I'll admit I was wrong," Dani said. "This one is the better one."

Bree smiled and ran her hands down the soft fabric. The dress was ivory in colour and clung to her slender body. It was strapless and the bodice was covered in small white beads that had been sewn into the silk fabric. The dress fell in soft folds to her ankles, and she gathered the material up in her hands and stared at the dark blue shoes on her feet.

"Do you really think I should wear these shoes?" she asked.

"Something blue remember?" Dani grinned.

"I already have something blue." Bree stared at the ring on her finger.

"That doesn't count," Dani said dismissively.

"I'm not sure I can walk in these," Bree said. "They're so high." She took a few wobbling steps forward and Dani giggled.

"You have some time to practice before the wedding. Now, what do you think of this dress?" Dani stared critically at herself.

"I think they're perfect. What do you think?" Bree turned to Sophia.

"I like it." Sophia was wearing a long-sleeved, dark blue dress with an empire waist cut. The dress stopped just below her knees and a wide ivory ribbon was sewn into the material beneath her breasts. Dani stepped forward and tied the ribbon into a bow at her back, and then turned so Sophia could do the same to her dress.

The curtain to the small changing room at the back of the store was drawn back and Leta came skipping out. Sophia had to press her lips together to stop from laughing. The young girl was wearing a white satin dress. It was covered from collar to hem in small and shiny stones. Based on the price of the dress, Sophia knew they couldn't be real jewels, but they sparkled and shone in the dim light and she understood why Leta had been so taken with the dress when she found it among the others.

"It's so pretty!" Leta crowed as she ran her hands over the small stones. "Please, Bree, can I wear this for the wedding? Please, please, please!"

Dani was staring horrified at the bright and garish dress. "Leta, I think that dress might be um, a bit too much for the wedding."

Leta's face fell. "But I love it. I sparkle when I twirl." She twirled in a circle, and the dress glittered so brightly that Sophia squinted.

Leta gave Bree an eager look. "It's so pretty, Bree. Don't you think?"

Before she could reply, Dani handed another dress to Leta. "It's too flashy for the wedding, Leta. Try this one on instead please."

Leta stared sadly at the plain blue dress in Dani's hands. "It doesn't sparkle."

"It's not supposed to," Dani said. "This is Bree's day. If you wear that dress, everyone will be looking at you. We want them to be looking at Bree."

Her bottom lip trembling, Leta gave Sophia a quick look. Sophia nodded at her and the little girl sighed in disappointment and reached for the dress. "Aye."

"Hold on." Bree crouched in front of Leta and took her hands. "If this is the dress you like best, then this is the one we'll buy."

Leta gasped. "Truly?"

"Aye. You look beautiful in it," Bree said.

Leta squealed with delight and threw her arms around Bree. "Thank you, Bree!"

"You're welcome." Bree kissed the little girl's cheek and patted her gently on the bottom. "Go and change. The boys will be getting impatient for us to finish."

Leta nodded and ran back into the change room. Dani gave a small moan of dismay. "Bree, what are you thinking? That dress is hideous."

Bree laughed. "Leta loves it and I like making her happy."

Dani sighed as she reached behind her and undid the bow at her back. "Maybe I can peel off some of those awful stones without her noticing."

"Where is he?" Bree gave James a worried look and he kissed her forehead.

"He said he wouldn't be long."

Dani stood in the back of the wagon and peered down the long road that led into the town. They had met the others at the edge of town, but Kaden wasn't with the two brothers. "Where did he go anyway?"

Nicky shrugged. "He just said he had one last thing to buy and that he wouldn't be long."

Sophia shifted on her horse and tried not to let her nerves show. Kaden was probably fine. She was more concerned that he had decided not to stay for the wedding after all. She hoped not. It would break Bree's heart.

Just Bree's?

She ignored the small voice in her head as Leta piped up. "Maybe he decided not to stay for the wedding."

"He would not leave without saying goodbye to me." Bree bit her lip nervously and then looked at James. "Would you go and look for him, my lord?"

He nodded. "Aye."

"I'll come with you." Nicky swung down from his horse as Bree gave him a grateful look.

"Thank you, Nicky."

Before he could hand the reins to Sophia, Dani sighed with relief. "There he is."

Kaden was walking quickly toward them and Bree waved at him. He waved back and, holding the pockets of his coat, jogged the rest of the way.

"Where have you been?" Bree asked.

"I had one last thing to buy," he puffed.

"What?" Leta asked.

"Something for you." Kaden winked at her.

Leta stared at him. "What is it?" She looked at his empty hands and he grinned and stood next to the wagon.

"Perhaps you can guess."

Leta stared at him for a moment, her eyes dropping to the pocket of his jacket when it twitched. "Your pocket just moved!"

"Did it?" Kaden said.

"Aye, it -"

She gasped loudly when a kitten poked its tiny head out of the pocket and meowed.

"It's a kitten! A kitten!!" Leta shouted. She reached out eagerly as Kaden pulled the kitten out of his pocket and handed it to her.

She held it carefully and rubbed her face against its soft grey fur. "It's so cute."

"Aye. I thought it could live in the barn and eat those rats that scare you so badly." Kaden grinned at her.

She giggled when the kitten batted at her long hair. "Is it a boy or a girl?"

"It's a boy."

She handed the kitten to Dani who took it with a small smile and placed it in her lap. Leta stared solemnly at Kaden for a moment, and then leaned over the side of the wagon and hugged him. "Thank you, Kaden. I like him very much."

Kaden patted her back. "You're welcome, Leta."

He untied Bandit from the back of the wagon and swung into the saddle. He nudged him over to where Sophia sat on her horse as James clucked to the horses and the wagon began to move.

"That was very nice of you." She smiled at him as they followed the wagon.

He grinned at her and arranged his coat carefully around him. "I have something for you as well."

There was another soft mew and he reached into his other pocket and pulled out a second kitten. This one was a light orange with dark orange stripes, and it hissed when Sophia reached for it.

"This one has a temper." He grinned. "It reminded me of you."

She gave him a mock glare and plucked the kitten from his hand. She held it in front of her, eyeing it carefully, and it hissed again. She tucked it into her jacket, wincing a little when it dug its claws into the skin above her shirt, and Kaden laughed.

"He likes you."

"Aye." She pulled the kitten's claws from her skin and tucked it further down. It curled into a ball against her stomach and stared balefully at her, its eyes glowing in the dimness of her jacket.

"He'll make an excellent hunter," Kaden said.

She smiled at him. "Thank you so much, Kaden."

"You're welcome, Sophia."

A small, sweet shiver went through her when he said her name and her smile widened. He flushed a little and said gruffly, "There were only two left. I thought this one might be lonely if I took its brother away."

"That was thoughtful of you."

He glanced at her again. "And I – I thought you might like him."

"I do - very much." Her cheeks reddened when she realized Dani staring at them.

The young girl had a look of misery on her face and she quickly glanced down at her lap before Sophia could say anything. Sophia sighed. There was yet another reason she couldn't let what was happening with Kaden continue. Dani had fallen for Kaden and she had no wish to hurt her cousin's feelings. She and Kaden had no future, but her cousin was human. Kaden would be better off with Dani.

The kitten dug its tiny claws into her abdomen, and she reached inside her jacket and rubbed its soft head. It retracted its claws and purred loudly, and she sighed before urging her horse to move faster.

CHAPTER 10

"Happy Birthday, Kaden!" Leta sang out as she ran into the barn. She jumped at him and he caught her, throwing her up in the air and grinning when she squealed with delight.

"Thank you, Leta." He held her gently and she kissed him on the cheek. His gift of the kitten had completely won over the little girl, and in the week since they had returned from town, she had become increasingly friendly with him.

"Where is Hogan?" She looked around the barn for the grey kitten.

"I believe he's in the hayloft with Piper. They're sleeping on my bed."

Leta made a face. "Piper's mean. He's always scratching me."

Kaden grinned. While Hogan was friendly and sweet, the orange kitten was very particular about whom he liked and didn't like. So far, he would only allow Sophia and himself to hold him. He hissed and scratched at anyone else who came near him.

His grin faltered. Sophia had been avoiding him since

they had returned from town, and he was more hurt by it then he wanted to admit. Each night when he closed his eyes he was tormented by visions of Sophia's breasts. He couldn't stop remembering the way her nipples had hardened in his mouth, and the sound of her voice moaning so sweetly. He pushed it from his mind and smiled at the little girl in his arms.

"Be brave, Leta." He kissed her soft cheek and set her down. "Go on and see if you can make friends with Piper."

She scurried up the ladder to the loft as the door opened and Doran, followed by Maya, came into the barn.

"Happy Birthday," Doran said as they stopped in front of Kaden.

"Thanks." Kaden smiled at the two of them.

"Have you seen Nicky?" Doran asked.

"Aye, I believe he is in the other barn with Evan and Ian," Kaden replied.

"Thanks. We're on watch in a few minutes." Doran kissed his mother on the cheek and left. Maya smiled at Kaden.

"How is your birthday, Kaden?"

"Fine, so far. I'm looking forward to dinner tonight."

Maya grinned. "Marian has been in a state all morning. She always gets herself worked up when she's cooking a special dinner. I don't know how many times Avery has told her that it doesn't matter, whatever she cooks always turns out delicious, but Marian worries anyway."

"She really has nothing to worry about," Kaden laughed. "I like everything she cooks."

Maya smiled and then gave him an oddly nervous look. "I have a birthday present for you, Kaden."

"You didn't have to do that."

"I wanted to. It's a bit of an unusual gift."

He stared curiously at her as she straightened her jacket

nervously. "I wondered if you would allow me to teach you to read and write."

He flushed and looked at the floor uncomfortably. "How do you know I cannot read or write?"

"Sophia mentioned it to me. No one else knows, and we don't have to tell them. I can come to the barn to teach you."

He didn't reply and she hurried on. "I'm a good teacher, and I've taught adults before. I taught Renee and Nadine, as well as Laura, to read and write."

"Maya, I -"

"If you rather I didn't, that's fine too," she said. "I just thought I would offer. I enjoy it and with the wedding coming up, we'll be staying with Avery and Tristan for a while longer. It's more than enough time to start teaching you the basics."

He finally looked at her and she smiled tentatively at him. He cleared his throat. "I – I would very much like to learn. Thank you, Maya. It's very kind of you to offer."

She smiled. "Good. We can start tomorrow if you'd like. I'll come by the barn after breakfast."

"Thank you," he repeated as there was a loud shriek from the loft.

"Piper! Owch! Stop that right now!"

Leta stuck her head over the side of the loft and stared down at Kaden. "Kaden, Piper is biting me. Will you come up and get him for me please? I want to play with Hogan."

"Aye, I'm coming." He grinned at Maya before he started up the ladder of the loft.

SOPHIA SMOOTHED HER DRESS DOWN AND TOOK ANOTHER gulp of wine. She'd already had three glasses, and she had a feeling she'd need at least another two to get through the evening. Marian's birthday dinner for Kaden had been impressive. Roasted duck, smoked venison, and heaping piles of potatoes and vegetables had filled the large table they'd brought into the common room.

They'd spent the last few hours eating and drinking in celebration of Kaden's birthday and, glancing around the room, she could see she wasn't the only one who'd had too much to drink. Bree, her cheeks flushed with colour, was laughing at something Nicky was saying to her. In the far corner, James and Doran were having a contest to see who could drink a glass of beer the fastest.

Her father and Ian roared with laughter when Doran, in desperation, tipped his glass over his head and opened his mouth wide. Sputtering and gasping, he allowed his grand-mother to pound him firmly on the back.

She sighed and stared into the fire. She'd spent the last week avoiding Kaden. At the time she thought it had been the right thing to do. Now, watching as her cousin giggled and flirted with Kaden, she wished bitterly that she had claimed him for herself.

Her coldness to him had first puzzled and then hurt him. She could see it in his eyes. After a day or so, he avoided her as studiously as she avoided him. She took another drink of wine as Dani's voice drifted to her.

"You don't know how to dance, Kaden? I'd be happy to teach you. Why don't we start right now?"

There was the quieter sound of Kaden's voice, but she couldn't tell if he was agreeing to the dance lesson or not. She straightened her back and told herself not to turn around. She didn't need to see Kaden pressed up against her cousin.

"Hello, my sweet Sophia."

"Hello, Mama." Sophia smiled faintly at her mother.

Avery put her arm around her waist. "Why are you standing by the fire all by yourself?"

Sophia shrugged. "Just tired I guess."

"Are you still having nightmares?" Avery brushed a strand of Sophia's hair back that had come loose from her braid.

"Not every night," Sophia replied. "I'm fine, Mama. Really."

Avery squeezed her waist. "You're looking lovely tonight. It's been so long since I've seen you in a dress."

"It's a special occasion."

"Indeed, it is." Avery glanced behind them. "I'm so happy for Bree that Kaden seems to be starting to trust us."

"Aye, it's good for Bree," Sophia said.

"Not just Bree perhaps?"

Sophia sighed. "There's nothing going on between the human and me."

"No? Because you have the same look on your face when you watch your cousin touch Kaden, that I did when I watched Victoria touch your father."

Sophia grimaced at the mention of Victoria. "It's not the same, Mama. Victoria was a terrible person and Dani is not. She deserves to be happy with someone like Kaden."

"Aye, perhaps she does. But I do not think that Kaden would be happy with her."

Sophia shrugged. "He might be. She is a human, she's kind and pretty, and she's obviously very fond of him. Why wouldn't he be happy with her?"

"Because she is not you, sweet Sophia," Avery said.

"Mama," Sophia gave her a look of exasperation, "what Kaden wants from me is something that Dani is more than willing to give him."

"And yet he has not taken it from her," Avery replied. "In

fact, he does what he can to discourage her. Dani is young and very…determined. She sees what she wants to when it comes to Kaden."

Sophia drained her glass of wine and gave her mother a miserable look. "I don't know what's wrong with me, Mama. I've never even been attracted to a human before, and now I want a human who hates Lycans."

"I don't believe he hates us," Avery said. "He may still not trust us fully, but he doesn't hate us."

"I don't want to hurt Dani."

Avery took Sophia's chin in her hand and gave her a stern look. "Do not use Dani as an excuse."

"I – I'm not."

"You are," Avery replied. "Kaden has no interest in your cousin, and you know that."

Her gaze softened and she stroked Sophia's cheek. "As a child you were so very much like Leta. Did you know that? You were brave and headstrong and so full of joy. You are still brave and strong and I'm proud of the woman that you have become, but I believe that it would serve you well if you could capture some of the joy you had as a child. You are too serious, my love. Life is meant to be enjoyed. You are too worried about your family and their happiness, to take your own."

She stood on her tiptoes and kissed Sophia's forehead. "We love you very much and we want you to be happy. If being with Kaden makes you happy, then you can't let that slip away without giving it a chance."

"And when Kaden leaves after the wedding?" Sophia asked. "When he leaves and breaks not only Bree's heart, but mine, what then?"

Avery smiled at her. "Kaden will not leave after the wedding."

"You're wrong, Mama," Sophia replied. "He will leave, and I'll be alone."

Before Avery could reply, Tristan joined them. "What are you two talking so seriously about?"

Avery smiled at him. "Nothing, my lord."

Tristan grinned and reached around Avery to squeeze her ass. "Are you getting tired, girl? I think we should retire for the night and leave the celebration to the children, don't you?"

He winked at her and Sophia rolled her eyes as Avery smiled. "Do you not have to go on watch, my lord?"

He shook his head. "No. Jeffrey and Martine are on watch now, and Ian volunteered to take my shift with Leo."

She took his hand. Then I think retiring for the night is a very good idea."

Tristan kissed the top of Sophia's head roughly. "Good night, sweet Sophia."

"Good night, Papa. Good night, Mama."

"DID YOU HAVE A GOOD BIRTHDAY, KADEN?" BREE, HER cheeks bright red and her thin body swaying, asked.

"Aye Bree, I did. The best I can remember." Kaden smiled at his sister.

"Good. I'm so -" She hiccupped loudly before dissolving into giggles.

Kaden laughed as James joined them. They were the last three in the common room and he watched as James lifted Bree into his arms.

"Come, little one, you've had too much to drink and it's time to tuck you into bed."

"I have not," Bree said indignantly. "I only had one beer."

"Aye, and two glasses of wine. Plus, I saw you drinking those shots of liquor with Nicky in the corner," James said.

Bree giggled. "They tasted funny."

She suddenly pounded on James' back. "Put me down! I need to have a birthday drink with Kaden!"

Kaden laughed. "I think you've had enough. You're going to have a headache in the morning as it is."

"No, I won't. James will heal me. Won't you, my love?" she said.

"Aye, little one. I will." He smiled at her and she leaned out of his arms toward Kaden.

"Happy Birthday, Kaden. I love you." She put her thin arms around his neck and hugged him fiercely.

He patted her back and kissed her on the cheek as James said goodnight and carried her out of the room.

He sighed and glanced around the room. His gaze landed on the scarf that Sophia had been wearing around her neck, and he crossed the room and picked it up from the couch. He brought it to his face and inhaled deeply. It smelled like her and he looked around guiltily before shoving it into his pocket. He drained the last of his beer and headed for the door. Dani stepped into the doorway and he swallowed his groan of dismay.

"Hello, Kaden."

"Hi, Dani."

"Did you have a good birthday?"

"Aye, I did. Thank you."

She stepped closer, keeping one hand behind her back as she trailed the fingers of her other hand along his arm. "I never gave you my present."

He frowned. "You didn't have to get me a present."

"I wanted to." She gave him a nervous smile. "Close your eyes."

"Dani, it's late."

"Please. It's a surprise," she pleaded.

He sighed and closed his eyes. He grunted with surprise when Dani pressed her lips against his. His eyes popped open as she pushed her tongue into his mouth. He pushed her away gently and she pouted at him in disappointment. "Why do you push me away?"

"You are too young for me."

"No, I'm not." She glared at him. "Tell me the truth. You do not want me because you want my cousin."

He hesitated and then grimaced when tears flowed down Dani's cheeks. He patted her back awkwardly when she flung herself into his arms. "She is a Lycan. You hate Lycans," she sobbed.

"I don't hate them, and it's not because of Sophia," he replied.

Dani gave a shuddering sigh. "I like you, Kaden. I know I could make you happy if you would just give me the chance. I may not have much experience, "she blushed, "but I am more than willing to learn."

Her hand began to wander to his crotch, and he grabbed it and held it away. "I'm sorry, Dani. I feel nothing more than friendship for you."

"Aye, because you are in love with Sophia."

"No, I'm not."

She laughed bitterly. "Of course, you aren't."

"I'm sorry, Dani," he repeated.

She rested her head against his chest for a moment and sighed deeply. "I know. If you – if you change your mind, you know where to find me."

She pulled away from him and wiped the tears from her face before leaving the room. He dropped into one of the chairs in front of the fireplace. He was an idiot. He had been without a woman for over four years and yet he had no interest in Dani, even after she had made it more than clear she wanted him in her bed.

He stared blindly into the fire. He wanted Sophia and if he couldn't have her, he'd rather have his own hand instead of another woman. He dropped his head into his hand. He really was an idiot.

CHAPTER 11

Weaving a little, Sophia returned to the common room. She squinted in the glow of the fire, looking for the scarf she had left behind.

"I thought you had gone to bed."

She screamed breathlessly and whirled around. She caught a glimpse of Kaden's face, stumbled back and tripped over her own feet. She landed on the floor with a hard thud and stared up at the ceiling, giggling softly.

"Are you all right?" Kaden's face, creased with worry, appeared over her.

"Aye." She giggled again and he raised his eyebrows at her.

"You're drunk."

"I am not," she protested.

"How much wine have you had tonight?"

"I don't remember."

He held his hand out. "Here, I'll help you up."

She shook her head. The room was spinning just the tiniest bit and she didn't feel like sitting up. "No, thank you. I'm going to sleep right here tonight."

He tugged her to her feet with a hard yank. She swayed and snickered as she bumped into him. "Oops."

"You *are* drunk," he said accusingly.

"Just tipsy." She patted his cheek. "You should be the one feeling tipsy. It was your birthday party after all."

"Why have you been avoiding me?" he asked.

"I haven't been," she said. "It's been a very busy week with um, wedding preparations."

"Liar." He scooped her up, holding her against his chest as he left the common room.

"Whee!" she whispered. She traced her fingers over his cheek as he carried her to her bedroom. "Why are you still here? Why aren't you tucked away in your bed in the rat-infested loft?"

"Dani cornered me before I could leave. She wanted to give me a birthday gift."

Sophia stiffened a little and dropped her hand from his cheek. "What was her gift?"

He didn't answer. He pushed open the door of her bedroom, letting it shut softly behind him, and carried her to her bed. He tried to set her down, but she put her arms around his neck and held tightly to him. "What was her birthday gift?"

"It doesn't matter."

"Tell me," she insisted.

"A kiss."

She glared at him. "And how did you enjoy your birthday gift from my pretty little cousin?"

He smiled. "Are you jealous, Lycan?"

Kaden grinned when Sophia shook her head vehemently. "No, I am not jealous."

"Are you certain?" He sat down on her bed, settling her on to his lap. Her dress had ridden up a bit, and he stared at the unfamiliar sight of her bare thighs. He was itching to touch them, to stroke her skin with his hand, and he made himself look away.

"Positive." She squirmed against him. "Thank you for bringing me to my bedroom. Goodnight, human."

He tightened his grip on her and stared at her mouth. "You sound like you're jealous."

"I'm not." She glared at him. "What do I care if you kiss Dani? I'm sure it was pleasant enough for you. She is your type, is she not?"

"And what is my type?" His hand gripped her knee and stroked her warm skin.

"Human, of course," she said.

He slipped his hand under her dress and rubbed her smooth thigh.

"Please don't do that," she whispered.

"Do what?"

"That." She looked down at her lap and he traced his fingers over the top of her thighs.

"How do you know what my type is, little Lycan?"

"Stop calling me that. I'm not little." She scowled at him.

"Aye, but you are a Lycan."

"And you're a human," she snapped. "Why are you not in my cousin's bed right now? She's made it perfectly clear she's more than willing to spread her legs for you."

He leaned toward her, his gaze dropping to her mouth. "Perhaps I did not care for your cousin's kiss the way you think I should have."

"What do you mean?" she whispered.

"Dani may be human but that does not automatically make her my type."

"What – what is your type?"

He studied her face. "Dark hair and dark eyes." He dropped his gaze to her breasts. "Full breasts with the prettiest pink-coloured nipples that harden in my mouth."

She moaned, and he squeezed her thigh. "Soft skin. A mouth that spits insults at me one moment and begs me to kiss it the next."

"I – I don't beg you to kiss me," she replied.

"Aye, not yet you haven't." He grinned arrogantly at her and could see the way it made her bristle.

She shoved at his chest. "I'm tired. Good night, Kaden."

"You haven't given me *your* birthday present yet, Sophia," he said.

"I - I told you I would not kiss you."

"No, you said you would not beg me to kiss you. There's a difference," he said.

She flushed. "I don't even like you. I'm not giving you a kiss as a birthday present. Go and find my cousin. She'll be more than happy to give you another."

He shifted her on his lap until his erection pressed against her ass. She gasped and stared wide-eyed at him.

"It's not a kiss I want from you," he said.

She snorted and he could smell the sweet scent of wine on her breath. A twinge of guilt went through him. Sophia was drunk and he was taking advantage of that. He was about to lift her off his lap when she squirmed again, and her ass brushed firmly against his cock. He groaned and forgot about his guilt as she rolled her eyes.

"Human or Lycan – you're all the same," she said. "Always thinking about how you can convince a woman to suck your cock. Although," she pursed her lips at him, "I'll admit I've never been given the 'it's my birthday' excuse before."

He moved one hand to her head and gripped the end of her braid. He pulled her head back and ent his mouth to her ear. "Wrong again, little Lycan."

She shuddered when he licked the curve of her ear. "What I want from you is not a kiss. Nor is it that beautiful mouth of yours wrapped around my cock. But," he paused and dipped his tongue into her ear, "I won't deny that I've spent more than one night picturing you on your knees in front of me."

She moaned and her hands clutched at his shoulders as he slipped his hand further up her skirt and traced the tops of her thighs. "What I want for my birthday is to have you sitting on my face. I want to lick your sweet pussy until you come screaming all over my face."

SOPHIA FROZE AS THE SWEETEST PULSE OF DESIRE SHE HAD ever felt, went through her. "I – I don't scream."

"You will," he promised.

His hand was on her panties and when he lifted her and tugged them down over her hips, she didn't stop him. He pulled her panties down her legs and she kicked them off her feet.

He laid back on her bed, twisting her body until she was straddling his hips, and grinned at her. When she didn't move, he stroked her thighs under her dress. "My face, little Lycan – sit on it."

She hesitated and his grin widened. "I promise I don't bite."

Sophia's pulse was pounding, and she was so turned on she could barely think straight. It had been too long since she had felt something other than her own hand between her thighs and gods, she wanted to feel his tongue on her. She knew Kaden didn't like her. She knew he was only using her and that, despite what he said, she would end this night on her knees in front of him, but she didn't care. The thought of his tongue tasting her was intoxicating. She was scrambling her way up his broad body, his big hands steadying her, before she even realized she was moving.

She planted her knees on the bed on either side of his head, her lower legs and feet braced against his chest, and moaned when he gripped her thighs. He winked at her before his head disappeared under the material of her dress. He tugged on her legs and she lowered herself down.

She sucked in her breath at the first touch of his tongue against her pussy. His hands slid up the inside of her thighs, and he used his thumbs to part her already-wet folds. His breath was hot against her, and she arched her back when he licked her clit with his tongue.

He used the tip of his tongue to swipe repeatedly over her clit until she was moaning and grinding her pussy against his face. She leaned back, resting her hands on his abdomen and thrusting more of her pussy into his mouth. His tongue, his deliciously hot and surprisingly stiff tongue, dipped into her. He probed at her tight opening and she moaned again. He licked and tasted every wet and dripping inch of her until she was writhing and twisting above him. Only his strong hands on her legs kept her from falling over, and she moaned in frustration when he pushed her upward and away from his mouth.

"Feel like screaming yet?" His voice was muffled, and she bunched her dress up around her hips, looking down at his dark head tucked between her thighs. His face was wet with her juices and he stared up at her, his blue eyes glinting in the firelight.

"Kaden," she moaned.

"Aye?" He kissed her inner thigh. "What do you want, Sophia?"

"Less talking, more licking," she demanded.

He grinned again. "Whatever you say, little Lycan."

She watched as he buried his face between her legs, and his hot tongue licked at her clit again. He sucked it into his mouth, rubbing it with his tongue while he pulled at the swollen nub with his lips, and her fingers twisted and tore at the fabric of her dress.

She was close to coming, her hips gyrating and twisting against his face as she fought to stay quiet. His tongue caressed and danced across her hot and swollen flesh, and she realized that Kaden was right. She was going to scream. She couldn't keep it in, not with the way he was nuzzling and sucking on her clit with a firm, relentless pressure.

She arched her back and threw her arm over her mouth, muffling her loud scream as she climaxed explosively on his face. She moaned into her arm as the last of her orgasm shuddered through her before she rolled to her side. She collapsed on the bed with a soft groan as Kaden sat up and leaned over her.

His mouth and chin were dripping with wetness and she had a moment of embarrassment before his mouth was on hers. He kissed her deeply, until the taste of the wine had been replaced by her own, and then pulled back.

She was sleepy. The combination of her orgasm and the wine she had drunk was making her feel light-headed and weak. She felt him kiss the tip of her nose, and then he tugged her dress down before pulling the covers out from under her.

He tucked her into bed, and she moaned when he couldn't

resist cupping one firm breast through her dress. Her nipple was hard against his palm, and he made a soft noise of regret before tucking the covers around her.

"Kaden?" she muttered.

"Aye?"

"Happy Birthday."

He kissed her mouth once more. "Thank you for the birthday present, Sophia."

CHAPTER 12

"K aden?"

"Aye?" He left the stall where he was brushing Samson and winced when Piper raced out from an empty stall and leaped at his leg. He climbed his thigh, his razor-sharp claws stabbing through his pants and into his skin.

"Gods be damned!" He pulled the tiny kitten off his leg and glared at it before rubbing its head roughly and setting it on the ground. It tore down the aisle of the barn and leaped onto his brother. Hogan meowed loudly and the two kittens, rolling and tumbling on the ground, disappeared into another empty stall.

Kaden rubbed at his leg as Evan grinned. "Still glad you bought the kittens for my sisters?"

"I'm starting to have my regrets."

Evan laughed. "Be glad you weren't at the house when Leta brought Hogan in the other night. Tia took one look at him and went nuts. They went crazy in the common room. They broke one of Mama's favourite bowls and Hogan climbed the wall and knocked a picture right off of it. When

Tia finally cornered him by the fireplace, Hogan scratched up her face something fierce before Dad could get them apart."

The boy's face was lit with amusement. "Then Leta started crying and having fits over Tia's face. Bree finally sent for James to come in from the barn and hold Tia until she healed."

Kaden shook his head with amusement as Evan looked around. "Have you seen Ian?"

"Aye, I believe he went ice fishing at the lake."

Evan's grin widened. "Really? I hope he catches something. It's been forever since we've had fish."

"I was just going to go and see if he had caught anything. Would you like to join me?"

"Aye, I could do that."

As they walked towards the lake, Kaden glanced at Evan. He was quiet and spent most of his time reading or drawing. He wondered if the boy knew how lucky he was to have a ready supply of paper. Paper was considered a luxury, and until he had started living with the Lycans he had never seen more than a scrap at a time. He tucked away the wages that Tristan paid him weekly, but at least twice a week he would pull out the bills and just stare at them. He would stroke the paper and marvel at the way the ink was pressed into it.

This morning when Maya had begun their lessons, she not only had books to teach him with, but she also had a bound book of plain paper for him to practice his writing. After she had left, he had spent quite a bit of time just touching the book of paper, flipping through its pages and smelling its good clean smell.

Evan glanced at him. "I heard that Aunt Maya is teaching you to read."

Kaden twitched in surprise and his face reddened. "How do you know that?"

Evan shrugged. "I'm quiet. People forget I'm in the room and say things that are supposed to be a secret. I overheard Sophia asking Aunt Maya how it went this morning."

He gave Kaden a quick look. "I won't say anything. Aunt Maya said you didn't want anyone to know. Why not?"

"It's embarrassing," Kaden said.

"Not that embarrassing. It's not your fault you grew up without having someone to teach you."

"Aye." Kaden changed the subject. "How was your sister feeling this morning?"

"What do you mean?"

"Both she and my sister had a bit too much wine last night."

Guilt flooded through him. He had allowed his lust for Sophia to control him last night. He had woken this morning and immediately felt ashamed of how he took advantage of her drunkenness. He needed to apologize to her, but he hadn't quite worked up the nerve.

Bullshit. You're avoiding the apology because you're afraid you'll take one look at her and be begging her to let you fuck her. Or at the very least, give her a repeat performance of last night.

He drew in a shuddering breath of need as he remembered the way she had tasted. She had been so wet and ready for him. He had no trouble picturing how she would look with her legs spread wide as her warm, wet core eagerly accepted his cock.

"Kaden?"

He cleared his throat. "Aye?"

"Are you all right?"

"Aye. What did you say?"

"I said Sophia is fine. In fact, she's in a better mood today than she has been in weeks. She must have had fun last night."

"What do you mean?" Kaden could hear the guilt in his voice.

"I mean that she must have had fun at the party last night." Evan gave him a strange look. "Are you sure you're all right?"

"Fine," he muttered. They were at the lake now and he waved to Ian. The old man was standing motionless at the large hole he had cut through the ice. A fishing pole was in one hand, and he waved back as Evan and Kaden stood on the shore for a moment.

Evan stepped on to the ice. "Let's join him."

Kaden hesitated. He couldn't swim, and the thought of crossing the ice with the cold water just below his feet made him nervous.

"Why don't we wait for Ian to come to shore?" he suggested. He could see the man setting his fishing rod down and reaching for the bucket stowed carefully behind him.

"Are you scared?" Evan asked without malice.

Kaden shrugged. "I can't swim."

"Well, it's not like you're going to fall into the -"

The young boy shouted in alarm as there was a loud, sharp crack. Kaden watched in horror as the ice broke around Ian's feet and he plunged into the water.

"Ian!" Evan screamed. He started to slide onto the ice and Kaden yanked him back.

"Go to the house! Find your father and your brothers! Go, Evan!"

His face white, Evan ran for the house. Slipping and sliding on the slick ice, Kaden made his way towards the flailing Ian.

"Hang on, Ian! I'm coming!" he shouted.

"Kaden!" Ian gasped as he slipped under the surface of the water. He popped back up a few seconds later, coughing and sputtering as he tried to heave himself up onto the ice.

Kaden fell to his knees. He lay flat on his stomach and slid his way toward Ian. All around him, the ice was creaking and groaning, and he swallowed down his panic and moved grimly forward. "Hold on Ian! Hold on!"

"I can't! Kaden, help me!" Ian shouted. The panic and fear in the old man's voice gave Kaden a rush of adrenaline and he slid faster as, with a final desperate look of terror at him, Ian disappeared under the water.

"Ian! No!" Kaden screamed. He slid to the edge of the broken ice and thrust his arm into the water. The coldness turned his arm numb almost immediately and he waved it around frantically under the ice. He was steeling himself to duck his head into the water when his hand brushed against something. He grabbed it and yanked hard as he squirmed and wiggled his body backwards.

He gave a shout of surprise when the large black wolf surfaced. Its eyes were closed, and its tongue hung limply from its open mouth. Kaden hesitated and then dug his cold fingers into the shaggy pelt of the wolf and heaved it onto the ice.

He shoved it as hard as he could, and the wolf slid limply across the ice. Kaden followed it, sliding like a snake on his belly, until he was a few feet from the icy water. He staggered to his feet and stared in disbelief at the wolf lying at his feet.

He was reaching for the beast when it suddenly coughed. Water poured out of its mouth and it gagged and coughed again before opening its eyes. They were a golden yellow and they stared wearily at Kaden.

"Ian?" Kaden whispered in disbelief. He backed up as the wolf whined and tried to gain its feet. "Ian, why didn't you -"

There was another loud crack and Kaden shouted as the ice broke around his feet. He dropped like a stone into the cold, black water and his breath whooshed out of his lungs in a hard rush. Panic flowed through him and he grabbed onto the edge of the ice before he could sink. It broke in his hands and he struggled and flailed to keep his head above the water.

The water was so cold. It was seeping into his bones, turning his arms and legs numb and stealing his breath from him. He slipped under the water, swallowed a mouthful of it and struggled to the surface, coughing and gasping for breath. His jacket was weighing him down and he tried to struggle out of it, but it clung to him wetly. He was going under again, he could feel it, and he took one last deep breath before the water slipped over his head.

He was tired. The cold and the heaviness of his clothes were working against him as he tried to thrash his way back toward the rapidly-shrinking circle of light above him. His lungs were burning, and his limbs were suddenly, incredibly heavy. He stopped fighting for the surface and watched with a numb disinterest as the light grew fainter and his breath released from his nose in a steady stream of bubbles.

A figure appeared in the circle of light. He watched as it dove into the water and swam toward him with long, powerful strokes. Sophia's pale face floated in front of him and she grabbed the collar of his shirt and yanked him toward her. Her hands grasped his face and her mouth descended onto his. He parted his lips and she blew a hard breath of air into his burning lungs before wrapping her arm around his chest and shoulders.

She yanked hard on the rope that was tied around her waist and then wrapped her legs around his hips, clinging tightly to him as they were pulled upward. In less than a minute they'd been hauled out of the water and were sliding across the frozen lake. Nicky, James and Tristan were standing a few feet from the shore and pulling on the rope that was tied around Sophia's waist.

"Kaden!" Sophia cupped his face as they were tugged across the cold ice. "Take a breath, honey. Come on, one big breath for me."

He opened his mouth and sucked in a whooping, gasping, lungful of air. His body was shaking violently as Sophia, her lips blue and her face white, smiled at him.

"Good, honey. Take another breath. In through the nose, out through the mouth, remember?"

They were at the edge of the lake now and when Nicky reached for Sophia, Kaden forced his numb arms and legs around her. He clutched her tightly, refusing to let her go, and James wrapped a blanket around the both of them.

"Ian," Kaden rasped out.

"He's all right," James said. "Uncle Marshall, Doran, and Evan have taken him into the house." He pulled on Kaden's shoulder. "Kaden, let go of Sophia."

"No." He shook his head and Sophia, her teeth chattering so hard she could barely speak, pressed her mouth against his in a brief kiss.

"It's all right," she soothed. "Let me go, honey. My brothers cannot carry us both, and we need to get into the house where it's warm."

Bree knelt beside him and squeezed his shoulder. "Let go, Kaden."

He let go reluctantly and Avery wrapped Sophia in a separate blanket. Tristan picked her up and carried her toward the house as James and Nicky hauled him to his feet.

"Can you walk?" Nicky asked.

He nodded yes, took a step forward and would have fallen if it wasn't for James and Nicky.

"Kaden, we can carry you. Just -"

Evan appeared leading Bandit. The horse snorted nervously as Evan pulled on his halter. "I thought we could bring Kaden to the house on Bandit."

"That was good thinking, Evan." Nicky clapped him on the back before turning and helping James hoist Kaden onto the horse.

Kaden closed his eyes, water dripping off of him in a steady stream, as Bree squeezed his shaking leg. Nicky tugged on Bandit's halter and led the horse toward the house.

HE STOOD IN THE DOORWAY AND STARED AT THE OLD MAN. HE was lying in bed with his eyes closed but after a moment he said, "Hello, Kaden."

"Hello, Ian. How are you feeling?"

Ian opened his eyes and sat up as Kaden sat in the chair beside the bed.

"Good. The lady Avery was kind enough to lie down with me for a while." Ian gave him a tentative smile.

"Why didn't you tell me you were a Lycan?"

"You never asked."

Kaden sighed and stared down at his hands. "You should have told me."

"I didn't think it would make a difference. We're friends. What does it matter if I'm a Lycan?"

"It matters because…" Kaden gave him an angry look.

"Because why?"

"I thought you were human, and you let me believe that." Kaden rubbed his hand through his hair.

"Aye, I suppose I did. I'm sorry for that, Kaden, but I liked being your friend," the old man said.

"I like being your friend as well," Kaden replied.

Ian reached out and took his hand, squeezing it once before releasing it. "Thank you for saving my life."

"It scared the hell out of me when you fell into the water," Kaden said.

"You and me both," Ian said. "I'm sorry that you nearly died trying to save me. How do you feel?"

"I'm fine."

"The lady Avery told me if it hadn't been for Sophia, you would have died."

"Aye. She saved my life." Kaden glanced at him and Ian frowned at the look of shame in his eyes.

"What's wrong, Kaden?"

"I don't know. I just – I used to think that Lycans weren't capable of caring for anyone but their own kind. And then Sophia risked her life twice for us - first to save Bree and then to save me. I guess I'm ashamed of the things I've said and thought about them."

"They understand why you felt that way," Ian said.

"Aye, I guess." Kaden sighed. "I'm tired, Ian. I'm going back to the barn. I'll talk to you later, all right?"

"Aye. Thank you again, Kaden." Ian reached out and squeezed his arm.

"You're welcome. I'm glad you're all right."

"WHERE'S KADEN?" SOPHIA ASKED BREE. IT WAS JUST after dinner and Kaden hadn't joined them to eat.

"He's in the loft. He said he wasn't hungry."

She gave Sophia a nervous look. "I'm worried about him. He says he's fine, but he's been acting strange all day. I don't know if it's because he almost died, or because he didn't know that Ian was a Lycan or...

She sighed. "I tried to convince him to stay in the house tonight. It's cold and the barn isn't that warm, but he refused. He said he wanted to be alone."

Sophia stood and Bree frowned. "Where are you going?"

"To talk to your brother."

"I don't know if that's a good idea, Sophia. Kaden is, well, he needs time to process things. If you push him to talk about it and he's not ready, he'll just close himself off from you."

"I need to talk to him, Bree." Sophia grabbed her cloak and left the room.

The air was cold, and she drew her cloak around her as she ran to the barn. She shoved the door open, climbed the ladder to the hayloft and peered into the room. Kaden, wearing just a pair of pants, was sitting on the side of his bed with his back to her. It was cool in the hayloft and she could see the goose bumps on the broad expanse of his back.

She hoisted herself up and stood quietly for a moment. He didn't move and she cleared her throat. "Kaden? Honey, are you all right?"

He jerked and whipped around, her scarf falling from his hands as he stared at her with wide and startled eyes.

She walked toward him. "I know what happened today was frightening, and I know you're surprised about Ian, but he had the best intentions."

He stood and nearly ran to her. She took a step backward and then his hands were on her cloak and he was unbuttoning it and pushing it from her body.

"Kaden -"

He slammed his mouth down on hers, his tongue pushing past her lips to stroke at hers urgently. She moaned and threw her arms around him, pressing her body against his.

His hands fumbled at the buttons of her shirt before he made a low noise of need and tore open her shirt. The buttons flew off and scattered to the floor, as he yanked her shirt from her body. He cupped her breasts, groaning at the hardness of her nipples against his palms, and kissed her again.

She returned his kiss, her tongue twisting and tangling with his as she reached for the button on his pants. She unbuttoned them and pushed them down his hips. He was naked underneath them and she took his erect cock in her hand and squeezed firmly. Wetness was surging between her legs. His frantic need for her had ignited her own fire for him.

She stroked him and he cried out and arched his hips into her hand. She dipped her head and licked his thick neck as she kicked off her boots. He tore at the button on her pants, and she reached down and helped him unbutton them before wiggling out of them. He raked her panties down her legs and then lifted her, pulling both her pants and her underwear off of her feet.

He left them crumpled on the floor as she wrapped her legs around his waist and rubbed herself against his cock. She moaned as his cock slid across her wetness and he groaned and moved to the bed.

He dropped her on the bed and looked down at her with savage hunger. She stared at his thick cock jutting out proudly from his body, and wetness pooled between her thighs. He hesitated as a look of confusion and doubt crossed his face. She parted her legs, smiling with satisfaction when his eyes dropped to her exposed and glistening sex.

"Please, Kaden," she whispered.

With a soft groan, he dropped to his knees between her legs. He pushed her thighs wide and entered her with a single thrust. She moaned and arched her body upward, taking him deep inside of her warmth. He was thick and hard, and as her body stretched around him, he propped himself above her on his elbows. She stroked his face, feeling the rough stubble under her palm, before kissing him on the mouth.

"Sophia."

His voice was raspy with desire, and she shuddered under him. He kissed her with rough urgency, one hand cupping her breast as he moved within her. She hooked her legs around his waist and met each of his thrusts as his tongue mimicked the movement of his cock.

"You're so warm," he whispered against her mouth.

She moaned in reply, and he reached between them and rubbed her clit with the pads of his fingers. They were rough against her skin and she shivered with pleasure.

"Oh, Kaden," she whimpered as he rubbed firmly in small, tight circles.

"Come for me, Sophia," he whispered as he rubbed her clit again. "I want to feel you coming around me."

His voice was enough to push her over the edge and she cried out, her body shaking and shuddering around his cock as she climaxed.

He plunged in and out of her, his breath coming in harsh, hot pants, as her core squeezed tightly around him. He whispered her name repeatedly as his body stiffened and he thrust deeply into her one final time. She wrapped her arms and legs around him, covering his face and shoulders and upper chest with soft kisses as he trembled madly before collapsing against her.

CHAPTER 13

She woke to find him staring at her.

"Hi," she said.

"Sophia, I..."

She realized with a jolt of panic that he was already regretting what had happened between them. Her heart dropped into her stomach at the thought that this was it between them, and in desperation she pressed her mouth against his. She kissed him hard, pressing her tongue against his lips until he opened them, and she could slip it into his mouth. He returned her kiss, his hands tightening on her hips, until he pulled back with a soft groan.

"Sophia, we need to talk."

"Not yet, all right?" she whispered. "Don't think – just feel. It's been so long for both of us. Can we not, just for tonight, make each other feel good?"

"Aye," he said.

She kissed him again and he ran his hand down her bare back to her ass. He squeezed it, rubbing her soft skin as he pressed her against his naked body. Sophia nuzzled her face into his neck and nipped at the stubble-covered skin.

He groaned and she smiled to herself before running her hands over his broad back. She traced the network of scars and he frowned at the look on her face. "What?"

"I'm sorry that my kind did this to you." She leaned forward and kissed one of the wide scars on his chest.

He shrugged. "It doesn't matter."

"It does," she insisted. "The cruelty they -"

She shrieked loudly, her back arching, before she scrambled over Kaden's broad body. She peered around him as Kaden clapped a hand against his chest.

"Gods be damned, little Lycan! Are you trying to give me a heart attack?"

She glared at the small orange kitten who was sitting on the bed staring innocently at her.

"Piper!" She growled at him, her eyes flashing green, and he hissed at her in reply before washing his face with one white-tipped paw.

"I thought he was a rat." She shuddered all over before peering at the floor of the loft.

Kaden laughed. "If it makes you feel better, I've never seen a single rat in the hayloft. Besides, both Piper and Hogan are big enough to catch them now."

She stared at the small kitten. "Really?"

"Aye, I watched each of them kill a rat yesterday."

She looked around the floor of the loft uncertainly as Piper brushed up against Kaden and purred. She leaned off the bed and picked up her scarf from the floor. "I wondered where this had gone."

He cleared his throat. "I uh, I found it the night of my birthday. I was going to bring it back to you."

She smiled and pushed him forward a bit so she could examine the scars on his back. "That was nice of you."

"I'm very nice." He reached behind him to stroke her lean

thigh as Piper jumped off the bed. She bent her head and pressed her mouth against a scar on his back. He shuddered and she licked from one shoulder blade to the other as he groaned.

She kissed and licked each one of his scars, paying special attention to the mass of scars that covered his lower back. Even as he moaned and squirmed beneath her warm tongue, her heart was hurting at the sheer amount of scarring on his back. She marveled at the strength he must have needed to survive it.

"Gods, little Lycan," he suddenly moaned. "Please stop."

"I'm sorry, does it hurt?" she asked.

He shook his head. "No, but I'm going to come all over the sheets if you don't stop."

She grinned and licked from the base of his spine to up between his shoulder blades. He made a soft groan of need and turned to face her.

"My turn," he whispered.

He tugged her over until she was lying on her stomach. He straddled her hips and massaged her lower back with his hard hands. She could feel his cock rubbing against her ass, and she reached behind her and took it in her hand. She stroked it lightly, and he arched his hips into her hand before taking both her hands and resting them against the bed.

He started his own slow, meandering path of warm kisses down her back. He tasted and licked her soft, smooth skin until she was trembling and twisting beneath him. When he bit her ass lightly, she cried out and arched up off the bed. He pushed her down with a gentle hand on her back and moved down until he could lick and nip the backs of her thighs.

"Gods be damned, Kaden," she moaned as his warm tongue licked the back of her knees. She jerked and ground her pelvis into the bed. She could feel wetness coating the inside of her thighs and she pushed her thighs apart eagerly when he knelt between her legs.

He rubbed and caressed her ass until she thought she would go mad with need. "Touch me, Kaden!"

"I am touching you, little Lycan." There was a hint of laughter in his voice and she twisted her head to stare at him.

"On your hands and knees, Sophia," he demanded.

She shuddered all over and obediently lifted her body until she was resting on her hands and knees. He reached between her legs, running his hand over her soaking wet pussy until she cried out and pushed herself onto his hand. He rubbed her clit and she made another soft, moaning cry.

He guided his cock to her wet slit and pushed into her. She arched her back as he gathered her long dark hair in one hand and tugged. She lifted her head, staring at the rough walls of the barn as he thrust back and forth. His hard cock surged in and out, sending waves of shuddering desire through her as she moaned and thrust her pelvis at him eagerly.

"Harder, Kaden," she murmured.

He dropped his hands to her hips and, holding her tight, plunged in and out of her. She gasped and made small breathless cries of pleasure as he fucked her hard and fast. She lifted her ass, silently inviting him to slide deeper within her, and he muttered her name as his pelvis slapped against her in a quickening rhythm.

She reached between her thighs and rubbed her swollen clit. She controlled her urge to shift as she shouted his name and climaxed. He thrust into her, his hands clamping down on her hips, and came deep inside of her. She collapsed against the bed and he rolled onto the bed beside her, panting harshly.

She turned to face him, and he smiled and kissed her mouth gently before pulling her into his embrace. She rested her head on his chest, tracing the scars with gentle fingers as he rubbed her back. She closed her eyes and listened to the solid beat of his heart beneath her ear.

"BREE? ARE YOU ALL RIGHT?" JAMES KNOCKED ON THE bathroom door.

"I'm fine," Bree called back. "I'll be right out."

He waited patiently outside the bathroom door until she came out. He frowned at her.

"You're pale. Were you throwing up?"

"Aye," she replied, brushing her hand across her mouth. "My stomach is a little upset."

"Come back to bed." He led her to their bedroom, and she crawled under the sheet and quilt. He stretched out behind her and put his arms around her, nuzzling the back of her neck affectionately. Warmth surged through her and the nausea in her belly disappeared as he stroked her upper chest.

"Better?" he asked.

She nodded. "Thank you, honey."

"You're welcome." They laid in companionable silence for a while. Bree watched as the sun peeked over the horizon, her thoughts turning to Kaden. She hoped he was feeling better this morning.

"What's wrong, little one?" James kissed her cheek.

"I'm worried about Kaden. He nearly died yesterday, and he found out that Ian was a Lycan." She sighed. "I should have told him Ian was a Lycan."

"It wasn't your information to tell, Bree. Ian could have told him," James replied.

"I guess." She smiled at him before admiring the ring on her finger. "I can't believe we'll be married soon."

"Aye," he pulled her closer, "and then you'll be stuck with me forever."

She laughed. "Stuck isn't the word I would use, James."

He grinned at her. "I suppose not. Speaking of being married, we should start thinking about what kind of house you would like."

She stared out the window. "Aye, I suppose."

He turned her gently to her back and stared down at her. "What?"

"Nothing."

"Tell me, little one," he said.

She shrugged. "I guess the thought of living away from Mama and the rest of your family makes me a little sad."

He stared thoughtfully at her. "You do not dream of having your own home?"

She shrugged again. "I don't know. Not really, I guess. Is that strange?"

He shook his head, but she continued anyway. "Maybe it's because I've always wished for a big family. Or maybe it's just because living here with your family has been the happiest time of my life. I love all of them so much."

"They love you too." James kissed the tip of her nose and rested his forehead against hers.

"Do you think we could find something close to them?" she asked timidly. "I don't want to be too far away from Mama or from Leta."

James smiled at her. "Little one, we can stay here for as long as you'd like. We don't need to find our own house until you're ready."

"But will your parents not want us to find our own place once we are married?" Bree asked.

James laughed. "You forget that Lycans live in packs, Bree. We are happiest when we are together."

"Truly?"

"Aye. Trust me – no one in my family will find it strange if we live here after we are married."

She smiled happily at him. "Thank you, James."

He nodded. "In fact, I could talk to Dad about building a house on his lands. The property is large enough that we could build our own place within walking distance of this one. That way we can have our own space, but you'll still be close to Mama."

Her eyes widened with delight and she hugged him impulsively. "I would love that so much. Do you think Tristan would agree to it?"

"Aye, I know he would."

She hugged him again and then crawled over him and began to dress. He tucked his hands behind his head and watched with interest as she pulled her nightgown over her head.

"You know," he said thoughtfully, "if we had our own place, you wouldn't even have to wear clothes. That's one argument for building our own home."

She giggled and finished dressing. "Aye, except I would freeze to death."

He sat on the side of the bed and pulled her between his legs, kissing her chest. "I'll keep you warm enough."

She kissed the top of his head as his hands squeezed her ass playfully. "Come back to bed, Bree."

She gave him an apologetic look. "I thought I might check on Kaden."

He squeezed her ass once more and then released her. "Do you want me to come with you?"

She shook her head. "No, that's fine. I think it might be better if I talk to him alone. I know he's upset."

"I'll see you at breakfast then?"

"Aye. Thank you, my love."

"For what?" he asked.

She smiled. "Just for being you."

Kaden groaned and threaded his hands through Sophia's long dark hair. "Gods, little Lycan. Do you know how many times I've dreamed about this?"

Sophia looked up at him, her mouth red and swollen, and grinned. "Is it as good as you imagined?"

"Better," he groaned again. "Occasionally in my dreams, I might have worried about your teeth."

She burst out laughing and squeezed her fingers around the base of his cock. "Don't worry, human. I have a firm 'no teeth' rule when I'm sucking cock."

His hands tightened in her hair when she slid her mouth over his cock again. He watched as she sucked the head lightly, her hands stroking his shaft with firm, long strokes. Sophia on her knees with her mouth around his cock, and the early morning light shining on her perfect tanned body was not a sight he would ever forget.

She took more of his cock into her mouth. The feel of her warm, wet tongue as it licked along his shaft was almost enough to make him come. He moaned as she sucked enthusiastically.

He jerked in alarm when Bree's voice floated up to him. "Kaden? Are you awake?"

He cleared this throat, giving Sophia a frantic look as she sat back on her heels and grinned up at him.

"Aye, Bree. I – I'm awake."

Sophia rubbed her thumb over the head of his cock. He

glared at her and tried to pull away, but she tightened her hand around his cock and held him firmly.

"Can I come up and talk with you?"

"Now is not a good time, Bree," he called.

His sister sighed and he gave Sophia another look of panic when he heard Bree start up the ladder. "Kaden, I know you're upset. You need to talk about what happened yesterday."

"Bree, we can talk about it later. I just, I need a few minutes," he said desperately.

"You can't avoid me forever," Bree said. "Why don't you come for a walk with me and we'll -"

"Bree, perhaps Kaden could take a walk with you after breakfast," Sophia said.

Kaden groaned and slapped his face into his hand. There was a moment of silence and then Bree, her voice coloured with a mixture of amusement and embarrassment, said, "Aye, that's fine."

"Thank you, Bree," Sophia said cheerfully.

"Um, you're welcome," Bree replied. "I'll see you both at breakfast then?"

"Aye, you will," Sophia said.

Kaden made another low groan as Sophia took his cock into her mouth again. It had started to soften during his conversation with his sister, but at the feel of Sophia's hot mouth, it stiffened immediately. Dimly, he heard the sound of the barn door closing and he wrapped his hands in Sophia's hair and tugged her mouth away.

"Sophia, you should not have said anything."

"Why not?"

"Because I think we should keep this between the two of us. I'm not sure it's wise for everyone else to know."

She smiled at him. "Kaden, it will be impossible to keep

it between the two of us. My family are Lycans. The moment you are around them, they'll know we've mated. They'll smell it on the both of us."

He groaned with embarrassment and she rubbed his hip. "Do not worry about it."

"Sophia, I'm sorry but we need to talk about what's happening between us."

She nodded. "I know. But first, I'm going to suck your cock until you come in my mouth. Then you're going to make me come. Then we'll talk."

He moaned as she leaned forward and licked his cock. "I don't want to take advantage of you, little Lycan."

"You're not," she said. She looked up at him, her eyes glowing a light green. "You're not the only one who has dreamed about this, Kaden. Only, in my dreams you do a lot less arguing."

CHAPTER 14

Terrence knocked lightly on Draken's bedroom door.

"Enter."

He took a deep breath and opened the door. He stood on the threshold as Draken climbed out of the bed. Naked, Draken crossed the room and took his pants from where they were draped on the chair. He slipped into them and poured himself a glass of wine.

"You've been gone a long time, Terrence."

"You gave me a difficult task."

The Lycan snorted. "Is that your way of saying you failed?"

"No."

Draken returned to the bed and shook the woman still curled under the covers. "Leave us."

"My lord, I thought you wanted me to spend the night with you," she pouted.

"I said leave us!" Draken snarled, his eyes glowing a dark red.

The woman whined, her own eyes lightening to a bright yellow, before she slid from the bed. Draken gave her an impatient look as she pulled her clothes on quickly. He pushed her away when she tried to kiss him, and she gave another high-pitched whine.

"Do not be angry with me, my lord," she whimpered.

"Go quickly before you feel my claws on that pretty back-side of yours," he said.

Without looking at Terrence she left the room, shutting the door behind her.

Draken rolled his eyes. "Gods, they're all the same. Whining, simpering fools." He stared blankly at the darkness outside his window for a moment. "It's why I want her, Terrence. She's…different. She wouldn't whine for my attention and lie under me like a dead cow."

"Aye, my lord."

Draken sat down in front of the fireplace and nodded for Terrence to join him. The Lycan sat in the chair next to him and cleared his throat.

"Tell me why it's taken you so long." Draken sipped at his wine.

"I couldn't go too closely to their home. They undoubtedly are keeping watch for us, and I couldn't risk the chance of them catching my scent."

"No, I suppose not."

"There is a town about half a day from their home. I stayed there for a few days and -"

"This town - is it mostly humans or Lycans?"

"Humans. But they seem to be ambivalent to Lycans. There were a few Lycans living in the town itself."

Draken took another sip of wine and Terrence shifted in his chair. "The Lycans showed up in the town while I was there."

Draken stared into the fire. "Did they see you?"

He shook his head. "No. The slave is marrying the Red."

"Is she now? And how did you find this out?"

Terrence shrugged. "It was easy enough to conceal my scent in a town full of humans and horses and other Lycans. I followed them for a while. The slave was trying on dresses and there was talk amongst them about the wedding."

"Was she there?" Draken asked.

"Aye, my lord. She was."

Draken's nostrils flared and he finished his wine in two large gulps. "How did she look? Is she as beautiful as I remember?"

"Aye."

Draken smiled. "I dream about her, Terrence. Every woman I have taken to my bed pales in comparison to her. She is meant to be mine. I can feel it in my very bones."

Terrence gave Draken an alarmed look. He had known the Lycan for many years, and he had never seen him react this way to a woman. She had turned into an obsession for his pack leader, and he felt a trickle of fear slither down his spine.

"My lord, I know you are determined to have this Sophia, but it will be very difficult to take her. I do not believe it is wise to risk the lives of your pack over her. These Lycans are – are powerful. We were lucky to survive our last encounter with them."

Draken's face turned red and a low snarl emitted from his chest. "This is twice now you've tried to tell me what to do, Terrence."

"My lord," Terrence said, "I'm only trying to do what is best for our pack. Your need for the Lycan has blinded you to –"

With a growl of rage, Draken leaped from his chair. He grabbed Terrence around the throat and lifted him out of his chair. He squeezed brutally for a moment and then threw him across the room. Terrence crashed into the wall and crumpled to the ground. Draken loomed over him, his face covered in hair and his eyes glowing bright red.

His body enlarged and the seam of his pants ripped with a soft purring noise. "I will have this woman as mine. Do you understand, Terrence?"

Coughing and choking, Terrence nodded as Draken crouched over him. "We leave for this town first thing tomorrow."

"My lord?" Terrence whispered.

"We will wait in the town for them to return. When she does, we will take her and kill the others."

"They may not come back," Terrence whispered again.

"They will return," Draken growled confidently. "I will wait for years if I must."

"Hello, Sophia."

"Hello, Mama."

Avery laid down on the bed behind Sophia and put her arm around her waist before kissing the back of her head.

"What's wrong, my love?"

"Nothing," Sophia said.

Avery didn't reply and Sophia leaned into her mother as Avery stroked her dark hair.

"Mama?"

"Hmm?"

"Did you fall in love with Papa right away?"

"Perhaps not right away but it did not take very long," Avery said.

They were silent for a while and then Avery asked, "Did

something happen with you and Kaden? Things seemed awkward between the two of you at lunch."

Sophia sighed. "I was worried about him last night and so I went to the hayloft to check on him. I just wanted to make sure he was okay, to – to comfort him, you know?"

"Aye, I do know," Avery replied.

"I comforted him and then this morning we…"

"Did you have a fight, my love?" Avery asked.

Sophia shook her head. "No. I almost feel like it would have been better if we had. We were both very calm and matter-of-fact about why it wouldn't work between us. We agreed that it should be a one-time thing and that was it."

"Do you love him?"

"I don't know. I hardly know him."

"I think you know enough," Avery replied.

Sophia rubbed at her forehead. "I know that when I realized he was under the ice, when I thought he would drown, and I would never hear his voice or touch him again, I thought I would go mad. Is that love, Mama?"

"I believe it is," Avery said.

"It doesn't matter. I already agreed we couldn't be together."

Avery squeezed her tight. "He will change his mind, my love."

"He won't. He's still leaving after the wedding," Sophia said miserably.

"How do you know that?"

"He told me this morning. He said it was one of the reasons why we couldn't – couldn't continue. He'll only be here for a little longer."

"I'm sorry." Avery kissed her cheek. "There's still a chance he'll decide to stay. You cannot give up hope."

Sophia sat up, squirmed past her mother and pulled on her boots.

"Where are you going?"

"For a run."

"It's almost dinner," Avery reminded.

"I'm not hungry," Sophia said with a faint smile.

Avery stood and hugged her. "Be careful in the forest, my love."

"There has been no sign of Draken. I am half-convinced he will not return," Sophia replied.

Avery shook her head. "He'll be back. Promise me you'll be careful and that you will not go far."

"I promise, Mama."

KADEN STOPPED AT THE END OF THE HALLWAY. EVAN WAS standing outside of the storage room and rattling the handle. He frowned when he heard Leta's muffled voice.

"Evan! This isn't funny! Let me out right now!"

"Leta, be quiet!" Evan said. "Just give me a minute."

"It smells in here!"

"I know, I know. I've lost the key."

Leta's scream of outrage reverberated behind the closed door.

"Calm down, Leta! It has to be around here somewhere." Kaden watched as Evan checked his pockets and then dropped to his hands and knees in the hallway and searched the floor.

"Evan!" Leta pounded on the door again. "I'm telling Papa!"

Kaden walked down the hallway and stopped in front of Evan. "What's going on?"

"Oh hey, Kaden." Evan gave him a nervous grin as Leta pounded on the door again.

"Kaden! Help me! Evan's locked me in the storage room, and it smells in here!"

Kaden frowned at Evan. "Evan, let her out."

"I've lost the key," Evan said sheepishly.

Kaden tried the door handle and then studied the thick, wooden door. "When did you have it last?"

"I swear it was in my pocket but now it's gone." Evan continued to search the floor.

"Kaden, please help me!" Leta hollered.

"Just stay calm, Leta. We'll have you out in a minute."

"What in the gods name is Leta carrying on about?" Vivian appeared in the hallway and frowned at Kaden and Evan.

"Hi, Grandmamma," Leta said plaintively through the door. "Evan's locked me in the storage room."

"Evan." Vivian gave him a disappointed look and the young Lycan flushed.

"I didn't mean to. I accidentally lost the key."

Vivian sighed. "Oh, Evan."

Kaden pushed on the door. It was solid and he leaned experimentally against it. It didn't budge and he stepped back as Vivian said, "Perhaps we could cut through it with an axe."

"Is there no spare key?" Kaden asked.

"No, I don't believe so. I didn't even know it locked."

She stared sternly at Evan. "Go and find your father and tell him what has happened please."

Evan nodded. "Yes, ma'am."

"Wait." Kaden grabbed Evan's arm before he could leave. He stared thoughtfully at Vivian's hair. It was piled on top of her head in a fashionable bun and she patted it self-consciously.

"What?"

"Do you have two hair pins that I can borrow, Mrs. Williams?" he asked.

She blinked at him. "Aye."

She plucked two pins from her hair and handed them to him. He knelt at the door and inserted the pins into the lock. He wiggled them with careful concentration, moving them gently back and forth in the lock for a few minutes until there was a soft click.

With a smile of triumph, he turned the door handle and the door opened. Leta came barrelling out and hugged him. "Thank you, Kaden! Thank you so much!"

"You're welcome, Leta." He patted her back as Evan grinned at him.

"Where did you learn to do that?"

Kaden shrugged. "You pick up things."

"Will you teach me?" Evan asked as Leta punched him in the arm.

"I'm telling Papa on you!"

"It was an accident, Leta." Evan ruffled her hair and she growled at him, her eyes lightening to green, before stomping down the hallway.

"I'm still telling on you!"

"Aww, c'mon Leta…"

Evan trailed after her and Kaden suppressed a grin as Vivian shook her head.

"Thank you, Mrs. Williams." He handed her back the hair pins and she tucked them into her hair before eyeing him carefully. "Are you in love with my granddaughter?"

He stared at her, shocked into silence by her forwardness.

"Well?" She gave him an impatient look.

"Mrs. Williams, I -"

"Call me Vivian," she said.

"Vivian, I'm sorry. I'm not really comfortable talking about this."

"Aye, I suppose it's really none of my business is it?" she said amiably enough.

She stared shrewdly at him. "When Tristan was young, I used to imagine what type of future he would have. I wanted him to be happy. I wanted him to find love and have children of his own. I believed he would be happiest with a Lycan. Our family had been nothing but Lycans for generations, and I saw no reason for that to change."

She smiled a little. "Of course, my husband was a fair bit more open-minded than I. He was friends with humans and Lycans alike and when Marshall's parents died, we took him in, even though he was half-human. We took Marshall in because it was the right thing to do. I did not expect that I would grow to care for and love him as much as I loved my birth child."

She leaned against the wall and studied her hands for a moment. "Still, I expected that Tristan would find love with a Lycan and when I realized that he had fallen for a human, I was against it. I liked Avery, I did, but deep down inside I believed that humans were not capable of feeling the emotions that Lycans did."

Vivian studied him for a moment. "Lycans live in packs. They spend their entire lives loving and protecting the members of their pack, and I did not believe that humans would ever understand that. I did not trust them to understand the Lycan way. I wanted my granddaughter to be raised by a Lycan mother. I wanted her to grow up strong and proud of who she was."

She sighed. "I look back at my behaviour and at how I thought, and I am ashamed. You mistrust and fear the Lycans, and it's understandable why. No one blames you for that,

Kaden. I, however, had no reason for my dislike of humans other than pure ignorance."

"You seem to like humans well enough now," Kaden said.

"Aye, I do. Avery and Maya changed my mind. Their love for my sons opened my eyes to the realization that humans can and do love as fiercely as Lycans. Your sister is another example of that."

She smiled at him. "I want my granddaughter to be happy. Being with you, being around you, makes her happy. I can see it on her face. I can smell it on her."

He blushed and she smiled again. "I am a much different person than I used to be, Kaden. I've learned to love and trust humans like I trust my own kind. I know that your situation is different from mine and you have many reasons for not trusting my kind, but I hope that you'll consider staying with us after the wedding. You make my sweet Sophia happy, and that makes me happy."

She hesitated and then patted Kaden's arm. "Will you think about staying?"

He stared at the floor. "I'm not sure it would be a good idea, Vivian. I am not like my sister. She trusts and loves more easily than I do."

"Fair enough," she said. "Will you be joining us for dinner tonight?"

"Aye."

She held her arm out. "Walk an old Lycan to the dining room, would you?"

He nodded and took her arm, leading her down the hallway.

CHAPTER 15

"Have you seen your sister?"

Nicholas looked up from the chess game he was playing with Doran. "She went for a run."

Kaden frowned. "What do you mean?"

Nicholas moved a chess piece and grinned at Doran. "Checkmate."

Doran groaned as Kaden sighed impatiently. "Nicholas, what do you mean?"

"I mean she went for a run in the forest. We Lycans like to do a little thing called exercise."

"She went alone?" Kaden scowled. Sophia had not been at dinner and although they had ended things amicably enough this morning, he couldn't help but worry that she was upset with him.

"She'll be fine," Nicky said. "She's tougher than you think, human."

"You should not have let her go alone," he said.

Nicky laughed. "You know as well as I do that Sophia does what she wants."

Kaden swore softly and stomped from the room. He

stopped in the hallway when he heard Doran say, "He's got it bad for her."

"Aye, he does," Nicky agreed. "I suppose she could do worse in a mate, although I never pictured Sophia falling for a human."

Muttering another curse under his breath, Kaden stalked outside. He jogged through the yard and into the forest. Leo and Jeffrey were on watch and they nodded to him as he approached them.

"Have you seen Sophia?" he asked.

"Aye, she went for a run a couple of hours ago," Leo said.

"Thanks." Kaden started into the woods and Jeffrey put his hand on his shoulder.

"You can't go in there."

"You let Sophia go alone," Kaden snapped.

"Aye," Jeffrey said affably, "but she is a Lycan."

"So?"

"She can take care of herself," Jeffrey said.

"So can I." Kaden took another step and grunted with anger when Jeffrey's hand tightened on his shoulder.

"It's not safe," he repeated.

"Let go of me, Lycan," Kaden said.

Jeffrey gave him a hard look. "And if I do not, human?"

Before Kaden could reply, Leo rested his hand on Jeffrey's arm. "Let him go, Jeffrey."

"Leo -"

"He can take care of himself. Let him go."

"Fine." Jeffrey released Kaden and took a step back. He shook his head as Kaden disappeared into the trees.

KADEN HIKED QUICKLY THROUGH THE TREES. IT WOULD BE dark soon and his worry for Sophia gnawed at his belly. He cursed to himself. The minute he found her he would turn her over his knee and spank the hell out of her. His groin stirred at the thought of Sophia across his lap, her naked ass ripe and full, and her low voice begging him to touch her.

He snorted loudly. What had happened between him and Sophia was finished. He had wanted to fuck her, and he did. Continuing to fuck her wasn't something that could happen, no matter how much he wanted her. He would –

There was a soft growl and he turned to see the brown wolf staring at him. He hesitated and then took a step forward. "Sophia?"

She growled again and he put his hands up. "I'm sorry. I was worried about you. You shouldn't be out here alone."

He took a step backward when the wolf bared her teeth at him. "Sophia? What's wrong? I thought -"

The wolf snarled loudly and stalked towards him. His heart pounding, Kaden backed up slowly, his hands held out in front of him. "Just calm down, honey, all right? Don't -"

The wolf crouched to attack. He gave a startled shout and stumbled back, tripping over his own feet and falling onto his ass. Kaden scrabbled backward as another wolf, this one three times the size of the brown wolf, appeared. It was grey in colour and its snout was lifted in a silent snarl. It stalked towards the brown wolf, a growl emitting from deep within its chest, and the smaller wolf lowered its head and whined uneasily.

The grey wolf barked loudly and snapped its teeth. The smaller wolf whimpered and then backed away into the trees. It turned and loped off as Kaden released his breath in a harsh rush and collapsed on his back. He peered up into the trees as the grey wolf stood over him. It looked down at him and he stared into its jade eyes.

"Gods, I hope you're Sophia," he muttered.

The wolf made a chuffing sound and he cringed as it leaned its head down. It licked his cheek and he closed his eyes. There was a quiet pop and then he felt the naked weight of Sophia straddling his abdomen.

"Hello, Sophia."

"Hello, Kaden."

He opened his eyes and stared into her dark ones. They were filled with amusement, and she wiped away a smudge of dirt from his cheek.

"Kaden?"

"Aye?"

"Why were you trying to talk to that wolf?"

"I thought it was you."

She snorted. "You thought that puny little wolf was me? It wasn't even a Lycan for the gods sake. It was just a regular wolf."

"I've never seen you in your Lycan form. How was I to know that it wasn't you?"

"Lycans are bigger, stronger, and smarter than regular wolves. Regular wolves are afraid of us." She licked her lips and her eyes turned the green of her wolf.

"Is that why it ran away from you?" Kaden asked.

Her eyes glowed. "It tried to take what is mine. It's lucky I let it run. I should have ripped its throat out for trying to harm what belongs to me."

She growled lightly, her nostrils flaring with anger, before she closed her eyes and shook her head. When she opened them, they were their normal dark brown.

"Why are you out here anyway?" she asked suddenly.

"I came looking for you. You shouldn't be out here by yourself."

"I can take care of myself."

"Aye, so I keep hearing," he muttered.

He was uncomfortably aware of Sophia's naked heat against the muscles of his stomach. He shifted under her as she unbuttoned his jacket. She pulled it apart and rubbed his chest through his shirt.

"What were you going to do when you found me?" she asked as she unbuttoned his shirt.

He groaned when she ran her hands over his naked chest. He stared at her breasts and forced himself to keep his hands at his sides. Her nipples were hard, and her skin was covered in goose bumps.

"Are you cold, little Lycan?" he asked.

"No." She ran her thumb over his flat nipple and then traced his collarbone with the tips of her fingers. "What were you going to do when you found me?"

"Spank you," he muttered hoarsely.

Her eyebrows rose up and then she laughed. "Do you really believe I would allow you to spank me?"

He didn't answer and she leaned over him, pressing her breasts into his chest. She rubbed her pelvis against his naked stomach, grinning when he moaned.

"Is that what you want, human?" she whispered into his ear. "Me bent over your lap, my naked ass in the air so you can spank it?"

"Sophia," he moaned and gripped her thighs in his hands, squeezing them firmly as she kissed his thick neck.

"Aye, Kaden?"

"We – we agreed not to do this, remember?"

"Aye, I remember." She bit the firm flesh of his shoulder and rubbed herself against him again. "But that was before you went traipsing through the woods like little Red Riding Hood."

"Like who?"

She grinned at him, her white teeth flashing in the growing darkness. "An ancient's tale. They told it to their children to frighten them. Red Riding Hood was a little girl who was afraid of the big bad wolf."

His fingers tightened on the firm flesh of her thighs. "Are you calling me a girl?"

"The way you keep denying me what is rightfully mine is starting to make me wonder."

He pushed her back until her pussy was directly above his erection and ground his pelvis against her. "Be careful what you say to me, little Lycan."

She pressed herself against his erection, her wet heat making him groan again, and then sat up. She cupped her breasts, running her thumbs over her nipples and smiling when his eyes darkened with lust.

"Why? Are you going to spank me?" she asked.

He groaned when she pulled tightly on her nipples, making her back arch with pleasure. His hands moved to her ass and he squeezed it roughly as he rocked his pelvis against hers.

"I'll make you a deal, human." Her hands left her breasts and went to the buttons on his pants. She flicked them open one-by-one and then leaned over him. "I'll consider letting you spank me one day if," she pulled his cock through the opening in his pants and squeezed it firmly, "you give me what is mine right now."

"Sophia, we shouldn't," he rasped out as his hips rose in time to the firm strokes of her hand.

"Aye, perhaps not," she agreed before leaning over and kissing him hard on the mouth. She plunged her tongue into his mouth, darting and flicking it against his tongue, before tearing her mouth from his.

He panted and moaned under her as she stroked his cock. "If you don't want to fuck me at least let me use your cock to make myself come."

He watched, his breath heaving in and out of his chest in harsh pants, as she reached down. She parted the lips of her pussy with her fingers and used her other hand to rub his cock against her wet clit. He cried out as she made a low moaning noise and arched her back.

"Should we fuck, Kaden? Are you ready to give me what is mine?" she panted.

"Aye. Oh gods, aye," he groaned.

She lifted her pelvis, slid her hand to the base of his cock, and thrust herself down onto it. They cried out in unison, and he gripped her hips tightly as she rocked up and down on his cock.

She braced her hands on his chest and rode him hard. She growled loudly, her eyes turning green, when he reached up and cupped her wildly-bouncing breasts. He pulled hard on her nipples and she leaned over him. Her eyes glowing brightly, she kissed him. He returned her kiss, thrusting his tongue between her lips as he thrust his cock deep inside of her.

He cupped her ass as she bounced up and down. She moaned and reached between them. She rubbed her clit hard and he gave a loud cry of pleasure, his hips bucking upwards, as her pussy tightened around him and she shuddered wildly.

She lifted her head to the sky and howled. He thrust his hips and let his own climax take over. He pumped furiously into her as her fingers raked over his chest leaving shallow, bloody furrows.

She crumpled against him, her pulse pounding in her ears

and her entire body trembling. He wrapped his arms around her and burrowed his face into the warmth of her neck as she stroked his hair gently. She touched his chest and stared guiltily at the traces of blood on her fingers.

"I'm sorry," she whispered.

"It's fine." He kissed the top of her head and stared up at the sky through the trees.

Darkness was nearly upon them and he could see the faint light of the stars. She rubbed his chest and he pulled her closer. Not sleeping with Sophia was turning out to be more difficult than he could ever have imagined. He tried to tell himself it was because he wanted her body and nothing more, but as she placed a gentle kiss on his scarred chest, he knew it was a lie.

CHAPTER 16

"What are you doing, my love?"

Tristan crouched next to Leta. It was just after breakfast and she was sitting cross-legged on the cold ground of the yard, her hands cupped together as she rocked back and forth. She was staring with hard concentration at her hands, her brow furrowed, and her lips set in a determined line.

"Leta?" He put a warm hand on her back.

"I found it in the yard, Papa. It has a broken wing." She opened her hands slightly so he could peer between them. He could see the small sparrow sitting in the palm of one hand, its left wing held out at an awkward angle.

Leta closed her hands around the bird and resumed her rocking as Tristan rubbed her back. "What are you doing?"

"I'm trying to heal it," she said. Her entire body tensed, and she grunted a little with the effort.

"Leta -"

"I know I'm a healer like Mama. I know it!" she said fiercely. "I can feel it in my bones, Papa."

He sat down next to her. "My love, I have no doubt that someday you'll be a healer like your mama. But it will not happen until later. You know that the gift of healing doesn't happen until you are older. Your brother's healing ability did not show up until he was in his teens. Remember?"

"I know," she sighed. "But I want it to happen right now, Papa. I want to heal."

He kissed the top of her head as Avery came out the back door. She wrapped her sweater tight around her body and joined them.

"What are you two doing out here?" she asked. "It's freezing out."

Tristan smiled at her as she squeezed his shoulder affectionately. "Leta found a bird with a broken wing."

Avery sat on the other side of Leta. "Let me see."

Leta opened her hands and Avery peered at the tiny bird. "Poor little thing."

"I'm trying to heal it, Mama," Leta said solemnly.

"Are you now?" Avery kissed her forehead. "That is very kind of you."

"It's not working," Leta said. "I know I can heal, Mama. Why won't it work?"

"You are not old enough yet, my sweet Leta," Avery said. "Here, let me see it."

Leta carefully handed the bird to Avery. Avery cupped it in her hands and Leta crawled into his lap, resting her head on his broad chest and linking her fingers with his. They sat in silence for a while, Leta humming a quiet tuneless song under her breath, until Avery smiled at her.

She opened her hands and Leta leaned forward to study the bird. It was sitting in the palm of Avery's hand, its broken wing now straight and smooth. Leta smiled delightedly as the bird stood and shook itself. It walked to the end of Avery's fingers, shook itself again, and then flew up and into the air.

Leta, her hand shading her eyes from the sun, watched it fly for a few minutes and then turned to Avery.

"Someday I'll be able to do that too, Mama."

"I know you will." Avery smiled at her as Tristan stood and offered his hands to them. He pulled them into a standing position and kissed Avery gently on the mouth before leading them both into the house.

KADEN SIGHED AND STARED BLANKLY AT THE CHESS BOARD IN front of him. It had been two days since he had gone to the forest to look for Sophia, and since then he had avoided being alone with her. He'd realized quickly after that night that he couldn't be alone with her. His willpower, his ability to resist her, was pretty much non-existent. He was leaving after the wedding, and it wasn't fair to her to continue to sleep with her.

And why exactly are you leaving after the wedding?

He jerked a little. Why *was* he still planning on leaving? He trusted the Lycans now didn't he? He searched inwardly and realized with a twinge of regret that no, he didn't trust them. He hated that he didn't and hated that he still didn't entirely believe they wouldn't turn on him. Despite everything they had done for both him and Bree, he couldn't get past his belief that deep down the Lycans considered them as slaves.

Even Sophia, the night in the forest, had told him repeatedly that he belonged to her. He felt a throb of lust deep in his belly. It certainly hadn't bothered him at the time – he'd enjoyed the way she so clearly claimed him as her own. She had driven off the smaller wolf because it tried to take what was hers.

Another shiver of desire went through him. He'd spent his entire life taking care of first his mother and then his sister. He'd grown used to being the one who took care of others, and even the few women he had slept with had a certain quality to them. They had a type of weakness and a craving to be protected that appealed to his need to keep others safe. Sophia wasn't like that. In fact, she'd proven numerous times that she was more than capable of taking care of herself.

Did that bother him? For the first time in his life he had met a woman who didn't need him to keep her safe. And when she wasn't saving his life, she was acting like it was her right to have sex with him. His cock hardened in his pants as he remembered the way she'd ridden him in the woods. It had turned him on when she told him he belonged to her. He rubbed his head angrily. He didn't want it to turn him on, he didn't want to feel like he belonged to her, but gods be damned he did.

He belonged to her and she belonged to him. He knew that to the very core of him. It was exactly why he needed to stay away from her, and why he needed to leave after the wedding. He may trust Sophia, but he wasn't sure he would ever trust the rest of her family. He had trusted Ian and look where that had gotten him. He wasn't angry with Ian and he understood his reasons, but it didn't negate the fact that the old Lycan had been lying to him the entire time.

He thought briefly of asking Sophia to go with him but knew immediately she would never do so. She was bound to her family both by love and the need to be in a pack. She would never leave them.

"Gods, Kaden, are you ever going to make a move?" Nicky asked impatiently.

"I'm thinking," Kaden replied. "I've only just learned how to play – give me a minute."

"It's been nearly five," Nicholas pointed out before giving him a teasing grin. "Perhaps you don't have the knack to play chess, or perhaps you need to play against a weaker opponent."

"I think you're doing great." Dani smiled brightly at Kaden and leaned against him, putting her arm around his shoulders.

Kaden sighed. The girl had left him alone for a few days after his birthday, but his near-death experience had renewed her crush. For a moment he wished Dani was Lycan, if only so that she would know that he had slept with Sophia.

She brushed her hand down his arm, squeezing the thick muscles gently. "Don't let my cousin get to you, Kaden. He beats everyone at chess – even Dad and Uncle Tristan."

He smiled uncomfortably and leaned away from her. She gave him a hopeful smile. "Would you like to go for a walk with me?"

"Um, that's nice of you but -"

"Get away from him, cousin." Sophia's low voice, almost a growl, interrupted him. She had entered the common room and was leaning against the wall, her eyes burning balefully at them.

Dani glared at Sophia. "Mind your own business, Sophia."

She turned back to Kaden. Will you come for a walk with me, Kaden?"

He shook his head. "No, Dani. I already told you that I -"

"He's mine, Dani," Sophia said.

Dani sighed impatiently. "No, he is not. He's a human, not some pet that you can claim as your own." She scowled at Sophia. "He can make up his own mind about what or who he wants."

"Did you not tell her, Kaden?" Sophia walked toward

them. "Did you not tell my pretty little cousin that you belong to me?"

"Be quiet, Sophia," Kaden said.

She ignored him and smiled at Dani. "I've had him inside me, cousin. It is my name he cries out when we are in bed together."

Dani turned white and she stared at Kaden in shock. "You said it was not because of her. You said you were not attracted to her."

Kaden's stomach twisted. "Dani, listen to me. I told you -"

"He does not want you," Sophia said. Her eyes were bright green and filled with a terrible blank light. "He does not -"

"Sophia, leave!" Kaden shouted at her as Nicky stood and strode to his sister. He shook Sophia's arm roughly.

"What is wrong with you?" he said.

Sophia stared blankly at him for a moment. The light died in her eyes and a look of regret and horror crossed her face as she turned to her cousin. "Dani, I – I'm so sorry. I did not mean to say those things to you."

Her slender body trembling and tears dripping down her face, Dani turned away. Kaden hesitated and then put his arm around her. She leaned against him, burying her face in his chest as Sophia gave him a look of shame.

"Kaden, I'm so sorry."

"Go on, Sophia," Kaden said. "Leave us alone, please."

Nicky pulled on her arm. "Come with me, Sophia."

She nodded, her face pale and sick looking, and allowed her brother to lead her from the common room.

Kaden rubbed Dani's back. After a moment she lifted her head and stared up at him, her eyes wide and wet with moisture.

"Is it true, Kaden? Have you slept with Sophia?"

"Aye. I have."

"You told me it wasn't because of her."

"It isn't," he said truthfully. "Sophia is not the reason I am not attracted to you."

"I don't believe you," she said.

"It is the truth," he said. "I'm sorry, I know you have a crush on me, but I don't feel the same way. It has nothing to do with you. You're sweet and beautiful, and you'll make someone who isn't me very happy someday."

She laughed a bit bitterly. "Aye, perhaps."

"You will," he said. "Besides, I'm leaving soon."

"Are you? Even after sleeping with my cousin?" she asked.

"I am."

"Does she know that?"

"Aye, she does," he said.

"Don't take this the wrong way but I'm glad you're leaving," she said. "It hurts too much to have you here, knowing that you'll never love me the way that I love you."

"You don't love me," he said.

"Aye, I do. As does my cousin."

"Sophia definitely doesn't love me," he said.

She laughed, a short sound full of genuine amusement. "I may be a human, but I've been around Lycans my entire life. Her need to make sure other females know you belong to her is not because of lust. A Lycan does not feel the need to claim someone unless they believe the person is their mate."

Kaden stared silently at her and she shrugged and walked towards the door of the common room. "Like it or not Kaden, she loves you."

"DANI?"

"What is it?" Dani didn't turn around as Sophia entered her bedroom.

"I'm so sorry, honey. I shouldn't have said what I did. I don't know what came over me," Sophia said.

When Dani didn't reply, she said, "Please, Dani. I'm so sorry. I do not want this to come between us."

"Come between us?" Dani turned and frowned at her. "You have never thought of me as anything more than your silly little human cousin. What do you care if you've hurt my feelings?"

"That isn't true," Sophia replied. "I love you, and I do not believe you're silly. I think you're sweet and wonderful, and I feel terrible for hurting you the way I have."

Dani stared in surprise at Sophia. The Lycan's tanned face was pale and she had tears in her eyes. In her entire life, Dani didn't think she'd ever seen Sophia cry. She sighed and hugged Sophia roughly. "I know. I'm sorry too."

"You have nothing to be sorry about," Sophia's voice was muffled against her shoulder.

"Aye, I do," Dani replied. "I knew how you and Kaden felt about each other, and yet I still tried my best to seduce him. I wanted him to be with me."

"If you believe that he'll be happy with you, I will step aside," Sophia said.

Dani laughed. "Bullshit, cousin. You nearly ripped my head off for putting my arm around him."

Sophia gave her a miserable look. "I don't know what's wrong with me. I feel like I'm going crazy."

Dani wiped the tears from Sophia's face. "You're in love. Isn't it great?"

"Aye, wonderful," Sophia said with a soft sigh.

CHAPTER 17

She climbed the ladder to the hayloft. He was standing near the bed and he didn't turn to look at her.

"Why are you here?" he asked.

"I came to apologize," she replied.

He didn't answer and Sophia took a few steps forward. She wanted to touch his broad back but she could see the tension in his body and so she clasped her hands together instead. "I'm sorry, Kaden. I should not have said what I did."

"It's not me you should be apologizing to, Lycan. It's your cousin," he said.

"I have already apologized to Dani."

He stayed silent and she sighed. "Kaden, will you please look at me?"

He turned around and glared at her. "You knew she had a crush on me, and you still rubbed it in her face that we had slept together. Why? I didn't take you to be cruel."

"I don't know," she said honestly. "I saw her arm around you and I – I just…"

"You just what?" he demanded. "Just had to lay your

claim on me? I don't belong to you, Lycan. I am not weak like my sister, and I do not need someone to take care of me."

"Your sister is not with James because she's weak and needs someone to look after her," Sophia said. "She's with him because he loves her, and she loves him."

"Aye. But if she did not, it wouldn't matter would it? James has decided she belongs to him and that's all there is to it. And now you're trying to do the same to me. I am not a Lycan, I'm human and I don't need you to protect me."

"I know that, Kaden. Lycans are – well, they are protective and possessive of -"

"I know exactly what you are. You take what you want without thinking about others."

Her temper flared and she glared at him. "You weren't complaining two nights ago when I saved your ass from the wolf and then let you fuck me."

He scowled at her. "I would have been just fine, Lycan. The only reason I was out there was because you were dumb enough to go into the woods by yourself. Have you forgotten that Draken is still out there? Have you forgotten that he's determined to have you?"

"No, I haven't forgotten!" she said. "But I am more than capable of taking care of myself."

"Aye, because you did that so well the first time Draken took you," he mocked. "If it had not been for me, you would have died that day."

Her face flushed red and her hands clenched into fists. Her eyes flashed dangerously at him. "You may have saved my life that day, but it doesn't mean I need your protection."

"Of course not. You do just fine taking care of yourself," he muttered.

She arched her eyebrows at him. "Tell me, human – what

bothers you more? That I don't need you to protect me or that you like the idea of belonging to me?"

She'd forgotten how quick he could be. He had crossed the room and pushed her roughly against the wall before she could react. He stared angrily at her as he pressed her against the coarse boards of the barn wall.

"I don't belong to you."

"You do," she argued.

He made a snorting noise of displeasure and leaned forward until his face was only inches from hers. "I will never be a Lycan slave again. Do you hear me? I won't let you try and control me."

She gave him a look of astonishment as hurt trickled through her. "Is that what you think I'm trying to do?"

He shrugged. "Is it not?"

"No!" She scowled at him. "You honestly still believe that I would keep a human as a slave?"

"What do you expect? You keep telling me that I belong to you," he replied.

She shook her head in disbelief. "I know you're not stupid, human. Why do you keep pretending you are?"

His hands bit into the soft meat of her arms and he gave her a little shake. "The gods help me, little Lycan. I will spank you."

"You mean you will try," she said.

His gaze drifted down to her breasts, his hands squeezing around her arms, and she put her mouth to his ear. "When I say you belong to me it does not mean I think of you as my slave. It means that no one else, including my pretty human cousin, gets to touch you or kiss you. It means that my mouth is the only one allowed to suck on that thick cock of yours."

He groaned, and she quickly unbuttoned her pants before taking his hand. She spread her thighs and pushed his hand inside of her pants. His face flushed and he shoved his hand between her legs, cupping her pussy before sliding his middle finger into her.

She moaned and wiggled on his hand. "It means that only you are allowed to touch," she leaned forward and licked his face with her warm, wet tongue, "to lick, and to fuck my pussy." She ground herself against his hand and smiled with delight when his control snapped.

He yanked at her pants and underwear, tearing them down past her boots and ripping them off her feet. Her shirt was next, yanked over her head so quickly that she heard the soft purr as the collar ripped. Wearing only her boots, she stood in front of him. His eyes raked over her body and he pulled his shirt over his head, dropping it to the floor before unbuttoning his pants and pulling his cock free. He pushed her back against the wall and grabbed her thighs in his large hands. He lifted her easily and she gave a soft hiss of pain when the bare skin of her back scraped across the rough boards.

He shoved his cock deep inside of her as he gripped her ass. She wrapped her limbs around him, her fingernails digging into his back as he thrust back and forth.

He stopped and she made a moan of need. "Kaden, please."

He stared at her. "Perhaps it is you who belongs to me, little Lycan."

"Aye, I do," she said immediately. "I'm yours, Kaden."

He stared at her in surprise and she leaned forward and kissed him on the lips. "I belong to you and you belong to me. Say it."

"I belong to you," he whispered.

She gave him a smile of such sweetness that his heart opened to her fully and completely. She tightened her limbs around him and kissed him again. He returned her kiss and carried her to the bed. She clung tightly to him as he lowered her to the mattress and propped himself on his elbows above her.

"Sophia -"

He hesitated and she kissed his neck. "What is it, Kaden?"

He smiled at her. "You're so beautiful."

She blushed and he kissed the tip of her nose before moving slowly within her. She moaned softly, her eyes drifting shut as he plunged in and out of her in a steady, slow rhythm. She squeezed her inner muscles around him, and he gasped, his hips thrusting against her.

She opened her eyes and smiled at him. "You make me feel so good, honey."

He kissed her hard on the mouth, his tongue stroking hers, before he buried his face in her neck and lost himself in the sweet warmth of her body.

"BREE?" AVERY KNOCKED WORRIEDLY ON THE BATHROOM door. "My love? Are you all right?"

Bree opened the door, her face pale and dark circles under her eyes. "I'm fine, Mama. Just a bit of the stomach flu, I think."

Avery frowned and took her hand. "Come with me." She led Bree to the common room and sat down on the couch. She opened her arms and Bree cuddled into her. Almost immediately, she felt better, and she rested her head on Avery's shoulder.

"Thank you, Mama."

"You're welcome, my love. You should have told James

you weren't feeling well. He would have healed you before he left with his father on watch."

Bree shrugged. "He did hold me for a while this morning until I felt better. I guess he didn't hold me long enough."

Avery stiffened against her. "James held you earlier?"

"Aye, he did. But the nausea came back after a couple of hours."

Bree sighed and snuggled in closer. Her stomach was no longer nauseous, but she was incredibly tired. She closed her eyes as Avery stroked her long, blonde hair.

"Bree, how long have you been throwing up for?"

"I don't know. Off and on for a few days."

"When was the moon full for you last?" Avery asked.

Bree frowned up at her. "What?"

Avery smiled. "Sorry, after years of living with Lycans I've picked up more than my fair share of their phrases. When was the last time you had your period?"

Bree thought about it for a moment. "I don't remember. I haven't been very regular over the last two years."

"Aye, I suppose not. They Lycans starved you, it's no wonder you weren't regular," Avery said.

"Why are you asking me this, Mama?" Bree sat up and stared curiously at her. "What do my monthlies have to do with…"

She stared wide-eyed at Avery before glancing down at her flat stomach. "No, I can't be. It's not possible. We're not even married yet."

Avery smiled. "You do not need to be married to have a baby, Bree."

Bree stood and paced back and forth in front of the fire. "I - what will James say? We've never even talked about children. What if he's angry?"

Avery stood and pulled her to a gentle stop. "Bree, you're

being silly. James loves you. He will be thrilled. Trust me. The real question is – how do you feel about it?"

Bree placed her hands on her belly and looked up at Avery. "I'm having a baby."

"Aye, my love. You are."

"I'm having a baby!" she nearly shouted it and then hugged Avery impulsively.

Avery laughed and returned her hug. "I take it you are pleased then?"

Bree nodded. "Aye, I am. I mean, I'm surprised, and it doesn't feel real to me yet, but…"

She gave Avery a wide, beaming smile. "I'm having a baby, Mama."

"You must tell James right away." Avery smiled at her.

"Tell me what?" James, a glass of water in one hand and the leg bone of a rabbit in the other, entered the common room. He stared curiously at Avery and Bree before taking the last bite of the smoked rabbit meat. Tia was dancing around his feet, her tail wagging excitedly at the sight of the rabbit bone, and he tossed it to her. She pounced on it and carried it to a spot in front of the fire. She gnawed at the bone as Avery dropped a kiss on Bree's forehead.

"I will talk with you both later." Avery kissed James on the cheek before leaving the room.

James glanced at his mother's retreating back before moving across the room to Bree. "What's going on with Mom?"

He looked at Bree's flushed face. "What's going on with you, little one?"

"I – I have some news." Bree was suddenly nervous, and she cupped her elbows to keep her hands from shaking.

James frowned and set his glass of water down before

folding her into his embrace. "What's wrong? Are you still feeling sick?"

She shook her head. "No. Well, not at the moment."

"What do you mean?"

She took a deep breath. "I'm pregnant."

He jerked against her and his eyes dropped to her flat stomach. "You're pregnant?"

"Aye. At least, Mama thinks I am. I've been feeling sick in the mornings for a while now and I missed my last period."

He stared silently at her and she gave him an anxious smile. "I might not be. I'm not very regular to begin with and I could just have the flu, but it doesn't feel like the flu."

He still didn't reply, and she swallowed thickly. "James, are you – are you angry with me?"

He blinked. "What? No, of course not."

He surprised her by suddenly dropping to his knees in front of her and raising her shirt. He kissed her bare belly, his lips warm on her skin. "Hello, baby."

She ran her fingers through his hair, and he smiled up at her. "You're having my baby."

"Aye, I am," she replied.

He stood and lifted her up, hugging her fiercely before kissing her hard on the mouth. "You're having my baby!"

"James, hush!" she scolded him. "It's too early to be telling everyone!"

"Right, of course." He carried her from the common room and down the hall.

"Where are we going?"

"To bed," he replied.

She smiled and nuzzled his neck. "I'd like that."

"You're going to bed to rest, little one. You're too pale and you're tired looking."

She rolled her eyes. "You certainly know how to flatter a girl, James."

He grinned as he carried her into their bedroom and set her gently on the bed. "Crawl into bed, Bree."

She shook her head. "Not unless you come with me."

"You need rest. I know you're still not feeling well."

She smiled and tugged his head down so she could place a kiss on his mouth. "Aye, and I know exactly what will make me feel better."

She pulled him on to the bed and straddled him before beginning to unbutton his shirt. "Will you help me feel better, my love?" She kissed a warm, wet path across his naked chest.

He groaned and gripped her hips in his large hands. "Aye, little one. I can do that."

CHAPTER 18

"Ian?"

"Aye, I'm back here."

Kaden stuck his head into the stall and smiled at the old man. "Sophia and I are going to town in the morning. Apparently, there are some last-minute wedding supplies needed and Sophia volunteered us to go. Do you want me to pick you up some new boots?"

Ian rested the shovel against the wall of the stall and stared at his worn boots. "If it's okay with you, I think I'll tag along. It's been a while since I've been to town."

"That's fine. We're dropping Martine off at her home on the way, and I believe Dani is thinking of going with us."

"Good, good." Ian gave him a hesitant look before scuffing his boot in the soft dirt.

"What?" Kaden asked.

"Are we good then, Kaden?" he asked.

"Aye, we are. I understand why you didn't tell me you were a Lycan," Kaden replied.

"I didn't mean to hurt you," Ian said.

185

"I know." Kaden clapped the old Lycan on the back and Ian winced.

"Careful. You're strong for a human."

Kaden laughed as Ian grinned at him. "So, you and the young Sophia huh?"

"Oh, uh – " Kaden stammered as Ian grinned again.

"Don't try and deny it. I can smell her scent all over you."

Kaden shook his head. "There are some things about living with Lycans that I will never get used to."

"Planning on staying on after the wedding, are you?" Ian asked.

"I don't know," Kaden admitted. "We haven't talked about long term. I told her earlier that I was leaving after the wedding, even after we slept together, and she seemed fine with it."

"Fine with it?" Ian frowned. "That doesn't sound like the Sophia I know."

Kaden didn't reply and Ian picked up the shovel. "What time are we leaving tomorrow?"

"Just after dawn. We want enough time to get back home before dark."

"Sounds good." Ian began to shovel out the stall and Kaden headed to the back of the barn.

"You know," Sophia's head popped up over the ladder leading to the hayloft and Kaden couldn't conceal his grin of happiness, "you could come to my bedroom and then we wouldn't have to worry about being eaten in our sleep by rats."

Kaden laughed. "I told you - I've never seen a single rat up here."

She stretched out on his bed and petted the purring Hogan. "Aye, you do keep saying that."

She flinched when Piper jumped up beside her, but he simply butted his head against her face and joined his brother in purring. She petted the orange cat and smiled at Kaden as he sat in the armchair and pulled off his boots with a low grunt.

"Seriously, my bed is much more comfortable than yours."

He stripped off his shirt and joined her on the bed. "Aye, I suppose it is. But you're rather noisy in bed, and I'd prefer not to have the rest of your family knowing what I'm doing to you."

He lay on his back and she climbed on to him, straddling his hips and running her fingers through the tufts of hair on his chest and abdomen.

"They already know, human," she said with an impish grin.

"Aye, don't remind me. At dinner tonight your father was trying to burn a hole through my skull with his gaze alone."

She rolled her eyes and slapped him lightly on the chest. "He was not. My father knows I'm a grown woman."

"You're an adult but you're still his little girl. I don't blame him for wanting to beat the hell out of me. I'd be the same way with my daughter."

"Do you want children?" she asked suddenly.

"I do. What about you?"

"Aye. I love children."

She hesitated and gave him a strange look. He rubbed her lower back. "What?"

"Your sister is with child."

"What? How do you know? Did she tell you?"

Sophia shook her head. "No. Her scent has changed."

"Her scent?" He gave her a skeptical look.

"Aye. Lycans can smell when a female is with child. It's easier to tell with Lycan females, but I can smell the scent change on Bree. She carries a pup in her belly."

"She hasn't told me." He gave Sophia a hurt look.

She leaned over him and ran her hand through his thick hair. "She may not even know yet. The scent change is very subtle which means it's still quite early in the pregnancy. My father and brothers have not even picked up on it."

He took her hand and linked their fingers, staring quietly at them.

"I'm sorry. Should I have not told you?" Sophia asked.

He shook his head. "No, I'm glad you did."

He sighed and she slid off him and sat on the bed. She wrapped her arms around her knees as he sat up and leaned against the rough wall of the barn. He stared absently into space and didn't notice when she stroked his thigh.

After a few moments, she squeezed his leg. "I'd better go. Good night, Kaden." She kissed him lightly on the cheek and pushed Piper out of the way.

He reached for her hand. "Why are you leaving?"

"I get the feeling you want to be alone."

He didn't reply but he put his arm around her and tugged her against him. She rested her head on his chest as he stroked her back with the tips of his fingers.

The knowledge that his sister was pregnant had shaken Kaden to the core. How could he leave knowing that Bree was going to have a baby? He was going to be an uncle, and the thought that he would not see his new niece or nephew was bothering him more than he could articulate.

He stared down at Sophia's dark head. Who was he kidding? It was not just a pregnant Bree that made him desire to stay. The woman in his arms had become as important to him as his sister was. Sophia belonged to him and he belonged to her.

A small smile crossed his face. She belonged to him. He had never been in love before, but he had a sneaking suspicion that he was falling in love with Sophia. The thought should have frightened him. Her family were Lycans, and he had no idea if he would ever fully trust any Lycan but her. He wasn't frightened though. In fact, Sophia made him feel happy and content for the first time in his life. He cupped her face gently and she stared up at him.

"You belong to me," he said.

"Aye, I do," she replied.

He smiled and kissed her. She kissed him back eagerly and he cupped her breast through her shirt. She gave a soft moan of need, and he buried his face in her throat and pressed his mouth against the steady pulse at the base of her throat.

She belonged to him.

BREE MOVED QUIETLY THROUGH THE DARK HOUSE. SHE HAD been too excited to sleep, and she had laid quietly in the dark for a few hours, listening to James' steady breathing and thinking about the baby she was carrying. Finally, she had slipped out of their bed and made her way down to the kitchen.

She lit the cluster of candles in the middle of the table and moved to the cook stove. It was still warm, Marian liked to keep the fire going when it was this cold, and she set the kettle on it to heat before taking a mug and a teabag from the cupboard.

"Can't sleep?"

She made a startled gasp and whirled to see Vivian standing in the doorway of the kitchen.

"I'm sorry. I did not mean to frighten you."

Bree smiled at the older Lycan. "I did not expect anyone else to be awake."

Vivian shrugged and entered the kitchen. She pulled down her own mug and Bree added a teabag to it. "The older I get the less I sleep, it seems."

"I'm sorry."

Vivian shrugged again. "I don't mind." She leaned past Bree to grab the small canister of sugar. "I find that I -"

She stopped abruptly and inhaled before dropping the canister on the counter. She rested her hand on Bree's abdomen as she inhaled again. "You carry a pup in your belly."

Bree jerked in surprise. "How do you know that?"

Vivian smiled. "Your scent has changed. Does James know?"

Bree nodded. "Aye, I told him earlier today. I just found out. I didn't even know for sure. Mama said I was, but I thought it might just be the flu."

Vivian stroked Bree's belly and then reached for the teakettle. She poured the hot water into both of their mugs and carried them to the table. "Sit down, Bree."

Bree stared into the mug of steaming tea. Vivian took her hand and squeezed gently. "You are with child."

"You really can – can smell it on me?" Bree whispered.

Vivian nodded. "Aye. It's early, your scent is only slightly different, but I have no doubt that you're pregnant."

Bree couldn't stop the smile from crossing her face and Vivian gave her a delighted look. "I take it you are pleased?"

"Very." Bree pressed her hand against her stomach as she dipped her spoon into the mug and pulled out the teabag.

She set it neatly on the table and took a sip of the fragrant liquid.

Tia padded into the kitchen and whined softly, pawing lightly at Bree's leg. Bree picked her up and cuddled her gently, kissing her soft head and rubbing her ears.

"Congratulations, Bree. I'm very happy for you and for my grandson." Vivian took her own sip of tea.

"Thank you, Vivian." Bree gave her a nervous smile. James' grandmother still made her anxious and she didn't think she'd ever been alone with the Lycan before.

"You know, I don't believe I've ever told you how happy I am that you and James are getting married. I like you very much," Vivian said suddenly.

"Oh um, thank you," Bree said again.

"Perhaps now your nervousness around me will lessen?" Vivian raised one eyebrow at her.

"I'm sorry. I'm just -"

"It's fine," Vivian said. "You have your reasons for being frightened of Lycans, and I've been told I'm not the easiest Lycan to get to know."

Bree wasn't sure what to say to that, so she took another drink of her tea.

"Would you like a boy or girl pup?" Vivian asked.

"It doesn't really matter to me," Bree replied. "I just want it to be healthy."

Vivian laughed. "With James as its father, it will be healthy."

Bree grinned. "Aye, I suppose you're right."

Tia licked her hand and she petted the dog gently as Vivian smiled at her. "I hope you have a girl. A little one with blonde hair and as sweet and kind as you are."

Tears slid down Bree's cheeks and, embarrassed, she swiped them away with the heel of her hand.

"I imagine you would like me to keep this quiet for a while?" Vivian said.

Bree nodded. "Just for a little longer. We'll tell everyone after the wedding."

Vivian took another sip of tea. "You're going to make an excellent mother to your pup, Bree."

Bree rubbed her flat belly as Tia curled into a ball on her lap. "I hope so, Vivian."

"You will," Vivian replied with quiet certainty.

CHAPTER 19

Sophia yawned and stretched as the horses pulled the wagon steadily over the hill. She lifted her face to the sun, closing her eyes and inhaling deeply. It was a cold day, but the sun felt good on her face. She smiled at Kaden and he grinned back at her.

"The sun feels good."

"Aye, it does," he agreed as he slapped the reins lightly against the horses.

He glanced behind him. Ian was sitting in the seat behind him, his head nodding as he dozed, and Dani was stretched out and sleeping in the back of the wagon. She had Ian's jacket over her, and her head cushioned with her own jacket. Kaden turned back to Sophia.

"You look very pretty today, little Lycan."

She flushed prettily. "Thank you, Kaden."

Despite the coldness of the air, she was wearing a light green dress that hugged her full breasts and accentuated the curve of her hips. He had only seen her in a dress once before, the night of his birthday, and his cock stiffened as he remembered how the night had ended.

She adjusted the shawl she was wearing over the dress and wrapped it a bit tighter around her.

"Are you cold?" He reached for the jacket he had draped next to Ian.

She shook her head and stopped him from grabbing it. "No, you know I don't get cold."

He nodded and when she tried to let go of his hand, he held it firmly, linking their fingers together.

———

Sophia held Kaden's hand and stared at the buildings of the town in the distance. She tried not to let her moroseness show. She was in love with Kaden, she knew that without a doubt, and he would be leaving after the wedding. They hadn't spoken of it in days and she was afraid to bring it up. If she stayed quiet, she could pretend for a little longer that Kaden loved her in return and wouldn't leave her.

As they drove down the main road of the town, he squeezed her hand. "Are you all right?"

"Aye."

He gave her a troubled look and then lifted her hand to his mouth, kissing her knuckles gently. She looked behind her. Dani was starting to wake and quickly she leaned forward and kissed him on the mouth. He returned her kiss, one big hand cupping her face as they kissed, and she nipped him lightly on the lower lip before breaking away from him.

He winked at her as he pulled in front of the large stables at the outskirts of the town. As Dani yawned and sat up, Sophia lifted her head when a fleeting scent caught her attention.

"What is it?" Kaden asked.

"Lycan," she replied.

"There are Lycans who live in town." Ian's gravelly voice said from behind them. He had woken from his light doze and was looking around curiously.

She smiled at the old man. "Aye. You're right. I'm just being paranoid."

"I'm going to talk to the stable master. Kaden, I want you to meet him. He has forgotten more about horses than I'll ever know." Ian said. Kaden jumped down and quickly went around the wagon to lift Sophia down. She smiled her thanks as he lifted Dani down next.

"Thanks," Dani said without looking at him.

Sophia felt another trickle of guilt go through her. Dani was still hurt by the realization that she and Kaden were sleeping together, and it bothered Sophia more than she wanted to admit. She was not particularly close to her human cousin, but she did love her and had no desire to cause her pain.

"Come, Dani." She held her hand out to the young woman. "We will go and get the supplies that Bree needs."

Dani stood next to her but didn't take her hand and Sophia dropped it to her side before giving Kaden a weak smile. "We will meet you in half an hour at the restaurant."

Kaden nodded and as he and Ian turned toward the stables, Sophia gave Dani a cheerful smile. "Ready?"

"Aye." Dani glanced quickly at Kaden's retreating back before following Sophia across the street.

———

"My lord. She is here." Terrence entered the hotel room.

Draken whirled around and stared at him. "Are you certain?"

"Aye. I saw her myself."

"Is she alone?"

"No, my lord. There are two others with her."

Draken paced back and forth in front of the large fireplace. "Human or Lycan?"

"One is a Lycan, an elder, and the other is a female human."

"Good. When did you see them?"

"Just now. I watched until they arrived at the stables and then came straight back here." Terrence replied.

"We will kill the other two and take her. By the time the others find out she is missing, we will be at my home and I will have mated with her. The gods willing, she'll already be carrying my pup when her family arrives to try and save her."

"My lord -" Terrence hesitated and Draken gave him an impatient look.

"What is it?"

"The slave, Kaden, is also with her."

"Is he? How interesting," Draken said.

"I believe that the woman and the slave are – are together."

Draken's nostrils flared angrily and he stomped across the room towards Terrence. He cringed back as Draken stopped in front of him. "How do you know this?"

"They kissed, my lord."

Draken swore violently before pushing Terrence to the floor with a hard shove. "She is mine! How dare he take what belongs to me! I will kill him."

"Aye, my lord," Terrence whispered as Draken loomed over him. Draken was starting to swell, his fingernails lengthening and his eyes glowing a deep red as his anger grew.

He yanked Terrence to his feet, his fingernails ripping holes into the Lycan's shirt as he pulled him close. "Go to the forest and gather our brothers. We will kill the humans and the Lycan and take Sophia."

He shoved Terrence towards the door of the room. "Go, you fool! Quickly!"

"Dani?" Sophia gave her cousin a small smile. "I'm sorry."

Dani sighed impatiently as they left the store and walked down the street. "Stop apologizing, cousin. Kaden loves you and you love him. It's not your fault that I'm in love with him too."

"If you want to talk -"

"Stop, Sophia," Dani said sharply. "You're the last person I want to talk with about my feelings for Kaden."

"Of course. I'm sorry," Sophia replied.

Dani shook her head. "If you say you're sorry once more, I'll punch you. I swear I will."

Sophia smiled a little and Dani gave her a rueful look. "I just – I need time, cousin. I'll get over it with time."

A wave of depression washed over Sophia. Kaden would be leaving in just a few weeks. Perhaps she and Dani could nurse their broken hearts together. She rubbed at her forehead, a grimace crossing her face, and Dani frowned. "What's wrong?"

"Nothing. Just tired, I guess. We should hurry. It's almost time to meet Kaden and Ian at the restaurant, and then we need to drive the wagon to the store to pick up the supplies. Kaden wants to be home before dark," Sophia replied.

"Let's take the alley," Dani suggested. "It'll be faster."

"Aye, you're right." Sophia ducked down the alley. She moved quickly and Dani panted as she struggled to keep up.

"Gods, Sophia. Slow down. Not all of us have legs as long as yours," she complained.

Sophia laughed as she exited the alley. "I'm hungry and ready for…"

She trailed off as she gazed down the street, her face paling.

"Sophia? What is it?" Dani asked as she drew closer.

Without looking at her, Sophia made a shushing motion with her hand. "Be quiet, Dani. Stay in the alley."

"What? Why?" Dani whispered.

"Draken is here. He has Ian and Kaden," she muttered between barely-moving lips.

Dani made a soft cry of dismay. "Get back, Sophia."

"It's too late," she murmured.

"Hello, my pretty! Have you missed me?" Draken called.

"Stay there," Sophia whispered to Dani. "Don't let them see you."

"Sophia, no…" Dani moaned.

Her heart thudding and the coppery taste of fear in her mouth, Sophia stepped out of the alley and walked toward Draken. The street was dismayingly empty and she swallowed back her terror as she stared at Kaden. Both he and Ian were on their knees in the street. Ian had a gash over his left eye and Kaden's face was bruised and swelling. Draken was standing between them and he was swinging her sword idly in one hand.

"Is this your sword, my pretty one?" Draken drawled as she slowed to a stop twenty feet from them.

She didn't reply and he grinned at her. "I've never met Lycans who use human weapons before. What's the point?"

She continued to remain silent and a look of anger crossed his face before he glanced behind him. Sophia could see another ten Lycans gathered in a loose cluster behind them and he nodded to one of the bigger ones.

The Lycan stepped forward and Draken showed him the sword. "Have you seen Lycans use human weapons, Terrence?"

The dark-haired Lycan shook his head and Draken turned to Sophia, dismissing him completely. "I found this in the back of your wagon. I suppose there's no place to put a sword when you're wearing a dress."

He looked her up and down, his grin widening, and his blue eyes starting to turn red. "You look lovely today. Step closer, please."

"Stay where you are, Sophia," Kaden said.

Draken scowled and Sophia cried out in dismay when he drove the end of the sword handle into Kaden's back. Kaden gave a hoarse cry of surprise and pain as he was driven forward.

Ian growled as thick, black hair sprouted on his face. His eyes turned a dark yellow and his shirt began to tear along the arms as his body swelled.

"Shift old man and I'll gut you like a fish," Draken said.

"Don't, Ian," Kaden said as he straightened. "Stay calm."

"Sophia," Draken said. "Come to me."

Sophia took a step forward and Kaden glared at her. "No, Sophia. Run, right now."

"Listen to your mate, Sophia," Ian said. "The Lycan has gone mad. I can smell it on him. He'll kill all of us anyway. Go!"

Draken sighed irritably. "Shut up, old man."

He gripped Sophia's sword and with an almost lazy flick of his wrist, sliced Ian's head from his body.

Sophia stared in horrified shock as Ian's head fell to the dirt. His eyes were still open, and she watched the light fade from them. She howled with rage and sorrow as Kaden stared in disbelief at Ian's headless body. Ian's body stayed upright for nearly thirty seconds and then fell forward with a soft thump. Blood poured from the headless stump of his neck and pooled under his body as Kaden roared with anger and leaped to his feet. He dove at Draken and the Lycan snarled and grabbed the big man's throat. His fingernails dug into Kaden's neck and he squeezed tightly before forcing Kaden back to his knees. Sophia could see blood dripping down Kaden's neck, and she howled again as she took a few staggering steps forward.

"Get over here now or watch him die," Draken spat.

"Sophia, don't -" Kaden choked out before Draken squeezed again. Draken watched as Kaden's face turned purple before tracing the sword, its blade splattered with Ian's blood, across Kaden's chest.

"Do you want to watch him die as well, my pretty?"

Sophia shook her head and approached Draken. She glanced down at Ian's body, the tears pouring down her face. Draken smiled at her with false sympathy. "There, there, my pretty one. Don't cry. He was an old Lycan."

"I'm going to kill you," she whispered raggedly.

Draken's hand, which had relaxed around Kaden's neck, tightened again and Kaden made another choking, gasping noise. She could feel the shift happening, the colours around her sharpening and her muscles tightening. Her sense of smell heightened, and she took a deep breath, inhaling the tangy scent of Kaden's fear and the metallic smell of Ian's blood. It drove her need to shift higher. Draken would try and take Kaden from her. He would kill her mate if she didn't stop him.

"If you shift, I will kill your lover right here." Draken

held the tip of her sword over Kaden's heart. "Do you understand?"

Her body continued to swell as her teeth lengthened and sharpened. She growled low in her throat and Draken pressed the sword into Kaden's chest. Bright blood blossomed through his shirt. Sophia threw her head back and howled at the sight and smell of her mate's blood.

Dimly she was aware of people gathering in the street, and Draken's pack quickly surrounded the three of them. They growled and snapped at the town people who were drawing close, and the humans gave shouts of alarm before retreating.

She took a deep breath and willed herself to stop shifting. Draken eyed her coolly, nodding his approval when she stayed in her human form, and pulled the sword tip from Kaden's chest. Keeping his hand around Kaden's throat, he nodded to the Lycan called Terrence.

"The collar, Terrence. Put it on her."

Sophia, her gaze on Kaden, didn't resist when Terrence locked the silver collar around her throat. She didn't react when Draken released Kaden and pulled her roughly into his arms. Three members of his pack held Kaden firmly on his knees as Draken nuzzled and kissed her throat above the collar.

"You smell of him. His scent covers you," he said. "That you would mate with a human should disgust me, but it does not. Such is your power over me, my pretty Lycan. Soon enough, it will be my scent that covers your skin."

He reached down and rested his hand on her abdomen as she continued to stare at Kaden. "My pup that grows in your belly."

He took her cold hand in his and squeezed it. "Come, it is many days' travel to your new home."

He led her away as Terrence cleared his throat. "My lord, what do we do with the slave?"

Draken glanced back at Kaden. "Bring him with us, of course. We always have a need for slaves. Besides, it will please me to have him watch as her belly swells with my pup."

Terrence nodded and Sophia watched helplessly as they shackled Kaden's wrists with heavy chains and slipped a leather collar around his neck.

"Come, pretty one. You must forget about your love for the human. You belong to me now," Draken said as he led her towards the trees.

CHAPTER 20

The moment Sophia disappeared, Dani crept to the mouth of the alley and peeked out. When the long-haired Lycan decapitated Ian, she opened her mouth to scream. A hand clamped across her mouth and an arm circled her waist like a band of steel. She was yanked backward against a hard body and a low voice whispered in her ear. "Quiet, girl. If they discover you, they'll rip you to shreds."

She struggled against him, kicking and flailing wildly, but he dragged her further into the alley. He twisted her around and pressed her back against the building.

"Stop struggling! I will not harm you," he said.

She sagged against him, staring up at him with wide, frightened eyes as tears dripped down her cheeks. He loosened his grip on her and stared down at her tear-stained face. "Shh. Stay here,"

He peered around the building before stepping back. "What's your name, girl?"

She stared silently at him. He was only a little taller than her and he had light brown hair and hazel eyes. She knew instinctively that he was a Lycan.

"Your name," he prompted.

"Danielle," she whispered. She started to shake as the image of Ian's headless body popped into her head.

"Oh, Ian," she moaned before covering her mouth with her hand. The Lycan in front of her hesitated and then drew her into his embrace. He hugged her, rubbing her back as she trembled and cried silently.

She jerked away from him and made a break for the street when Sophia howled loudly. He cursed and hauled her back against him. "No, Danielle! Stay with me."

"I have to help them! I have to -"

"You cannot help them. Do you hear me? There are too many of them. They'll kill you or take you prisoner along with your friends." His grip on her was too strong to break and she moaned again and slumped against the building.

He looked cautiously around the side of the building, and Dani took a deep breath and peeked around his trim body. The Lycans were leading Sophia and Kaden into the forest, and a crowd of humans had gathered around Ian's head and body.

Dani started toward them and the man pulled her back roughly. She glared at him and punched him hard in the chest. He flinched and she drew back when his eyes glowed at her.

"Don't be afraid of me," he said.

"I'm not," she muttered.

"Aye, I suppose not." He leaned into her and inhaled deeply. "What is a human doing with Lycans?"

"My father is a Lycan!" she said hotly.

He frowned and inhaled again. "Yet, you are a full human. How odd."

She gave a trembling sigh. Her brief burst of anger had left her, and she was crying again. "Please, let me go. I have to get back to my family and tell them what's happened."

"Do you live here in town?" he asked.

She shook her head, staring numbly at him. "No. The Lycan is my cousin. Her family lives about half a day from here by horse."

He frowned at her. "You cannot travel home by yourself. It isn't safe in the forest, even if you stick to the road."

"I don't care. I have to go!" There was a note of hysteria in her voice and he rubbed her upper arms soothingly.

"Shh, Danielle. I will escort you home to your family."

She blinked at him. "I – why are you helping me?"

He shrugged. "I never could resist a damsel in distress. Let's go."

He led her down the alley and she gave him a nervous look. "Do you have a horse?"

He shook his head. "No. What need would I have for a horse? When we are out of the town, I'll shift, and you can ride on my back. It will be faster."

Dani nodded and followed him as he walked quickly towards the edge of town.

"What's your name?" She panted as she struggled to keep up with him.

"Andric."

DANI CLUNG TIGHTLY TO ANDRIC'S LIGHT BROWN FUR AS HE loped through the forest. After leading her from the alley, he had made one stop at the hotel. She had waited nervously in the street before he returned, carrying a large leather bag in his hand.

Without speaking, he'd taken her hand and led her out of the town. They followed the road, Dani tensing when they passed a wagon of humans heading toward the town, but

Andric smiled easily at them and spoken briefly with the eldest man. Half a mile outside of town, they moved into the thick trees, neither speaking until they were deep within the woods.

Andric dropped his bag on the forest floor and quickly unbuttoned his shirt. Dani, her face flushing, turned away.

"Where is your uncle's home?" he asked as he stripped off the rest of his clothes and stuffed them into the leather bag.

"Near the big lake. Do you know where that is?"

"Aye. I am familiar with the area," Andric replied. There was a low popping noise and he barked softly at her.

She picked up the leather bag, slinging it over her body as he crouched down. She climbed onto his back, sinking her fingers into his fur and hanging on tightly as he moved through the trees.

Now, she stared at the late afternoon sun. They had maybe another hour of travel to get to home, and she breathed a sigh of relief. She'd alternated between bouts of terror and disbelief over the last few hours and she was anxious to tell the others what happened. Her fear for Sophia and Kaden was making her feel nauseous, and more than once she'd wept silently as Andric carried her through the trees.

She realized that Andric was slowing down, and she slid off his back when he stopped completely. The fur on his neck was standing up and he was inhaling deeply. She felt a prickle of fear against the back of her neck. The forest was too silent. No birds sang and no small animals rustled in the underbrush.

She looked around fearfully as Andric nudged her toward a cluster of large trees. She slipped around them, leaning against the largest one as Andric shifted to his human form.

"What is it?"

He shook his head, pressing up against her and clamping

his hand across her mouth. He placed his mouth at her ear and breathed, "Gogmagog."

She stiffened and moaned quietly behind his hand. Adrenaline rushed through her and she stared wide-eyed at him. Gogmagogs were hideous human-like creatures who lived in the outskirts. They were rumoured to be over twenty feet tall and had the strength of thirty men. She had never seen one, had never even heard of one leaving the outskirts, but she knew the tales of them.

She was beginning to tremble wildly against the Lycan and when he tried to draw away, she put her arms around his naked waist and clung tightly to him. He stroked her hair and put his fingers to his lips. She nodded and they stared silently at each other as the minutes stretched out.

There was nothing but silence and she was just starting to relax when she heard the low grunt. Her fingers tightened on Andric's skin and he gave her a reassuring nod as he pushed her back into the undergrowth.

The grunting continued, a low and inhuman sound, and Dani and Andric clung to each other like frightened children when the ground shook under their feet. She stared up at the Lycan, her own fear increasing when she saw the fear in his eyes. He smiled reassuringly at her, but his hands tightened around her back when the grunting grew closer. It was rhythmic in sound, a loud grunt followed by a whistling breath as the creature inhaled. The bushes trembled and the creature made a thick, coughing noise before the sound died completely.

Dani held her breath. The whistling breathing and grunting was bad, but the silence was much worse. She strained to hear in the silence. Andric, a look of alarm on his face, was sniffing the air lightly.

A shockingly large hand covered in thick black hair, shot

through the bushes and grabbed Andric around the calf. It yanked hard and he was pulled from her grip and dragged away as easily as a child. She had one last glimpse of his pale face before he disappeared.

The Gogmagog roared with pleasure and Andric howled loudly before the air was filled with snarling and growling. She leaned down and picked up a large, thick branch from the ground as the Gogmagog roared again. This time it was tinged with pain and Andric made a howling sound of triumph that cut off abruptly. There was a loud thudding noise that made her cringe and then Andric was barking and the Gogmagog was making harsh grunts of frustration.

"Stop moving!" A thick voice muttered and all the hair on her arms stood up. The voice was gargled and almost too distorted to recognize as human. Andric growled again. Her hands tightened on the branch when the creature made a loud grunt of approval and Andric whined, a sound of hurt and fear that made her heart pound in her chest. She hesitated only briefly before stepping out from the cover of the trees.

Her mouth dropped open and she stared in repulsion and fear at the creature standing with its back to her. The legend was wrong, she thought numbly. The Gogmagogs were not twenty feet tall, but the beast towered at least twelve feet in height.

His hair was a rich black and it hung to his shoulders in a tangled mess of twigs and leaves. He had the fur of a bear wrapped around his massive body. The bear's head and claws were still attached to the fur, and she stared mutely at the sunken holes where its eyes used to be.

Andric was in his wolf form and the Gogmagog was holding his body high over his head. He raised his knee and she realized with horror that he was about to break Andric's back. She ran forward and swung the thick branch at the creature's exposed legs. It was like hitting the solid trunk of a tree, and she nearly dropped the branch when the shockwaves reverberated up the wood and into her arms.

The Gogmagog rumbled in surprise and looked over his shoulder. He grinned, revealing black and rotting teeth, and threw Andric against a large tree. There was a sharp crack and Andric whimpered quietly and collapsed on the ground.

The Gogmagog turned toward her. His chest was massive and his arms thick with muscle. He clenched his hands into fists, his knuckles cracking, and Dani screamed with terror and backed away. She raised the branch and swung it at the beast. He caught it deftly and ripped it from her hands. He broke it in half as easily as a twig and grinned again at her.

"Human," it whispered before reaching out and snagging her upper arms. Dani screamed again, the sound echoing in the forest, as he dragged her toward him. She kicked frantically at the massive creature's shins, but he shrugged off the blows easily.

He was bending toward her when Andric leaped onto his back. He scrambled up the Gogmagog, his claws tearing through the bear's fur to leave shallow bloody grooves in the beast's skin.

It screamed angrily and, still holding Dani by one arm, swung its other arm behind him and beat at Andric's body. Andric howled and Dani watched numbly as Andric scrabbled even higher and sunk his teeth into the side of the Gogmagog's throat.

She tried to yank her arm back, but the beast held it firmly even as Andric's teeth tore his throat open. Blood poured out of him, coating his chest and Dani's face and upper body. She struggled and writhed against him, keeping her mouth and eyes closed against the flood of hot liquid. The creature's grip loosened and when she yanked against his grip again, he released her. She staggered back, falling onto her ass and wiping at the blood covering her eyes, as the beast screamed again weakly and sank to its knees. The ground shook and it gave her a final look of dumb surprise before falling flat on its face.

She scrambled back on her butt, her heart pounding and her blood pumping through her veins. She couldn't stop her small gasps and whimpers and she swiped her arm across her mouth and eyes, trying to clear them of the blood. She collapsed on her back, staring up at the sunlight filtering through the trees. She moaned in fear when a hand dropped onto her stomach, but it was only Andric. He stared down at her.

"Danielle, are you hurt?"

She shook her head, grimacing at the drops of blood that flew from her hair and he helped her to her feet. He was holding his left arm against his side and he winced as he took a step back.

"You're hurt," she said.

"My arm is broken, and I think a few of my ribs as well," he replied. "I'll be fine by tomorrow. My body will heal itself."

"Aye," she whispered.

He looked her over, staring at the blood on her shirt, before rummaging through the leather bag. He took out his pants and shirt and handed the shirt to her as he struggled into the pants. "Take my shirt. Yours is ruined."

She took the shirt and glanced around him at the body of the Gogmagog lying on the ground. "Is it dead?"

"Aye." He pressed his left side gingerly and winced again.

"I – I've never seen one before. Have you?"

He nodded. "Aye, but never this far in from the outskirts and never one by itself. They travel in packs like we do."

"What is it doing here?" She wondered as she pulled her wet, sticky shirt over her head. She used the relatively clean back of it to swipe at the blood on her chest and abdomen. Anxious to get the shirt off, she realized too late that she was standing half-naked in front of the Lycan. Her face beet red, she turned around quickly and slipped his shirt over her head.

"Sorry," she muttered when she turned back.

He stared at her and then grinned boyishly. "I don't mind. I like a free-spirited girl."

She flushed even brighter and dropped her ruined shirt on the ground. "Can you walk on it if you shift back?" She pointed to his arm.

He shook his head. "No, I don't think so."

She slung the leather bag back over her body. "It's not much farther to my uncle's home."

"Lead the way home then."

She nodded and started past him. He caught her arm and lifted her grimy, bloody hand to his mouth. He kissed the knuckles gently. "Thank you for saving my life, Danielle."

A shiver went through her and she pulled her hand out of his grip. "I didn't, not really. You saved mine."

"Still, you're a brave little thing – for a human."

She blushed again but didn't object when he took her hand. "Let's go."

CHAPTER 21

"Andric?" Dani gave the Lycan a worried look. He had turned away from her and was coughing into the crook of his arm. "Are you all right?"

"Aye," he said hoarsely, without looking at her.

She made him turn around to face her and gave a sharp cry at the blood that coated his lips. Over the last forty minutes the Lycan had been slowing down. His breath was wheezing in and out of his lungs, and he kept his broken left arm clamped firmly against his left side.

"You're getting worse."

He shook his head and carefully flexed his arm. "No, it's a little better, I think. My arm isn't as sore."

She reached out and touched the blood on his mouth before showing her fingers to him. "You're bleeding inside."

"A punctured lung, maybe." He coughed again and nearly fell over.

"Put your arm around me." Dani pressed up against his right side and slipped her arm around his waist. "We are almost home. You can rest there and heal."

He gave her a tired look and leaned heavily against her as they stumbled through the trees.

"YOU'RE LYING, JEFFREY."

"Doran, I swear I'm not. She took off her shirt and there it was - a third nipple smack dab in the middle of her chest and pointed right at me," Jeffrey said earnestly.

Doran laughed and shook his head. "The last time you told me this story, the nipple was just above her belly button."

Jeffrey shrugged. "So, I'm not good with details. I never could -"

He stopped abruptly and straightened up from the tree he was leaning against. "Do you smell that?"

Doran, his face grim, nodded. "Aye. It's Lycan."

He inhaled again, a look of fear coming over his face, as he started into the trees. "Dani?"

"Doran, wait!" Jeffrey called quietly. "If they have her, we need to -"

"Dani!" Doran shouted. "Danielle, where are you?"

"Doran! Help us, quickly!"

He tore off into the trees, his body already beginning to swell as Jeffrey cursed lightly and went after him.

Doran, his blood surging in his veins and hair starting to sprout on his body, leaped easily over a fallen tree. He could smell Dani's fear and the scent of blood in the air and he started to growl. If they hurt his sister, if they tried to –

"Doran!"

He skidded to a stop, staring in surprise at his twin. Her blonde hair was caked and matted with blood. It had dried to maroon-coloured streaks on her face and arms and she was supporting a semi-conscious Lycan beside her.

"Dani! What happened?"

"Doran!" Dani began to cry, and she leaned the Lycan against a tree before nearly leaping into her brother's arms.

"What's going on? Where are the others?" He brushed her blood-soaked hair back from her face.

"Draken," she whispered. "He – he was waiting for us in the town. He took Kaden and Sophia. I couldn't stop them, Doran. There were too many of them and they would have killed me. I'm so sorry."

He patted her back as Jeffrey rubbed his hand across his face. "Gods be damned. We have to let the lord Tristan know right now."

"Aye," Doran said as he hugged his sister.

"Where is Ian? Did they take him as well?" Jeffrey asked.

Dani swallowed convulsively. "I – they killed him. The long-haired one, Draken, he just – just took Sophia's sword and cut off his head." She sobbed brokenly as Jeffrey staggered back.

"No," he whispered. His tanned face was pale, and he gave Doran a look of horror. "Ian cannot be dead."

"He is." The Lycan leaning against the tree replied. "I saw him kill the old man."

"Who are you?" Doran asked.

"His name is Andric." Dani's tears had left tracks through the blood on her face and Doran rubbed at the blood as she stared up at him.

"He saved my life in town and in the forest. There was a Gogmagog and it -"

"There are no Gogmagogs this far east," Jeffrey interrupted. "They do not leave the outskirts."

"It was a Gogmagog," Dani insisted. "I saw it with my own eyes. It is the beast's blood that covers me. Andric killed it, but not before it broke his arm and his ribs. I think he has a punctured lung. His arm is starting to heal but he is bleeding inside. He needs to see Aunt -"

There was a soft thud and the three of them turned. Andric had collapsed on the floor of the forest. Dani pulled away from Doran and knelt beside the fallen Lycan. "Andric? Andric, wake up!"

He didn't move and she gave Doran and Jeffrey a frightened look. "We have to get him to the house and to Aunt Avery. Quickly!"

When Doran hesitated, she scowled at him. "He saved my life, Doran. Help him!"

Doran and Jeffrey knelt beside the unconscious Lycan and lifted him. Dani followed as they walked quickly toward the house.

"MY LORD?"

"What is it, Terrence?" Draken asked.

He was sitting next to Sophia. She had pinned her long dark hair on top of her head, and he was gently stroking a few of the strands that had loosened and lay against her neck.

"Are you sure we should stop for the night? Is it not best to keep travelling?" Terrence asked.

Draken shrugged. "I am both tired and hungry. Why should we not stop?"

"Her family will come for her."

"They have no idea we've taken them." Draken smiled at Sophia. "Were they expecting you back today, my lovely?"

She refused to reply, and his nostrils flared angrily before he nodded to the Lycan standing closest to the kneeling Kaden. The Lycan squatted beside Kaden and placed his long, dirty fingernail against Kaden's throat.

"One word from me and he'll slice your lover's throat wide open," Draken said. "Do you want to watch his life blood soak into the ground?"

"Tomorrow," Sophia said. "We were spending the night in town and traveling back in the morning. They won't be expecting us until tomorrow afternoon."

"There, you see?" Draken said with satisfaction. "They are not expecting them until tomorrow, and it will take them at least another day to discover that they were taken. Besides, they may not even suspect that it is I who has taken them."

"Is it wise to believe her, my lord?" Terrence said. Sophia could see the look of disbelief that covered his face.

"Be quiet, Terrence. I grow tired of your complaining." Draken leaned in and nuzzled her neck. "You are so beautiful, Sophia."

She refused to look at him, staring instead at the bound Kaden across the campsite. They regarded each other steadily as Draken growled.

"Your obsession with the slave is ridiculous," he snapped. "Lycans who lower themselves to sleep with humans are no better than dogs!"

He grabbed Sophia's chin and turned her face toward his. "Why would you want the human when you have me? I will make your every wish come true, my pretty. He is useless and weak."

He jerked back in shock when Sophia spat in his face. "He is worth a thousand of you"

He slapped her hard across the face. Kaden roared with anger and jumped to his feet. Three members of Draken's pack immediately pushed him back to his knees as Draken snarled and stalked across the campsite. He grabbed Kaden's hair and yanked his head back. His eyes were a dark red and his fingernails had lengthened to razor-sharp points. He raised his hand over his head, ready to slit Kaden's throat, when Sophia's voice rang out.

"Stop!"

Draken turned to look at her, his body stiffening and a grunt of surprise erupting from his throat when he saw how close she was to shifting.

"Do not forget the collar around your neck," he warned.

She grinned at him, her teeth very white and very sharp. "I have not forgotten. If you kill the human, I will shift. I swear it."

"You wouldn't," he said.

"Shall we find out?" she replied.

He hesitated and her grin widened as hair appeared on her cheeks. With a snarl of anger, Draken released Kaden and stepped toward her.

"Enough. Calm yourself," he said.

She took a deep breath and pushed her wolf down. Her body returned to its normal size and Draken stared at the dents in her neck where the silver points inside the collar had pressed against her flesh. She heard Kaden give a shuddering sigh of relief.

"You would kill yourself over a human?" He stared at her in disbelief as her eyes faded from jade to dark brown.

"I will make a bargain with you," she said. "Release the human into the woods at dawn. Play your little game of hunt with him and if you are successful in taking his head, I will willingly join you in your bed."

"Sophia! No!" Kaden shouted.

She ignored him and continued to stare at Draken. "Do we have a deal?"

"Do you honestly believe the human will survive the hunt?" Draken asked. "There is but one of him and," he swept his arm around the campsite, "ten of my pack. It has been weeks since they hunted, and they are anxious to hunt again."

"Do we have a deal?" she repeated.

He grinned at her. "Of course, my sweet. I will do whatever it takes to make you happy. In the morning, we will release your human. When my pack brings back his head, you will be mine."

———

ANDRIC WOKE WITH A START. HE SAT UP STRAIGHT AND stared blankly around the room before climbing out of bed. His bag was sitting neatly on the floor and he quickly dressed. He rubbed at his side. The piercing pain had disappeared, and he breathed a sigh of relief. The pain had been incredible, like nothing he'd felt before, but it seemed he'd healed while he slept.

The door to the bedroom opened and a young, dark-haired girl peeked in cautiously.

"Hello." He gave her a friendly smile as she regarded him solemnly. "What's your name?"

"Leta."

"I'm Andric."

"I know. You saved Dani."

"She opened the door wider and leaned against the frame before inhaling deeply. "You're a Lycan."

"Aye, as are you." He gave her another friendly smile, but she stepped back into the hallway when he started towards her.

"Don't be afraid of me. I won't hurt you."

She looked at him disdainfully. "I'm not afraid."

She turned and disappeared down the hallway and he followed her with an amused grin. She led him through a maze of hallways before stopping in front of a doorway. He joined her and stared at the room full of humans and Lycans.

"Doran and Evan, you will go with Jeffrey to town and bring back Ian's body." A long-haired Lycan paced back and forth in front of the fireplace as he spoke. "Dani, are you sure they went north?"

Dani nodded. "Aye." The young woman was pale, and her eyes were swollen from crying, but she took a deep breath and straightened her back. "After they – they killed Ian, they took Sophia and Kaden north."

"Based on what Bree has told us about where Draken lives, that makes sense." Andric stared at the largest Lycan he'd ever seen. His hair was a dark red and he had his arm around the waist of a tiny blonde human woman. She was leaning against him, her face white and tears shining on her face.

Leta glanced up at him before walking into the room. "He's awake."

Andric stood just inside the doorway. A blonde woman with features similar to Danielle, walked over to him. She hesitated and then took his hand, squeezing it tightly. "Thank you for saving my child."

He nodded as Dani appeared next to her mother. "How do you feel, Andric?"

"Better. How long have I been sleeping?"

"Only an hour or so," she replied.

He frowned. His injury had been grave, and he was surprised that his Lycan healing had worked so quickly. "Only an hour?"

"Aye." He followed her gaze to the redheaded woman who was standing apart from the others. She was staring into the fire, her face pale and her arms folded across her torso.

The Lycan with the long dark hair cleared his throat. "My

name is Tristan. Thank you for your help. You are welcome to stay at my home until you are fully healed."

He stared around the room. "The rest of us will leave immediately. If we're lucky, we'll catch their scent and find them easily."

A shorter man stepped forward. "Brother, I don't believe we should leave the women unprotected. What if Draken has ordered other members of his pack to come here?"

Tristan nodded. "You are right, Marshall." He turned to a blond-haired man. "Nicky, you will stay and -"

"No!" the man shouted. "I am going with you, Dad. You cannot ask me to stay while my sister's life is in danger."

"Nicholas, your mother needs your protection. We -"

"I'm going with you." The redhead turned away from the fire.

"If Mama is going, so am I." The tiny blonde woman said.

The red Lycan shook his head immediately. "No, Bree. You're staying here." His hand rested protectively against her abdomen for a moment.

"He is my brother," she said. Andric was a little amused at the way she stared defiantly at the Lycan who was three times her size.

"Aye, and she is my sister," he said. "We will bring them back, little one. I promise you."

Tristan put his arms around the redheaded woman. "You're not going, Avery."

"I am," she replied.

"No, girl, you're not. You need to rest after heal -" He stopped suddenly and glanced at Andric before rubbing her back. "You need to rest."

"Tristan, you cannot tell me what to do." Avery glared up at him and tried to pull away.

He tugged her closer and stroked her long red hair. "We will move faster if we shift."

"You can carry me on your back."

"You will slow us down," he said gently.

Andric watched as the Red slumped against Tristan for a moment before turning and staring into the fire again. Leta crept over and wrapped her arms around Avery's waist as Tristan kissed the back of her shoulder and squeezed her hip before turning to the others.

"Nicholas, you -"

"No, Dad," Nicholas said. "I am going with you. Leo is here, and Doran and the others will be back by tomorrow morning. Dani said there were least a dozen Lycans. You'll need my help. You know you will."

"I would be happy to stay until you return," Andric said.

The man named Marshall stared at him suspiciously. "Who are you, and why are you so eager to help?"

"Daddy!" Dani glared at him. "Stop it. He saved my life, remember?"

"Aye, I remember," Marshall answered. "But it still does not explain why a Lycan is without a pack. Why were you in town?"

"My pack was killed by leeches two moons ago," Andric said. "I am travelling to Vanden. I have a cousin there."

"I'm so sorry, Andric," Dani said.

Marshall scrubbed at his face. "Maya, what do you think?"

Dani's mother studied Andric carefully for a moment. "We'll be safe with him."

Marshall stared at Tristan who gave him a slight nod as an older female Lycan stood up from the couch. "I may be old, Tristan, but I can still fight if need be. I will keep Avery and the others safe."

"I know, Mother." Tristan glanced around the room. "We leave in ten minutes."

THEY STOOD IN THE COLD SUNSHINE, STARING SOLEMNLY AT each other for a moment as Leta wrapped herself around Tristan's legs.

"Papa? Pick me up."

He bent and scooped her up, burying his face in her hair before kissing the top of her head.

"I love you, Papa."

"I love you too, Leta. Be good for your mama. I will see you soon." He kissed her again and set her down before moving to Avery. He pulled her into his arms and kissed her. She stared up at him and he brushed a strand of her hair away from her cheek.

"Tristan, if he hurts her…"

Her lips trembled and a tear slid down her pale cheek.

"Sophia is strong and smart and brave. She'll do whatever it takes to survive," Tristan said hoarsely.

He wiped away the tear from her face as she took a deep breath. "Be careful, my love."

"I will." He stepped away from her and she caught his hand, squeezing it firmly as behind them, James picked up Bree and hugged her.

"Tristan?" Avery refused to let go of his hand.

He looked back at her, his heart aching at the fear etched into her face.

"Bring her back to me," she said. "Promise me you'll bring my child home."

"I promise."

CHAPTER 22

Sophia stared calmly at Kaden across the camp. He smiled at her, but he was afraid. She could smell his fear. She looked around the camp. Just over an hour ago, Draken had retired to his tent. He had invited her to join him, and she had politely declined.

"Very well." He grinned, his eyes glowing at her, before lifting her hand and kissing her knuckles. "I'm willing to wait until tomorrow. Remember your promise, pretty one. When my brothers bring back the human's head, you will join me in my bed."

She hadn't replied and he'd kissed her hand a final time before disappearing into his tent. He was the only one with a tent. Two of the Lycans kept watch while the rest of the pack had shifted into their wolf forms and curled up on the hard ground. Only Draken's second-in-command, Terrence, had remained in his human form.

She suddenly stood and the two Lycans standing guard, growled in unison. She glared at the giant wolves, her eyes flashing at them and her hands in tight fists. "If he freezes to death in the night, you won't get your hunt tomorrow."

She moved to Kaden. Terrence held up his hand and shook his head as the Lycans stalked toward her. They whined uneasily and Terrence gave them a warning look. They sat down, staring suspiciously at Sophia as she sat on Kaden's lap.

His hands were chained behind his back, and she rubbed his arms briskly as she pressed her warm body against his cold one. She cupped his face and kissed him before moving her mouth to his ear.

"The Gallante River is only two miles north of here," she breathed. "It is wide and deep. Go to it. The Lycans won't be able to swim and will not go into the river after you."

"I can't swim either, remember?" he breathed back.

She kissed his warm mouth again. "You won't have to. Even going chest deep will be enough to deter them."

"I won't leave you."

She squeezed his bound arms. "You must. It is your only chance." She glanced at Terrence. He was staring at them and she placed her mouth closer to Kaden's ear. "My family will find you and save you."

"You don't know that," he murmured.

"I do," she insisted. "They'll come. Once you're with my family and safe, you can come back for me."

"Sophia -"

"Enough talking," Terrence said. "I will allow you your last night together but keep your mouths shut." He glanced nervously at Draken's tent.

Sophia stroked the back of Kaden's neck and stared at Terrence. "Your leader has gone mad. You know that don't you?"

"Aye, I do," Terrence said.

"Then why do you follow him so willingly into his madness? You and the rest of his pack are going to die. My family will come for us and believe me when I say they will show you no mercy."

Terrence sighed heavily before glancing at the two Lycans watching over them. "Your mate will die tomorrow. My brothers will chase him down like a dog and take his head. You will be forced to share Draken's bed and carry his pups. When your family comes for you, Draken will make you watch as he murders them one by one."

Sophia smiled bitterly. "The last time you met my family, you and your master ran like cowards in the night. Have you forgotten how easily we killed your brothers?"

Terrence shook his head. "No."

"Draken has," Sophia replied.

Terrence nodded. "Aye, his obsession with you has blinded him to the sorrow and death you will bring upon us."

Sophia gave him a look of bewilderment. The Lycan, although more stable than Draken, was obviously on the cusp of madness himself. "You speak in riddles, Lycan."

He smiled. "Aye, I suppose I do."

She turned away from him and touched the puncture wounds on Kaden's neck. They had scabbed over, but they looked sore.

"How is your chest?" She pulled his shirt open and looked down it. The wound from her sword had clotted and she ran her fingers over it.

"It's fine," he grunted.

"Do not be afraid, my love." She smoothed her hand over his hair.

"I'm afraid for you." He stared at Draken's tent.

"I can take care of myself."

"Aye." A faint smile crossed his face. "I have noticed."

He pressed a kiss against her throat. "I can't leave you, Sophia. Do not ask me to."

She rested her forehead against his. "You have to. Please. It is your only chance to survive."

He gave her a helpless look and she kissed him again. "Do not make me watch Draken kill you, human. Promise me you will run."

"Sophia -"

"Promise me," she insisted. "Watching you die will destroy me. Do you understand?"

"Leaving you here alone with Draken, knowing what he will do to you, will destroy *me*," he replied.

"Whatever he does, whatever he *tries* to do, will not matter. I belong to you. Nothing will ever change that," she whispered.

He leaned forward and gave her a brief, warm kiss. "I love you, little Lycan."

She drew in a trembling breath as tears slipped down her cheeks. "I love you too, Kaden."

"I should have told you before, but I was afraid. I never believed I would love a Lycan, love anyone, the way I love you," he said.

She stroked his cheek with her thumb. "I was afraid too."

"This is all very touching," Terrence said. "But tomorrow the human will die in the hunt and you," he gave Sophia a look of pity and regret, "will wish you were dead."

Sophia tucked her body against Kaden's and put her arms around him before smiling coldly at Terrence. "Before tomorrow is over, it will be you and your lord Draken who wish for death."

SOPHIA WATCHED AS DRAKEN STRETCHED DEEPLY BEFORE staring up at the cloudy sky. It was just after dawn and he yawned and squatted next to the small fire. "I believe it may snow today, Terrence."

"Aye," the smaller Lycan said.

Draken turned to her and Kaden. "It's time to say goodbye to your human lover, my pretty. My brothers are anxious to begin the hunt."

He grinned merrily at Kaden. "I will bring your head back to my home for the other slaves to see. They've been most unruly since you and your sister escaped. How is your sister by the way? Still fucking the Red? Perhaps I will pay her a visit after I kill the other Lycans. Do you think she would like that? Has she missed me?"

Kaden stared at him, his nostrils flaring angrily, and Draken laughed. "Who would have thought that both you and your sister would fall in love with Lycans? The irony of it is absolutely staggering, is it not?"

When Kaden remained silent, a dark look crossed Draken's face. "Answer me, human."

"You're going to die today," Kaden said.

Draken laughed. "The humans are so ridiculous, are they not, Terrence?"

"Aye, my lord," Terrence replied.

Draken stood and clapped his hands together briskly. "Unchain him."

Terrence unchained Kaden's hands. Kaden rubbed his wrists and then put his arms around Sophia's waist. He hugged her hard, burying his face in her throat and inhaling deeply as she put her mouth to his ear.

"Remember what I told you, my love. They will find you."

He nodded and kissed her deeply. She returned his kiss, threading her hands through his hair and holding him as they both ignored Draken's angry growl.

"I love you," she whispered against his mouth.

"I love you too, Sophia."

They clung to each other until Draken growled again. "Enough!"

He gave Kaden a baleful look. "I will allow you an hour's head start. You should thank me for my generosity."

Kaden ignored him and kissed Sophia again. "I will see you soon."

She smiled at him and cupped his face. "Aye, you will."

"Go, human. Before I change my mind and take your head right now," Draken snarled.

Kaden kissed Sophia a final time and without looking back, jogged into the trees. He disappeared and Sophia took a shuddering breath. Fear was eating away at her stomach and she traced the silver collar around her throat before sitting down.

Draken's pack was pacing back and forth, whining and growling deep in their throats, and Draken held his hand up. "Patience, my brothers. You will have his head soon enough."

He took a deep breath and smiled at Sophia. "Now, how about we have some breakfast?"

SOPHIA STARED SILENTLY INTO THE FIRE AS DRAKEN SUCKED at the leg bone of a rabbit. Twenty minutes had passed since Kaden had disappeared into the forest, and Draken's pack was still pacing back and forth restlessly.

With a loud sigh, Draken threw the bone into the fire and wiped his hands on his pants. "Go on, then."

The Lycans yipped in response and Sophia leaped to her feet. "You said an hour!"

Draken laughed. "Aye, but I must admit that I am impatient to have you in my bed. The sooner my brothers bring back the human's head, the sooner I can have you."

"No!" Sophia leaped for the Lycan nearest her, but Terrence caught her neatly around the waist. She twisted against him, her fist catching him hard on the jaw and he gave a grunt of frustration before hitting her across the face. Dazed from the blow and weakened by the silver collar, she slid down his body and collapsed on the ground as blood flowed from a cut on her temple.

"Careful, Terrence!" Draken said. "That's the future mother of my pups, remember."

"Forgive me, my lord," Terrence muttered.

Draken nodded and stared at his pack. "You five go after the human. The rest of you stay."

They whined with disappointment and he curled his lip at them. "Do not argue with me. Go, and bring me his head."

———

KADEN, PANTING HEAVILY, LEANED AGAINST A TREE. HE HAD a stitch in his side, and he pressed his hand against it as he laboured to catch his breath. He had been running steadily for nearly thirty minutes, but there was no doubt in his mind that Draken would not honour the hour he had promised him.

He stiffened as he heard rustling in the bushes to his left and a low growling. He stood frozen for a moment and then took off again, his heart pounding in his chest. He could hear the river ahead of him and he forced his tired legs to pump faster. There was a sharp bark and he risked a quick glance behind him. Fresh adrenaline flowed through his veins at the sight of the two large, brown Lycans loping after him. They grinned at him, snarling and snapping their teeth, and he turned and ran for his life.

He could see glimpses of the river now, a bright ribbon of blue snaking through the trees as the growls of the Lycan grew louder. The trees were thinning, and he leaped over a fallen log as the sound of the river filled his ears. The ground was sloping downward, he could see the shoreline of the river, and he put on a burst of desperate speed.

There was a flash of black and he turned just as the third Lycan came out of the trees to his left and leaped for him. He caught it in his arms. The bulk of the Lycan drove him backward and they tumbled to the ground. They rolled down the slope of the river bank, the Lycan snapping and growling and Kaden screaming hoarsely. They hit the river with a cold, wet splash and Kaden screamed again as his foot slammed into a large rock jutting out of the water at the edge of the river. It broke his ankle with a loud, sharp snap and pain roared up his leg and into his pelvis.

River water flowed into his mouth and coughing and sputtering, he stumbled to his feet. He staggered, pain from his broken ankle was shooting up his leg, and he roared with shock and pain when the Lycan bit him on the thigh. The wolf's sharp teeth tore through his pants and ripped a chunk of muscle and flesh from his thigh. Kaden screamed and grabbed the Lycan's thick head. Gritting his teeth against the pain, he dragged the twisting, writhing Lycan deeper into the river.

They were waist deep now and before the Lycan could twist free and leap on him, he dropped on top of its muscular body and forced it under the water.

"The gods help me!" He screamed into the cold air as he laboured to keep the struggling Lycan under the water. On the bank of the river, four other Lycans snarled and howled with rage as they watched their brother drown.

The Lycan's struggles ceased and Kaden stood up,

balancing shakily on one leg. The dead Lycan floated upward, its eyes staring blankly at the sky, and the Lycans watching from the river bank howled in agony.

Two of them floundered into the water and, using the Lycan to balance, Kaden struggled deeper into the river. The Lycans yipped in fear and anger as he moved chest deep into the river. The pain from the broken ankle and the bite in his thigh was fading as the coldness of the water numbed his lower body. He balanced carefully in the quickly-flowing water as he stared at the Lycans on the shore.

As his teeth chattered and his body trembled, he grinned fiercely at them. "Afraid of a little water, are we? Come and get me, you mangy dogs!"

They howled in reply, pacing back and forth as Kaden turned and scanned the far side of the bank. He was safe for now, but he couldn't stay in the river forever. He'd freeze to death. He gritted his teeth and, steeling himself against the pain, pushed the dead Lycan away and took a step forward.

The adrenaline had seeped from his body, and the coldness of the water had numbed his ankle and fooled him into thinking that he could walk. As a bolt of searing pain shot up his leg, he screamed hoarsely and immediately lifted his foot. His other foot slipped on the slick bottom of the river and he plunged backward into the icy water. He swallowed a mouthful of water and panic flooded through him. He struggled to find purchase with his good foot as he thrashed in the water.

He was going to drown. The bottom of the river seemed to be made of ice and it was impossible to struggle to his feet. He was going to die and Draken would hurt Sophia. He couldn't let that happen. He couldn't –

A hand sliced through the water and gripped his arm. He

was hauled to his feet and, coughing and choking, he stared in disbelief at Nicky.

"We really need to teach you how to swim, human," Nicky said as he put his arm around Kaden's waist and dragged him toward shore.

Two of the Lycans on the shore were already dead and the other two were howling and shrieking as James and the others tore into them. Kaden watched numbly as the largest one, a giant black beast, bolted for the trees. James chased after him and leaped onto his back. As the Lycan opened his mouth to scream, James ripped his throat wide open and blood sprayed out in a gushing fountain. The Lycan made a gurgling scream and collapsed as James howled in triumph.

Nicky helped Kaden sit on the ground as Marshall, his white fur splattered with blood, snarled loudly and killed the last member of Draken's pack. Shivering and gasping for breath, Kaden watched numbly as Tristan shifted to his human form and knelt beside him.

He grabbed Kaden's arm and shook him. "My daughter! Where is she?"

"She's back at the camp. She made a bargain with Draken to try and save my life," Kaden gasped out.

"What kind of bargain?" Nicky asked as James, still in his Lycan form, approached them. He sniffed at the wound on Kaden's thigh and Kaden grunted with pain when the Lycan dropped his large body onto his leg.

Warmth tingled through his leg as Tristan shook him again. "What bargain?"

"She said she would go to Draken's bed willingly if his pack members succeeded in hunting me down and bringing back my head. She believed you would find me and save me."

He stared up at Tristan and Nicky. "How did you find me?"

Marshall had shifted and he crouched naked next to his brother. "Luck. Dani said they had taken you north. We've been running all night, trying to catch your scent."

"Dani's safe then?" Kaden asked.

Marshall nodded and Kaden gave Tristan a hesitant look. "Ian is dead."

"Aye, Dani told us." Tristan rubbed his hand across his face. "We must keep moving. How far away is the camp? How many Lycans are with Draken?"

"Two, maybe three miles. There are at least another six Lycans, not including Draken." Kaden winced as James pressed his body firmly against his leg. He reached out and touched the wolf's shoulder gingerly. "Thank you."

James barked softly as Tristan stood. "I'm going after her."

"Dad, wait!" Nicky grabbed his father's arm before he could shift. "You can't go on your own. As soon as James has healed Kaden's leg, we'll go together."

"We can't wait, Nicky!" Tristan said.

For the first time since he met him, Kaden could see Tristan losing his usual iron-clad control. He pushed at James' shoulder. "It's better. I can walk on it."

Nicholas shook his head. "It isn't, and you know it. We need to wait."

He squeezed Tristan's arm again. "Give us ten minutes, Dad."

Tristan took a deep breath as Marshall said, "He's right, Tristan. You cannot go alone. If we are to save Sophia, we must stay together."

Tristan sighed harshly and stared into the woods as Nicky let go of his arm. "Will they be on watch for us, Kaden?"

Kaden shook his head. "No. Sophia told them you weren't expecting us back until today and Draken believed her."

"Are you sure?"

"Aye. He's gone mad," Kaden said. "Ian -"

His throat closed to a pinhole and he swallowed painfully. "Before Draken killed him, Ian said he could smell the madness on him."

Nicky stared silently at him and Kaden gave him a sudden, pleading look. "I didn't want to leave her. She made the bargain with Draken before I could stop her, and she made me promise I would go for the river. She told me that once you found me, we could come back for her."

When Nicky didn't answer, he stared down at the cold ground. "I didn't want to leave her."

Nicky clapped him on the shoulder. "We know." He turned toward his father and his uncle. "We use their scent to cover ours."

They nodded and Kaden watched as all three of them shifted. He grimaced as they rubbed and rolled their large bodies across the bodies of the dead Lycans. He tapped James on his shoulder and the large wolf stared at him.

"I think it's better."

James stood and Kaden stared at his leg. The bite on his thigh wasn't completely healed but it had stopped bleeding. He flexed his ankle carefully, sighing with relief when there was nothing but a slight twinge of pain.

James was staring at him questioningly and he nodded. "It's good enough. Let's go."

The red Lycan turned and joined the others in rolling and rubbing against the dead Lycans. When they were finished, James crouched down on the ground. He barked impatiently at Kaden.

What he wanted was obvious, but Kaden hesitated. "Are you sure you -"

Tristan interrupted him with an angry growl and without another word, Kaden climbed onto James' back. He clutched the Lycan's fur as the pack moved swiftly through the trees.

CHAPTER 23

Sophia touched the cut on her temple. It had been nearly twenty minutes since the pack left, and she stared at the flecks of dried blood on her fingers before raising her knees and resting her forehead on them.

Her heart was pounding in her chest and she'd never been so frightened in her life. She had bargained for Kaden's life out of sheer desperation. She was frantic to stop Draken from killing him, and at the time she was positive her family would find him and save him. Now, doubt was creeping in and she could feel the hot tears wanting to leak down her face. If the Lycans caught up to Kaden before he made it to the river, he wouldn't have a chance. And if he did make it to the river, if her family didn't find him, he would freeze to death. She blinked back the tears. She couldn't think that way. Her father and brothers would save him. They had to.

The distant sound of howling brought a rush of adrenaline to her veins and she stared wildly into the trees. She inhaled deeply, her pulse pounding in her ears, as there was another faint howl. She cocked her head as Terrence gave the other

Lycans a quick look. That howl sounded like one of pain and she felt a thin thread of hope.

Draken grinned happily as the other Lycans regarded each other uneasily. Without speaking, he ducked into his tent. Ten minutes later he reappeared and stood in front of Sophia. He held his hand out.

"They have found him, my pretty one. Come, join me in my tent."

She shook her head. "No. They have not returned with his head."

Draken scoffed. "It is only a matter of time. Let's go. I grow tired of your games."

"Draken," Terrence said, "the howling sounded -"

"Enough, Terrence!" Draken shouted. He reached down and yanked Sophia to her feet. She punched him hard in the face and he roared with shock and hurt.

"You stupid bitch!" He grabbed the back of her neck with one hard hand. She struggled wildly but he dragged her to his tent and shoved her inside.

"Do not interrupt us!" he snapped at Terrence before following her in.

Sophia was waiting for him and she dove at him, grabbing his waist and trying to knock him off his feet. His body beginning to swell and his skin rippling, Draken snarled and grabbed her shoulders. He pushed her upward before slapping her viciously across the face. The blow knocked her off her feet and she fell to her hands and knees, panting loudly and her head ringing.

She stiffened, her nostrils flaring, when she caught a glimpse of her sword tossed carelessly beside the blankets of Draken's bed. It gleamed in the dim light, and she bowed her head and wept quietly.

"I'm sorry," she sobbed. "Please don't hurt me. Please."

Draken knelt beside her and petted her bowed head. "Shh, my pretty. I don't want to hurt you. Do what I say, and everything will be fine."

"I'm sorry, my lord," she whimpered. She sat up and rested her head on Draken's chest, curling her arms around his waist and clinging to him.

Draken smiled at her, his eyes changing to red, as he stroked the tendrils of dark hair that had loosened and curled against her neck. "That's my good girl."

"Please, can we take this off?" She touched the collar around her neck.

He shook his head. "No, my pretty. The collar will stay on until I know I can trust you."

"You can trust me, my lord." She smiled at him as he thumbed away the tears on her cheeks.

He laughed and pinched her chin. "Aye, I'm sure you want me to trust you, but I think a few more moons wearing the collar will be necessary. Don't you?"

"Whatever you say, lord Draken," she replied.

"I will take the collar off when I'm sure that you have forgotten all about that stupid, weak human and wish to be my mate." He kissed the tip of her nose. "You're so beautiful, Sophia."

"Thank you, my lord," she replied before looking at the floor of the tent.

He put his fingers under her chin and tipped her head up. "I have waited my entire life for someone like you, Sophia. When we arrive at my home, I will give you everything you have always dreamed of. Would you like that?"

"Aye," she whispered.

"Good." His eyes glowing, he dipped his head to kiss her. Before he could press his mouth against hers, there was a chorus of frightened howls and Terrence was screaming his name.

"Gods be damned!" Draken shouted. He thrust her away from him with a hard shove and stalked to the front of the tent. He stuck his head out the opening.

"Terrence! I told you not to -"

He stuttered to a stop, his eyes widening with horror as he watched his pack of Lycans being torn apart. Terrence, still in his human form, was backing away from Kaden. He gave a hoarse shout of fear and his body began to enlarge. Hair sprouted on his face and he snarled at Kaden. He turned to flee but Kaden reached out with terrifying quickness, his face a grim mask, and wrapped his large hands around Terrence's rapidly-swelling neck. Before the Lycan could shift completely, Kaden twisted his head roughly to the left. Terrence's neck broke with a quiet snap, and he slithered bonelessly to the ground as Kaden shouted Sophia's name.

"No," Draken whispered. He backed into the tent and turned quickly. Sophia was standing in front of him and his eyes widened with shock as a soft breathless gasp escaped from between his lips.

He stared wide-eyed at her before his eyes dropped to the sword embedded deep in his chest. Sophia, growling deep in her throat, twisted the sword and grabbed the back of his neck. She yanked him forward, the sword thrusting into his chest to the hilt, and grinned fiercely at him.

She wrenched the sword free and took a step back as he touched his chest. His hand was immediately drenched with blood and he stared at the bright red bloom of colour on his fingers before holding them out accusingly to her.

She grinned. A shudder went through him at the look in her eyes before his legs gave out. He collapsed to his knees and then fell forward onto his nest of blankets. Darkness was creeping over his vision and he turned his head, his eyes rolling upward in their sockets to stare helplessly at Sophia. She curled her lip at him as he whined feebly.

"For Ian," she said as she raised her sword high above her head.

"Please, don't," he begged.

SOPHIA IGNORED DRAKEN'S BEGGING. WITH A SOFT SNARL, she brought her sword down. The sharp blade whistled through the air and carved through Draken's neck. Sophia wrenched her sword free and grinned savagely into Draken's vacant eyes.

"Sophia!" Limping badly, Kaden barreled through the opening of the tent. He stumbled to a stop, staring in bewilderment at Draken's body before his gaze fell on Sophia.

"Hello, human," she said. Tears dripped down her cheeks as Kaden blinked at her.

"I – I'm here to rescue you," he said.

She grinned through her tears. "I told you I could take care of myself."

A huge grin broke out across his face and he limped toward her. "Gods, little Lycan. I love you."

Crying freely now, she wrapped her arms around his waist and buried her face into his neck. "I love you too, human."

He hugged her hard, kissing the top of her head and the side of her neck until she raised her face to his. They kissed deeply, clinging tightly to each other, as Tristan stuck his head into the tent. His face was pale, and he gave a hoarse shout of relief when he saw Sophia.

"Sophia!"

She broke away from Kaden and staggered to her father. "Papa!"

He hugged her fiercely, kissing her face numerous times before holding her away from him and looking her up and down. "Are you all right? Did he hurt you?"

He touched the cut on her temple and the bruise forming on her jaw as she shook her head. "No, Papa."

"Thank the gods." He hugged her again. "Thank the gods."

"James, I'm fine!" Sophia huffed impatiently as James continued to press his hands against her face. "Finish healing Kaden."

She sat down beside Kaden as James knelt on his other side and rested his hand on the bite on Kaden's leg. Warmth and tingling surged into his flesh and he gave the Lycan a grateful nod before turning to Sophia. He cupped her face, resting his forehead against hers before he reached up and plucked two of her hair pins out.

She looked at him in bewilderment as he winked at her. "Turn your head, little Lycan."

She turned her head obediently and he went to work on the lock on the silver collar around her neck. After a few minutes of patient probing, the lock clicked open and he pulled the collar from her throat. She sighed with relief and rubbed at her neck before unbuckling the leather collar around his neck and tossing it on the ground beside the silver one.

He smiled at her and kissed her as Tristan crouched beside them and squeezed Sophia's hand. "As soon as Kaden is healed completely, we'll head back for home. Your mama is worried to death."

"Aye, Papa," Sophia replied.

Kaden cleared his throat and she stared at him. "What is it?"

"There are other human slaves at Draken's home," he said.

She studied him for a moment before nodding and turning back to her father. "Papa, we have to help them."

Tristan sighed harshly before glancing at Marshall. "Aye, I know."

He stood and rubbed at his forehead. "We'll go to Draken's home and rescue the other humans. Marshall, you'll go home and tell the others what we're doing. Tell them we'll be home as quickly as we can."

Marshall nodded. "Aye, Tristan."

Tristan glanced at Kaden. "Can you lead us to Draken's home?"

"Aye, I can."

"How many more Lycans can we expect at Draken's home?" Nicky asked.

Kaden thought carefully. "At least another ten, maybe more. Draken's pack was large."

Nicky grinned delightedly at James. "We should have brought our swords."

Tristan squeezed Marshall's shoulder briefly. "Be careful, brother."

"I'll see you at home." Marshall kissed Sophia's forehead before stepping back and shifting. He barked once and loped away. Tristan watched until he had disappeared and then turned back to the others.

"We'll leave as soon as Kaden is healed."

CHAPTER 24

"Leta, it's almost dinner." Avery stuck her head out the back door and smiled at her. "Come in and wash up, please."

"Aye, Mama," Leta said as Avery disappeared inside the house.

She climbed to her feet and dusted the dirt from the palm of her hands before reaching into the pocket of her pants. She pulled out the piece of rabbit meat and held it high above her head as she stared at the small dog dancing around her feet. "Tia, sit."

Tia sat obediently and Leta smiled happily. "Good girl!"

She tossed the piece of rabbit meat and Tia snatched it out of the air, chewing it quickly before staring expectantly at her.

"That's all the rabbit meat, silly." Leta giggled. "You don't get any more until -"

She stopped and stared into the trees that lined the property. She lifted her head and inhaled before whispering, "Papa?"

There was a flicker of movement in the trees and then Tristan came striding out from them.

"Papa!" Leta shrieked with delight and tore across the yard. Tia, barking excitedly, followed at her heels. She launched herself at Tristan and, grinning broadly, he caught her and lifted her into his arms.

"Hello, sweet Leta. Have you missed me?"

Too excited to speak, she pressed loud kisses across his face as her siblings and Kaden appeared behind them.

"Oh, Papa. You've been gone so long. It's been moons," she said as she patted his cheeks.

He laughed. "It's been two weeks, my love."

Before she could reply, Avery stepped out into the yard. "Leta, I asked you -"

She stopped, her mouth dropping open as she stared at Tristan and Leta.

"Tristan?" She ran across the yard as Tristan, still holding Leta, moved forward to meet her.

"Tristan!" She threw her arms around him and kissed him. He returned her kiss, one strong hand threading through her hair to hold her firmly as she pressed herself against him.

"Mama, you're squishing me," Leta complained.

Laughing and crying, Avery rubbed Leta's back affectionately before looking behind Tristan's wide frame.

"Sophia!" She darted around Tristan and embraced Sophia before kissing her smooth cheek. "My sweet, baby girl. I was so scared for you."

"I'm fine, mama." Sophia hugged her hard as the rest of the family flowed out of the house and into the yard.

Kaden stood back and watched as the Lycans were reunited. Doran clapped Nicky on the back as Marshall embraced his brother. Maya hugged Sophia, her pale face shiny with tears, before she stepped back, and Vivian took her place.

Kaden grinned as Bree, her thin face glowing with happiness, was picked up by James. He smothered her face with kisses before setting her down and resting his hand against her stomach for a moment. She smiled up at him, clasping his hand as he murmured something to her. She nodded immediately and a look of relief came over his face. He bent and kissed her belly quickly. She stroked his thick, red hair before walking to Kaden.

Kaden bent and hugged her as she patted his back and kissed his cheek. "I'm so happy you're back."

"Me too." He smiled at her and she hesitated before wrapping her hand around his neck and tugging his head down. She placed her mouth to his ear.

"I'm pregnant, Kaden. We're telling the others after the wedding, but I wanted you to know first."

She was looking at him nervously and he gave her a broad smile. "Congratulations, baby sister. You'll make an amazing mother."

Relief crossed her features and she hugged him again. "Thank you, Kaden. I love you."

"I love you too, Bree."

She squeezed his hand and returned to James as Avery approached Kaden. "Welcome home, Kaden."

He hesitated only briefly before hugging the Red. She rubbed his back and whispered, "Thank you for saving her."

"I love her," he said.

"Aye, I know," she replied.

She hugged him again before stepping back. Dani was standing behind her, her hand clasping a short, brown-haired man's hand, and she gave him a shy smile.

"Welcome back, Kaden."

"Thank you, Dani."

"This is Andric. He helped me after Draken took you and Sophia. He saved my life, actually."

Kaden held out his hand and Andric shook it. "It's nice to meet you."

"It's nice to meet you as well," Kaden said

Andric put his arm around Dani's waist and kissed her cheek. Dani gave him an adoring look and Kaden breathed a sigh of relief. It seemed that Dani's crush on him was forgotten and he glanced over their heads, searching for Sophia.

She was staring at him as she hugged Evan, and she gave him a small smile. He felt a surge of love for her that was nearly overpowering in its simplicity, and he headed toward her as Nicky took his grandmother's arm.

"Come, Grandmamma, I will regale you with my tales of heroism while we eat dinner.

Vivian laughed and rolled her eyes. "I can hardly wait, Nicky."

———

"I'M SO SORRY, OLD MAN." KADEN STARED AT THE PLAIN wooden cross that marked Ian's grave. He sat cross-legged beside the grave and sighed deeply. It was early the next morning. Sophia had joined him in his bed in the hayloft last night, and they had spent most of the night either making love or holding each other silently.

They hadn't spoken about the future, and he had woken before dawn and slipped out of bed without waking her. He had brushed down Bandit, taking comfort in the familiar chore, before heading into the house. It was quiet and still as he had walked into the kitchen. Avery and Tristan were sitting at the table holding hands and talking quietly. He had stammered out an apology, but they insisted he join them. He sat with them for a few minutes before asking about Ian. Her face a mixture of sympathy and sorrow, Avery directed him to Ian's grave.

Now, he reached out and touched the wooden cross briefly. "I'm sorry," he said again.

Strong arms snaked around him and Sophia dropped to her knees behind him before hugging him. She rested her chin on his shoulder and stroked his chest.

"I miss him." His voice was rough with unshed tears and Sophia kissed his cheek, her own cheeks wet.

"Me too," she whispered.

He squeezed her hands and she slipped around him and sat in his lap. He buried his face in her throat as she stroked his broad back with her warm hands. "I'm so sorry, Kaden."

They sat silently for a few minutes before Sophia cleared her throat. "Your sister and my brother will be married in less than a week."

"Aye. She told me she was pregnant." He lifted his head and smiled at her. "She said they would tell everyone else after the wedding."

She stroked his face. "I'm glad she told you."

She paused and then smoothed her hand over his brow. "After the wedding I'll leave with you for Vanden."

"You would leave your family?" he asked.

"Aye. I love you, Kaden. I'll go wherever you go."

He kissed her fiercely, sliding his tongue deep into her mouth as she gave a small gasp of surprise. She kissed him back, threading her fingers in his hair, as he rubbed her lower back.

He pulled his mouth free and rubbed his thumb across her swollen bottom lip. "We're not going to Vanden."

She frowned at him. "Where are we going then?"

He shook his head. "We're not going anywhere. We're staying here with your family. I won't ask you to leave your family for me and since I can't be without you, I guess I'm staying right here."

He wiped the tears from her cheeks with his thumb as she smiled at him. "Truly, Kaden?"

"Aye. Your family will have to put up with me for a lot longer than they thought."

She laughed and kissed him again. "They'll be happy to hear that."

"ARE YOU NERVOUS, BREE?" KADEN ASKED AS THEY STOOD at the closed door to the common room. Behind it they could hear soft murmurs and quiet music.

"Only about walking in these shoes. I should never have let Dani convince me they were a good idea." Bree made a face and lifted the bottom of her dress to show him the blue shoes on her feet. "You'll make sure I won't fall flat on my face, won't you?"

He grinned and nodded. "Aye, I can do that. You look beautiful, Bree."

"Thank you, Kaden. Just between you and me, I feel a bit like a princess. Isn't that silly?" Bree said.

"It's your wedding day – you should feel like a princess." He straightened his tie and tugged a little at the collar of his shirt.

She grinned at him. "You're looking very handsome as well. Sophia won't be able to take her eyes off of you."

"Bree, I'm not leaving after the wedding."

"I know," she said a bit smugly.

He frowned at her. "How do you know? I haven't told anyone but Sophia."

"I knew you weren't leaving when James and the others brought you and Sophia back to us. I could see it in the way you looked at her."

"I love her."

"Aye, you do." She squeezed his arm. "Come, it's been nearly five minutes since Dani, Sophia and Leta walked down the aisle. James will think I have cold feet."

Kaden pushed open the door to the common room. The small gathering of family and friends stood, and he lifted Bree's hand to his mouth and kissed her knuckles. She was staring at James, her face lit with a happy glow, and she smiled briefly at Kaden before returning her gaze to James.

"Are you ready, Bree?" Kaden asked.

"Aye, I am."

CHAPTER 25

"**C**ongratulations, James."

Bree watched as a tall, thin Lycan shook James' hand.

"Bree, this is Rory Barton and his wife Jade. My father and his father, Thomas, are old friends."

"It's lovely to meet you." Bree smiled at the couple. "Thank you for joining us today."

"Thank you for having us," Jade said. "The ceremony was beautiful."

Bree blushed. "Aye, except for the part where I tripped and nearly landed on my face."

Rory laughed. "Your brother kept you on your feet."

"Aye, thank the gods." Bree blushed again.

James winked at her and kissed the top of her head. "I thought it was adorable."

Loud laughter from the far end of the common room had all four of them turning their heads. Nicky, his tie and jacket discarded, and his shirt unbuttoned, was chugging a large mug of beer to the screams of encouragement of a crowd of young people standing in front of him.

Bree giggled when he drained the mug and grabbed a curvy, dark-haired woman and kissed her. There were shouts and whistles of approval and when Nicky finally released the woman, she staggered on her feet and held her hands to her glowing cheeks. Nicky winked at her and slapped her on the ass. She giggled and then jumped on to his back. Carrying her piggy-back, Nicky led the group out the far door and into the cold night. Bree could hear them laughing and howling happily as the door closed behind them.

"Oh, Christa," Jade said with embarrassment in her voice.

James cleared his throat. "Christa is Rory and Jade's eldest daughter. She and Nicky have always uh, gotten along very well."

"Oh," Bree replied. There was an awkward silence and then Bree smiled at the Barton's. "Is your father here, lord Barton?"

"No, I am afraid not."

"How is the lord Thomas?" James asked.

"Doing poorly, I'm afraid," Rory replied. "In fact, I meant to ask your mother if she would come visit him soon. He so enjoys seeing her and says that he always feels better after she visits."

"I'm sure she would," James replied. "She is very fond of your father."

Avery materialized beside them. "Rory, I was just coming to ask you how your father was doing." She squeezed Jade's arm affectionately. "I was sad not to see him here today. Come, join Tristan and me at the table. We haven't had a chance to visit with you at all."

She smiled at James and Bree before leading the couple towards the table where Tristan was sitting.

"What is wrong with Rory's father?" Bree asked.

"Old age. His Lycan healing powers have faded completely."

"Will your mother heal him?" Bree asked in a low voice.

James shook his head. "There is no cure for aging. She will sit with him and hold his hand. It will help him to feel better, help take away some of his aches and pains, but it won't heal him fully."

Before Bree could reply, Leta ran up to them. She twirled in a circle in front of them, her dress sparkling brightly in the small lights strung on the ceiling.

"Bree! Everyone loves my dress!" She said.

Bree laughed as James picked up his baby sister and set her in the crook of his arm. "So they should, Leta. You look very pretty today."

"I know," Leta replied. "But you look prettier, Bree."

"Thank you, Leta." Bree squeezed her leg as the music started up again.

James set Leta down and patted her bottom lightly. "Go find Evan and tell him to dance with you."

"Eww, gross!" Leta made a face. "I'm not dancing with Evan! I'll ask Papa to dance with me." She skipped away as James took Bree's hand.

"Will you dance with me, Mrs. Williams?"

"I would love to, Mr. Williams." Bree smiled up at him and then squeaked with surprise when he picked her up and carried her to the middle of the room. Holding her close, her feet dangling around his shins, he swayed to the music. She wrapped her arms around his shoulders and kissed him lightly on the mouth.

"This has been the happiest day of my life, James," she said.

He smiled at her. "Mine too." He glanced around the

room as more couples began to join them in dancing. "When do you want to tell everyone about the baby?"

"I thought we would tell them tomorrow. What do you think?" Bree replied.

"Aye, that sounds fine with me."

Bree kissed him again before looking over James' shoulder. Her smile widened as she watched Sophia lead Kaden to the middle of the room. Her brother pulled Sophia close and they swayed together as she whispered into his ear.

"It doesn't look like your brother is leaving after the wedding." James had followed her gaze and she gave him a look of pure happiness.

"Aye. He told me earlier that he was staying. I'm so happy, James. I'm married to the most wonderful man in the world, my brother is staying, and I have a new family. Everything is perfect."

He nuzzled her neck affectionately. "Aye, little one. Perfect."

"GODS BE DAMNED, MY HEAD HURTS." LATE THE NEXT morning Nicky staggered into the common room. He slumped next to his brother. "Hold me, James. I beg of you."

Bree laughed as James snorted and rolled his eyes. "If I take away your hangover you'll never learn, Nicky."

"I've learned my lesson, baby brother. I swear." Nicky reached for him and James dodged away.

"Christa was disappointed when you didn't join the rest of us in saying goodbye this morning," James said.

Nicky waved one hand weakly in the air as the other hand rubbed at his aching temple. "She wasn't disappointed last night when I led her into the forest and let her ride the hell out of me. The girl nearly -"

He suddenly paused and gave Bree a look of embarrassment. "Uh, I mean we made love under the stars and it was beautiful and touching."

Bree laughed again. "Spare me the details, Nicky."

James snickered. "You need to be careful, brother. Christa is anxious to be married and she has her eye on you."

Nicky shook his head rapidly and then groaned at the pain. "I'm way too young to be tied down. I still need to sow my wild oats."

"If you sow any more wild oats, you'll be a farmer," Tristan remarked as he entered the room. He was followed by Avery, Leta and Evan, and Leta stared at her father curiously.

"Why is Nicky becoming a farmer, Papa?"

"He's not." Avery laughed. She held out her arms. "Come here, Nicky."

"Thank you, Mama." Nicky sighed gratefully as he embraced his mother. He rested his head on her shoulder as she stroked his short, blonde hair.

"Bree? I drew you something as a wedding gift. I didn't want to give it to you last night in front of everyone," Evan said.

She took the paper from him and studied it carefully. It was a pencil drawing of her and James and she hugged Evan delightedly.

"I love it, Evan. Thank you so much."

He blushed and ducked away as James ruffled his hair.

The front door banged open and Sophia and Kaden entered the common room. Their cheeks were red, and Bree shivered in the blast of cold air that accompanied them.

Avery, still holding Nicky, smiled at them. "You know, you don't have to stay in the hayloft."

"We know." Sophia held Kaden's hand and smiled at him. "I'm actually growing to like it up there. Even with Piper attacking me in the middle of the night."

"Better than a rat, is it not?" Kaden winked at her and she shuddered before poking him lightly in the chest. "The first time I see a rat in the hayloft, we're moving back into the house."

Vivian, followed by Marshall, Doran and Maya, entered the common room. "What's going on? Marian said you were looking for us."

"Aye, we are, Grandmamma." James said. "Where is Dani?"

"Right here." Dani hurried into the room with Andric. She was flushed and breathless. "Sorry, we were um, going for a walk."

Nicky snickered and her blush deepened as Marshall made a soft grunt of disapproval. Maya elbowed Marshall gently and gave him a pointed look before smiling at James. "What is it, James?"

James grinned at his family. "Bree and I have an announcement to make."

The others stared at them as Bree, suddenly nervous, looked down at her feet. James put his arm around her and kissed the top of her head. "Go ahead, Bree."

Bree licked her lips and stared at the group of Lycans and humans she had grown to love. She glanced briefly at her brother. He gave her a nod of encouragement and, squeezing James waist tightly, she smiled at her new family. "We're going to have a baby."

There was a moment of silence and then Leta squealed with delight. "A baby! You're having a baby!"

She ran across the room and latched onto Bree's waist.

She kissed Bree's abdomen and then hugged her. "Truly? You're having a baby?"

"Aye, I am." Bree grinned down at her and then Tristan was standing in front of them. She was surprised to see he had tears in his eyes, and he hugged her roughly, squishing Leta between them.

"Congratulations, little one," he said hoarsely before releasing her and hugging James. He clapped him on the back, making James wince, before stepping back and allowing the others to crowd around them.

As the others congratulated Bree and James, Tristan returned to Avery. She was standing by the fireplace and staring at her children with a small smile on her face. Tristan put his arm around her and kissed her.

"Did you know, girl?"

"Aye. I guessed it a few weeks ago. Bree and James asked me to keep it quiet. Are you upset with me?"

He shook his head. "No. We're going to be grandparents." He gave her a look of wonderment. "I can't believe it."

She grinned and stroked the grey at his temple. "You do not look old enough to be a grandpa, my lord."

"Nor you a grandmother. You are as beautiful as the day I met you, my love," he said.

She smiled at him. "Thank you. Perhaps we should sneak away and celebrate together."

He gave her a look of regret. "I would like that, girl, but I should check on the horses. Ian -"

He paused, pain crossing his face, and she cupped his face. "I'm sorry, my lord. I know how much you miss him."

"Aye, I do." He rested his forehead against hers. "I wish he -"

"Papa!" Leta squeezed her way between them and stared up at him. "Can I come to the barn with you?"

"May I, Leta," Avery said.

"May I, Papa?" Leta asked.

"Yes, my love. You may." He kissed Avery and then lifted Leta into his arms. He tugged the end of her braid. "But you'll have to brush Samson for me."

"I can do that, Papa," Leta said.

"Good." Tristan winked at Avery as he carried Leta from the common room.

―――――――

"Do you want a boy or a girl, Bree?" Dani asked. She was sitting on Andric's lap, stroking the Lycan's sand-coloured hair.

"It does not matter to me," Bree replied as she smiled at James. "Either is fine."

"I think she's having a girl," Maya said. "And I'm never wrong. I predicted each of my sister's babies and I was right each time."

Avery laughed. "Aye, but you were wrong about your own. You were certain you were having a girl."

"I did have a girl," Maya replied. "I just didn't realize she was hiding behind her brother."

She winked at Doran as Avery laughed again. "Aye, it was a bit of a surprise when five minutes after Doran arrived, you started shouting you needed to push again."

"Was that when Daddy dropped Doran?" Dani asked.

Her brother flushed. "The gods be damned, Danielle!

How many times do I have to tell you – Dad didn't drop me as a baby."

"No, but he might have juggled you a bit when your mother started pushing again." Avery grinned at him.

Marshall held his hands up. "In my defense, Doran was both goopy and slippery and Maya was squeezing my hand so hard I had lost all feeling in it. In fact, it hasn't been the same since."

He winked at Maya who rolled her eyes good-naturedly. Nicky stood and stretched. "As much as I enjoy hearing about my cousins' gross entrance into this world, I think I'm going to take a nap."

He squeezed his brother's shoulder. "Congratulations James and Bree. I'm very happy for you and I know -"

He stopped as Renee stepped into the common room. "M'lady?"

Avery glanced at her and frowned. "Renee? What's wrong?"

"There's a man here. He says he's here to speak to Nicky. He wouldn't tell us what his business was."

Avery glanced at Nicholas who shrugged. "Send him in."

Renee nodded and disappeared as James sighed. "It's probably the father of one of your many lady friends. No doubt she's with pup, and we'll be attending another wedding soon enough."

Nicky gave him a horrified look. "Quiet your tongue, brother! I have no wish to be a husband or a father."

"Aye, the string of broken hearts you have left scattered over a fifty-mile radius are testament to that."

Before Nicky could reply, Renee was ushering in a man and two women. The shortest of the women had a toddler strapped to her back and the child stared curiously at them over the woman's shoulder. The man was tall with silver hair and a close-cropped beard. His eyes were a dark brown and his face was weathered with deep lines.

Doran was standing next to Sophia and she heard the young man's sharp inhale. He was staring at the woman standing next to the man. She was stunningly beautiful. Her skin was light brown and her hair fell to her waist in dark waves. She was tall with lush curves, and her dark brown eyes regarded them calmly.

Kaden took Sophia's hand and leaned down to breathe into her ear, "Lycan or human?"

"The man and the dark-haired woman are Lycan. The short-haired woman is human," she murmured.

Sophia glanced at the human woman. She had light brown hair that was cropped into a pixie cut and she was dressed warmly in a thick jacket and pants that were too big for her. She was short and sturdy looking. Although not nearly as beautiful as the Lycan female, she had a unique look that Sophia guessed many men would find appealing. Her skin was pale, and she had full lips and beautiful eyes. Even from across the room, Sophia could see that the left one was blue and the right one was brown.

The child strapped to her back was the spitting image of her, and Sophia had no doubt that the little girl was her daughter. She was wearing a pink knitted cap and her cheeks were rosy from the cold. The child stared at her and Sophia smiled. The little girl immediately hid her face in the back of her mother's neck. The woman stroked the child's shoulder soothingly.

The silver-haired man stared at Nicky. "You are Nicholas."

"Aye," Nicky said. "Do I know you?"

"No. My name is Meridan. I am here on behalf of your father."

Nicky glanced at Avery who gave him a look of bewilderment.

Meridan cleared his throat. "I am here on behalf of your birth father."

"Papa?"

"Aye, Leta?" Tristan was crouching beside Bella, running his hands down her foreleg as she nuzzled at his hair.

"There's a strange carriage in the yard."

Tristan stood and glanced over the wall of Bella's stall. Leta was standing at the door to the barn. Hogan was in her arms and Piper was sitting a few feet away, his tail twitching as he stared at the young Lycan.

"A carriage?"

"Aye."

He joined her in the doorway, peering across the yard at the black carriage with the two grey horses hitched to it.

"Who is it, Papa?" Leta asked.

"I do not know. Let's go and find out, shall we?" He smiled at her and held out his hand and she let Hogan go before taking his hand.

He closed the barn door behind him, and they walked hand-in-hand in the cold sunshine towards the house.

"Will it ever snow, Papa?" Leta asked. "I want to go sledding."

"It will snow soon enough," Tristan replied. "When we are digging our way out of the house every morning, you will wish for green grass and flowers."

He stopped suddenly and lifted his head, inhaling before turning and staring into the woods to their left.

She giggled. "Do you remember when Nicky built me the

snow slide from the kitchen window all the way to the ground? That was so much fun. Do you think it will snow enough this year for him to do that again?"

There was a soft whooshing sound and Tristan made a strangled gasp of surprise. Leta squeezed his hand. "Papa?"

She stared at him as he studied the arrow sticking out of his chest. She dropped his hand and backed away as he reached for the arrow with trembling hands. He pulled it free with a hard yank and stared in bewilderment first at the bright blue feathers at the end and then at the blood coating the tip of it.

Leta's eyes widened as red liquid blossomed on the front of his shirt. "Papa?"

"Leta." He gave her a look of confusion as the patch of blood grew on his shirt. She gasped loudly when he slowly sank to his knees, his head dropping forward.

"Papa!" She crowded up next to him as he collapsed backward onto the ground. "Papa!" She shook his shoulder, her eyes wide with fright.

Tristan stared up at the sky. He watched a cloud drift lazily across it as the frantic beating in his ears began to slow. Dimly he was aware of Leta screaming, and he tried to turn his head to smile and reassure her, but his body refused to obey his mind's command. He continued to stare up at the sky as the beating slowed even further. He realized with faint puzzlement that the beating he heard was the sound of his heart.

I'm dying, he thought with a muted sense of surprise. He pictured Avery's face – her laughing green eyes and her pale skin, and the way her hair flashed like fire in the sun. He whispered her name as the sun dimmed in the sky.

He frowned in confusion. Why was the sun setting so soon? Darkness was creeping across the edges of his vision and as the beating of his heart slowed to a stop, he closed his eyes and whispered Avery's name one last time.

Want to read about Danielle and Andric's love story?
Check out "Alpha Moon" (Book Four, Red Moon Series).
This 30K novella takes place in the two weeks between
Kaden and Sophia's rescue and James and Bree's wedding.

PALE MOON EXCERPT

(BOOK FIVE, RED MOON SERIES)

Copyright ©2014 Elizabeth Kelly

Nicky held out his hand and watched as the snowflakes landed on his open palm. They melted quickly and he stared at the cloudy sky before dropping his gaze to the ground before him. The ground was stained with his father's blood, and he closed his eyes and took a deep breath before reaching for the shovel he had brought out from the barn.

He thrust the shovel into the hard ground, dug up a chunk of the blood-stained grass and transferred it to the wheelbarrow. As he dug, he couldn't stop thinking about the silver-haired Lycan's visit that morning.

***

Nicholas stared in surprise at the silver-haired Lycan standing before him. "My birth father," he repeated.

"Aye. He needs your help," Meridan said.

Avery moved to Nicky's side and took his hand. "How do you know his father?"

"We work for him." Meridan indicated the two women standing next to him.

"Why did he not come himself?" Nicky asked.

"Your father has been taken by the leeches deep into the outskirts. We need your help in getting him back."

"Why would I help a man who abandoned me as a child?"

"He only learned of your existence three moons ago. Your mother's cousin, Saredina, fell ill. Before she died, she sought out your father and told him about you. She told him that a Lycan named Tristan Williams had taken you and your sister away from the city. Your father was preparing to come here when he was taken by the leeches.

"If he was taken by the leeches to the outskirts then he is already dead," Nicholas said.

Meridan shook his head. "No. The leeches have not killed him. I can assure you of that. They are holding him prisoner."

"You're wrong. The leeches do not take prisoners," Nicky replied.

The female Lycan frowned at Meridan. "How can they not know? Do they not care what happens to their own kind?"

Meridan shook his head at the woman. "Quiet, Pavina. You forget that news does not travel as quickly in the country as it does in the city."

"What are you talking about?" James led Bree towards Kaden and Sophia, standing her close to her brother and giving Kaden a brief look. Kaden nodded and put his arm around his sister, holding her against him.

James stood next to Nicholas and Avery and gave Meridan a hard stare. "Tell us what you mean before I lose my patience."

"In the last year or so, there has been a surge in the number of humans that the leeches have taken. They have been turning the humans in an attempt to increase their own kind. Four moons ago it became clear why they were so desperate to increase their numbers. They needed larger numbers to take the Lycans. They've been abducting our kind and taking them to the outskirts."

"Why would they do that?" Avery asked.

"They are experimenting on them."

"What do you mean?" Nicholas frowned.

"They are attempting to make a hybrid of our kinds. Leech and Lycan mixed together. They believe they can use the Lycans to create a new race of vampires. They seek many of the Lycan's unique abilities, but what they desire most is the Lycan's ability to walk in the sun."

"The gods be damned," Avery breathed.

"Indeed," Meridan said. "If the leeches are successful in their quest, if they create a new hybrid of leech and Lycan, then we are all in grave danger."

"How do you know they have not already succeeded?" James asked.

Meridan shrugged. "We do not know for sure that they have not, but the rumour is that they are running into…issues."

Pavina snorted. "The leeches are ridiculous for believing they can create a hybrid. The Lycan gene is too powerful to be diluted by the leech's filth."

"What are the issues?" Nicky asked.

"Lycans who have been infected by the leeches die with a moon or two of being bitten. Their healing powers go into overdrive trying to destroy the leech's infection within their bodies. The constant attempt to heal takes an enormous toll on the Lycan. It saps their energy and strength and eventually kills them."

There was a horrified silence in the room and Meridan

sighed. "Despite their failure, the leeches do not seem to be giving up. More and more Lycans are being taken."

"Including my birth father," Nicky said.

"Aye. He was taken from the city nearly a moon ago. We are traveling to the outskirts to rescue him. Before he was kidnapped, your father confided in me about you and I made the decision to find you."

When Nicholas didn't reply, Meridan gave him a brief smile. "We have gathered many of your father's friends and employees to help us, but we could always use more Lycans. It will only become more dangerous the closer we get to the outskirts."

Nicky ran his hand restlessly through his hair. "You want me to help a man I've never met?"

"He is your father," Pavina said sharply. "What kind of Lycan leaves his own blood to die?"

"Hush, Pavina," Meridan said. "Nicholas, we believe there is a good chance that your father is still alive and has not been bitten yet. Your father is a good man, and there are many who are willing to risk their lives to save him. He is anxious to meet you."

Meridan paused. "If he has been bitten, then at least give him the chance to meet his son before he dies."

Nicky turned to his mother and her face paled at the look on his face. She cupped his face and gave him a frantic look. "Nicky, you do not know that they speak the truth."

"We're not lying!" Pavina snarled. She growled deep in her throat and her eyes turned a dark yellow as she took a step toward Avery and glared ominously at her. "You would be wise to hold your tongue, human. Not all Lycans are so complacent toward humans."

She shrank back against Meridan, her eyes widening with fear, when a chorus of low growls answered her. Every single

Lycan in the room began to shift, their eyes glowing fiercely as they stalked toward the three strangers. James and Nicky stood in front of Avery and used their large bodies to block her completely from the gaze of Meridan and the two women.

"Threaten our mother again and you will die in this room," James said. His beard was heavy on his face and his upper body had swelled to nearly twice its size. His shirt ripped across his shoulders with a low, purring sound as Meridan put up his hands in a calming gesture.

"Please, she meant no offense. Pavina speaks without thinking."

Nicky approached the female Lycan until he was standing only inches from her. He sniffed at her hair and then snarled under his breath. He bared his teeth at her, and a small whimper escaped her throat at the sight of his sharp fangs. She lowered her gaze to the floor.

"Keep your eyes on the floor. If you even look at my mother, I will pluck your eyes from your head and give them to her as a gift," Nicholas growled.

Pavina whined softly in submission as Nicholas continued to stare at her.

"Puppy!"

Nicholas turned to his right. The human female was standing frozen with fear, but the small child strapped to her back was giving him a look of pure delight.

"Puppy," she said again and before her mother could stop her, reached out and stroked the hair on Nicky's cheek with her small hand.

"Violet, no!" the woman gasped. She pulled the child's hand away and took a step back. "I'm sorry," she said.

Nicky cocked his head and stared into the woman's oddly-coloured eyes. He waited for her to drop her gaze like Pavina and when she didn't, he leaned in and inhaled. She smelled delicious, he thought hazily. Underneath the smell of her fear, there was an exotic blend of vanilla and jasmine and the good clean scent of her child.

"Hi, puppy," the little girl said, and her mother made a quiet moan of dismay.

Nicky, his body shrinking and the hair on his cheeks fading away, suddenly grinned at the toddler. "Hi, baby."

He gently pinched the girl's chubby cheek before stepping away. Sophia, Vivian and Evan had joined James and were standing in a tight cluster around Avery. They stepped back as he stood next to his mother. He put his arm around her and stared at Meridan.

"We speak the truth, Nicholas. I swear it," the silver-haired Lycan said.

He didn't reply and Avery squeezed his waist. "Nicky, we must speak to your father first. He is still in the barn with Leta."

"Aye, I know," he replied.

Avery turned to Evan. "Evan, go the barn and get your father. Go quickly."

"Aye, Mama." Evan started for the door of the common room. He paused, his eyes widening, when the faint sound of Leta screaming could be heard.

"Leta?" Avery whispered. She stood frozen for a moment and then bolted from the room.

ABOUT THE AUTHOR

Elizabeth Kelly was born and raised in Ontario, Canada. She moved west as a teenager and now lives in Alberta with her husband and a menagerie of pets. She firmly believes that a person can survive solely on sushi and coffee, and only her husband's mad cooking skills prevents her from proving that theory.

For more information about Elizabeth, check out her website at

www.elizabethkelly.ca

facebook.com/EKellyBooks

twitter.com/ElizabethKBooks

instagram.com/elizabethkelly_author

amazon.com/Elizabeth-Kelly/e/B00EOHZ0MS

bookbub.com/authors/elizabeth-kelly

ALSO BY ELIZABETH KELLY

Tempted Series

Tempted

Twice Tempted

Forever Tempted

Breathless

Tempted Trilogy (Books 1-3)

Red Moon Series

Red Moon

Red Moon Rising

Dark Moon

Alpha Moon

Pale Moon

Red Moon Bundle Books 1 – 3

Red Moon Bundle Books 4 – 5

The Recruit Series

The Recruit (Book One)

The Recruit (Book Two)

The Recruit (Book Three)

The Recruit (Book Four)

The Recruit (Book Five)

The Recruit Series Bundle Books 1-3

The Recruit Series Bundle Books 4-6

The Shifters Series

Willow and the Wolf (Book One)

Ava and the Bear (Book Two)

Katarina and the Bird (Book Three)

Porter's Mate (Book Four)

Bria and the Tiger (Book Five)

Rosalie Undone (Book Six)

The Dragon's Mate (Book Seven)

Rise of the Jaguar (Book Eight)

The Draax Series

Reign (Book One)

Rule (Book Two)

Rebel (Book Three)

Harmony Falls Series

Sweet Harmony (Book One)

Perfect Harmony (Book Two)

Forbidden Harmony (Book Three)

Redeeming Harmony (Book Four)

Individual Books

The Necessary Engagement

Amelia's Touch

The Rancher's Daughter

Healing Gabriel

The Contract

A Home for Lily

Saving Charlotte

Shameless

The Fairy Tales Collection

Broken

An Unlikely Seduction

Holiday Romance

The Christmas Wife

The Christmas Rescue

The Christmas Nanny

Sordid Games